Wonders & Wickedness

A Victorian Murder Mystery

Carol Hedges

Little G Books

Copyright © 2017 by Carol Hedges
Cover Artwork and Design by RoseWolf Design
Cover Photograph by Estelle Clarke

All rights reserved.

No part of this book may be used or reproduced in any manner whatsoever without written permission of the author except for brief quotations used for promotion or in reviews. This is a work of fiction.
Names, characters, and incidents are used fictitiously.

This edition by Little G Books (August 2017)

For Edward Archie

About the Author

Carol Hedges is the successful British author of 16 books for teenagers and adults. Her writing has received much critical acclaim, and her novel Jigsaw was shortlisted for the Angus Book Award and longlisted for the Carnegie Medal.

Carol was born in Hertfordshire, and after university, where she gained a BA (Hons.) in English Literature & Archaeology, she trained as a children's librarian. She worked for the London Borough of Camden for many years subsequently re-training as a secondary school teacher when her daughter was born.

Carol still lives and writes in Hertfordshire. She is a local activist and green campaigner, and the proud owner of a customised 1988 pink 2CV.

Diamonds & Dust is her first adult novel.

The Victorian Detectives series

Diamonds & Dust
Honour & Obey
Death & Dominion
Rack & Ruin
Wonders & Wickedness
Intrigue & Infamy

Acknowledgments

Many thanks Gina Dickerson of RoseWolf Design, for the superb cover. To the following people, who always encourage and support me: Terry, Shelley, the two Sues, Ros, Barb, Rosie, Val, Jo, Anne, Brenda and Sheila, my editors, not forgetting numerous friends on Twitter and Facebook ... many thanks.

Most of all, I owe a debt that is un-payable to all those wonderful Victorian authors whose work I have shamelessly plundered, paraphrased and pastiched. Without them, this book would never have been written. I thank them, albeit posthumously.

Wonders & Wickedness

A Victorian Murder Mystery

'What an amazing place London was to me when I saw it in the distance … I made it out in my mind to be fuller of wonders and wickedness than all the cities of the earth.'

Charles Dickens, David Copperfield 1849

'The message is that all things are connected ... who does not understand should either learn, or be silent.'

Dr John Dee, Philosopher & Alchemist

London 1864. It is mid-September and the beginning of evening, a time when day is balanced between twilight and dusk. The temperature has been dropping, and the fog that has been hanging about in alleys and cellars all day is moving back in for the night.

Fog finds its way up from the river and down from the sky, filtering like a melodramatic ghost through cracks and crevices. Tendrils of fog slip in around shutters, sliding into lighted rooms, where they make the candles crackle.

Pause awhile in Oxford Street, that great West End thoroughfare of commerce, lined with shops and edged on both sides with lamp posts that seem to run pell-mell down to the high arch of white marble that marks the beginning of Hyde Park, with its meadows and green rises of trees; its valleys filled with old tufted oaks with gnarled branches.

Not that any of this is visible now, on this particular fog-enwrapped evening. Indeed, to the man peering out through the heavy wooden shutters, it is like trying to see through pale grey velvet.

Afterwards, he thinks there might have been shapes out there, looming in the gloom, moving stealthily in the street, just beyond the blotched streetlights. A background noise of people, echoes of whispers, whispers of echoes. But then a great city like London is never really silent, day or night, is it?

The man's name is John Gould. He is a shop owner. Tomorrow he will celebrate the grand opening of his latest enterprise: a brand-new department store right in the centre of Oxford Street.

The new enterprise has a three-storey high frontage, with a classical portico. There are mahogany fittings throughout the store, an elegant staircase fronting the street, and a customer lift to elevate ladies and gentlemen by a gentle and pleasing process to the upper parts of the building.

There are plate-glass display windows, featuring the latest merchandise brought in from all over the world, and tastefully arranged by expert dressers to tempt in the passing trade.

It will be a store to rival anything London has seen so far, and he hopes its name will live on into the future long after he has gone. He has even designed the colourful street signage himself. It reads: *John Gould & Company: Never Beaten on Price.*

Tonight, Gould is taking a final stroll round the interior of the store, checking that all the shelves are stocked with a variety of goods, that all the wooden counters are clean and polished and ready for trading. Overhead, in a series of cramped dormitories, his serving staff are settling down for the night.

Tomorrow is going to be a day to remember. But not for the reasons he thinks.

***

Rumours can start from nowhere, but once they exist, they spread like wildfire. By first light, drawn by the invisible rumour magnet, a small crowd starts gathering outside John Gould & Company. Many are clearly the sort of people who might pass through the ornate black and gold double doors and purchase the goods for sale within.

Some are not. They are the people with incomes of dubious reliability, the sort who hang around in alleyways or lean against walls waiting for things to happen and hoping there will be opportunities. By early morning they have been joined by others, on the basis that a small crowd always attracts more crowd, because if there wasn't something worth looking at, there wouldn't be a small crowd looking at it in the first place, would there?

Thus, by the time John Gould, resplendent in shiny new top hat, sky-blue waistcoat, black frock coat and matching trousers, alights from his carriage, accompanied by Mrs Gould in forest green velvet and a fashionable bonnet, the press of people outside the store is such that the coachman has to flick his whip across various shoulders to clear a pathway to the entrance.

Gould strides through the waiting people, a pleased smile on his face. This is better than he could have hoped. He signals to the four burly store room men, who are waiting with long hooked wooden poles to remove the heavy wooden shutters.

They begin to do their job. A palpable air of excitement runs through the onlookers. Reaching the store entrance, Gould turns, and throws wide his arms in an expansive gesture of welcome.

"Friends, customers, this is indeed a great day."

The last window shutter is removed. There is an expectant pause, followed by gasps from those nearest to one of the windows. Someone at the front of the crowd cries out. Others nearby start shouting. There is consternation. Somebody screams. A woman faints. People at the back of the crowd start pushing forward.

Gould pauses, slightly puzzled. He had expected a degree of enthusiasm, but not exactly on this scale.

"I shall continue," he says, raising his voice and eyeing the crowd sternly.

"I think you'd be better off stopping and calling the police," a man in the crowd shouts back.

Finally, Gould senses that something is amiss. He steps out of the doorway. The crowd parts in a Red Sea manner to let him through. He approaches the first big display window, where a mock dining room has been arranged to show the select viands, tableware and household goods stocked in the shop.

Gould is very proud of this particular display. Three shop assistants laboured all day under the direction of the window dresser to set it up. Gould wanted it to convey that here is a genteel upmarket family emporium catering to the 'right' sort of customer.

He remembers the finished window clearly. It was a masterpiece. What he does not remember is a shirt-sleeved man sitting at the foot of the table, his head face down upon the oval mahogany dining table. He is clutching a carving knife in one outstretched hand, and his blood has stained the white damask tablecloth bright crimson.

***

Detective Inspector Leo Stride of Scotland Yard's detective division is a man in dire need of coffee and patience. Sadly, both are temporarily unavailable. The coffee is tantalisingly close though; he can smell its fragrant aroma coming from his favourite coffee stall outside Cox & Greenwood's.

The trier of his patience is a lot closer. Actually, it is standing right in front of him with its arms folded. It is clad in greasy corduroys, a black shiny hat, a tweed jacket that has seen better days but never participated in them, and the fixed eager expression of a man with a grievance.

"Yes, Mr Cretney," Stride says with a world-weary sigh. "How may I help you this morning?"

At least twice a week for as long as Stride can recall, Rancid Cretney, retired businessman and now active member of the Union of London Busybodies has managed to catch him on his way in to work. It is uncanny how the man seems to know exactly when Stride will be turning into Craig's Court.

Stride has tried varying his arrival times to escape him. No use. At some point on his journey, the man will always step out from behind a pillar, or from the midst of a crowd, waving his hand and demanding attention in a loud voice. It is uncanny and disconcerting. And a damn nuisance.

Rancid Cretney purses his mouth and assumes his 'concerned citizen' face.

"It's those people next door. Again. They bin moving about."

"And that is a crime, in your opinion?"

"It is when you do it at one in the morning. I could hear them through the wall."

Stride opens his notebook and takes a step back. Although Mr Cretney may have quit the feline provisions market some time ago, the smell of his former employment (and source of his first name) has yet to quit him completely.

"Could you be a bit more precise, Mr Cretney? What exactly did you hear?"

Rancid Cretney rasps his nails across his stubbly chin.

"It sounded like they was dragging something across the floor. Then there was some more of that chanting they do, and then it all went quiet. Then there was this shout, and someone slammed the front door and legged it down the street."

"Did you see who it was?"

Cretney draws himself up to his full height, which is slightly less than five feet.

"No, I didn't. Coz why? Coz I ain't a-going to go looking out of my window at one in the morning. Who do you think I am? I listened for a bit more, and when I didn't hear anyfink, I went back to sleep."

Stride closes the notebook.

"So, are you going to investigate?" Cretney asks. "Sounded very suspicious to me."

"Mr Cretney. This is the umpteenth time you have stopped me to complain about your neighbours. May I suggest that instead of wasting police time, you just go round, knock on their door and ask them what they're up to. Have you ever thought of that?"

There is a pause while Rancid Cretney, who is slightly hard of thinking, mentally processes this.

"I couldn't do that. I'm not some interfering busybody."

In the face of this palpable untruth, Stride is rendered speechless.

"I'm just a law-abiding citizen doing my duty," Cretney continues with an air of unctuous self-righteousness.

Stride ponders the truth of this. From his perspective as a detective, nobody is entirely law abiding; there is always the latent potential in every individual to commit some crime, even unwittingly. Meanwhile Rancid Cretney, an underdog who is never going to be an overdog however hard he tries, stands awaiting the outcome of his latest complaint.

"I shall get one of my officers to look into it," Stride says at last.

"You said that last week."

"Indeed."

"And the week before. So when can I expect somebody to turn up?"

"When I have an officer free. Now if you will excuse me, I am a very busy man and there are important matters to be dealt with. Good day to you."

Stride spins on his heel and heads swiftly for the front entrance of Scotland Yard before his ear can be bent with further complaints.

"Oi ~ I haven't finished," Cretney calls after him. "I pay my taxes. I know my rights. Something's going on in that house. I made a serious complaint. Another serious complaint. It's your DUTY to take it seriously!"

Alas, his words fall upon thin air. Muttering angrily about the farces of law and order, Rancid Cretney kicks a passing urchin into the gutter and goes to drown his grievances in a pint of porter at a local hostelry.

The bells of the city are chiming the hour as Detective Inspector Stride enters his place of work. Middle aged, with thinning hair, pouchy eyes and wearing a crumpled brown suit, he is known to his colleagues as a man with a fearsome reputation for bulldog tenacity, coupled with an equally fearsome ability to take on board more caffeine than is probably healthy.

Stride checks with the desk constable to see if anything interesting has been reported by the night shift. Nothing has. Then he slopes off to his small paperwork-heavy office, where Detective Sergeant Jack Cully is waiting for him.

"Morning Jack. I see you got in early as well," Stride observes.

"Violet is teething," comes the laconic reply. "You?"

"Painters."

They share a silent moment of communality at the altar of hard-pressed husbands.

"And worse luck, it looks like being a reading-the-paperwork sort of a day and I bloody hate reading paperwork," Stride growls, eyeing the reports piled on his desk with disfavour.

There is the sound of running feet in the corridor, and one of the day constables bursts in, ashen-faced, mud-splashed and out of breath.

"There's a dead man, sir. In a shop window in Oxford Street, sir. With a carving knife. It looks as if he's been ~"

But Detective Inspector Stride, his expression transformed from despair to delight, has pushed back from his desk, grabbed his hat and is already halfway out of the door before the man has finished blurting out his news.

***

The Victorian General Postal Service is the wonder of the age. Every day letters, packets, bills, newspapers, magazines, official documents, comestibles of a varied and sometimes unwholesome nature, together with sundry goods of all types, are dispatched from its grand porticoed headquarters in St Martin's-le-Grand.

There are between ten and twelve daily deliveries. From 7.30 am to 8.30 at night scarlet-coated postmen can be seen trudging the streets of London, which they will assure you are not paved with gold, but with very uneven setted stone and cobbles that play havoc with their boots.

Here is one such scarlet-coated postman now, stepping up to the door of a fine stuccoed four-storey townhouse in the exclusive enclave of a Georgian garden square in Bloomsbury, where Watch Boxes manned by constables serve to keep out undesirables.

The exterior canvas blinds of this house have been rolled up in deference to the passing of summer. A man is repainting the railings dark green, watched by a pretty servant girl who stands in the kitchen area looking up coquettishly.

The letterbox clangs. The letter lands on the tiled floor. It is picked up by the butler (yes, we are moving in the upper echelons of London society now). He checks the name and address, then places the letter on a silver tray and carries it to the queen of this particular urban castle, who is seated in her parlour, not so much eating bread and honey as dictating the week's menus to the cook.

Lady Meriel Wynward picks up an ivory letter-opener. Watched by the cook, she slits open the envelope and draws out a torn piece of paper. Still watched by the cook, Lady Meriel reads the words written thereon.

Then she reaches inside the envelope and pulls out a lock of dark hair, tied with a red ribbon. She utters a low cry, stands up, attempts a few faltering steps and faints dead away onto the richly carpeted floor.

From collops to collapse in under three seconds.

Curious, the cook picks up the sheet of paper and the lock of hair. Her eyes widen and she sucks in her breath sharply. Replacing them both carefully on the carpet by Lady Meriel's outstretched hand, she hurries away to find her master and relay the startling news to him.

***

We move on to another location. This is not an aristocratic townhouse in a leafy square, guarded by police-manned Watch Boxes. This is a small run-down row of cheap terraced houses off Carnaby Street at the back of Regent Street. Here, ladies of the 'soiled dove' variety rent places by the night, selling their bodies to men who fancy their company.

Also from these dingy fetid attic rooms come the beautiful hand-stitched ball gowns for rich young ladies selling their future to men who fancy a well-dowried wife. Same game, but with different rules, more money and better clothing.

And here, in the upper room of a soot-blackened house, a small furtive man has just lit a match under a trivet, upon which is placed a beaker of cloudy liquid. He has long white hair and beard, and a hooked nose that swoops down to thin pale lips.

Look more closely.

The man is wearing a black velvet doublet, black hose and a stiff white ruff. On his head is a small black skull cap that moulds to the shape of his head, ending just above his ears. He might have stepped out of some Elizabethan painting. It is an effect he has taken some trouble to cultivate.

Most of the time, the man goes by the name of Felix Lightowler, and runs a small antiquarian print and book shop close to the British Museum. The rest of the time, he is known to intimates, of whom there are practically none, as Master John Dee, a name he has adopted, along with the appropriate clothing, in honour of his hero: the Elizabethan mystic, seeker after esoteric knowledge and alchemist.

Lightowler's interest in alchemy and Dee started many years ago, when he bought up the library of a deceased Norfolk gentleman, a recluse, and found amongst the learned books on classical history and Biblical exegesis, a short hand-written tome by Erasmus Romanus, an obscure monk living at Westminster Abbey in the fourteenth century. It was titled *The Boke of the Nature of the Secrets of the Quintessence.*

Perusing its yellow pages, sprinkled with brown dots of mould and possibly vintage food stains, he had discovered a translation of Avicenna's great work on metals and their transmutation, along with hand-written notes describing the results of Romanus' own experiments.

The journey from interest to obsession is a lot shorter than people think. It wasn't long before Lightowler was haunting libraries and booksellers all over the country and abroad, seeking out astrological and alchemic texts and poring over the spidery writings that described the search for the Philosopher's Stone, which could turn any base metal into gold, and the Elixir of life that bestowed youth and immortality.

As a result of his efforts, he has now acquired a large collection of ancient esoterica, most of it written by the sort of people for whom daylight and sanity were alien concepts. And because nothing escapes the man in the street, he has also acquired a small collection of followers, attracted mainly by the lure of making gold, although they pretend it is the study of ancient texts that fascinates them.

The water in the beaker starts bubbling, emitting a cloud of grey steam. He removes it carefully, pouring the liquid into a china receptacle containing a small handful of brownish dried leaves, and allows it to infuse for a while. Then he adds some sugar, and sits down to enjoy his tea.

The tea drunk, Lightowler changes into his street clothes, which are of a plain, nondescript blending-in nature. He pulls on a top hat and long dark overcoat and sets off, slinking along the inside of the pavement and keeping his face averted from passers-by.

Lightowler reaches the shop, unlocks the door and prepares to open up for business. He takes down the shutters and hauls the bulks of books out onto the pavement. People heading for the British Museum, guidebooks in hand, pause to peer at the yellowing antique prints of classical scenes, or flick through the cheap second-hand books on London and its environs.

At the end of the day Lightowler will pack the books away, shutter up the shop and then return home, where he will await the arrival of the apprentice alchemists. Tonight, they are going to direct a *'Triall touching the Maturing of Metalls involving a Concoction or Disgestion'* and see if the end-result might be the production of gold.

A busy day lies ahead. Followed by an equally busy night.

***

Meanwhile, a short distance away in Oxford Street, Georgio de Lesseps, window dresser and 'departmental stylist', stands at the rear entrance to the display window, now covered from top to bottom with a black cloth to deter prying eyes.

"Nooooo," the dresser wails, wringing his finely-manicured hands. "The best patterned damask in London. There was nothing like it. And now someone is bleeding all over it."

"Has bled," Detective Inspector Leo Stride says. "Past tense. Bleeding would imply that the death took place quite recently, whereas I'm afraid the gentleman, whoever he was, is ex-sanguinated, as our police surgeon will no doubt tell us shortly. What do you think, Jack?"

Detective Sergeant Jack Cully nods.

"Sounds like the sort of word he'd use."

De Lesseps takes a fine lawn handkerchief from his silk waistcoat pocket and dabs at his eyes.

"Tone on tone floral sateen damask, completely reversible. And a set of matching table napkins. It took me months to find them. Look at them now ~ ruined. Completely ruined!"

Stride gently pushes him out of the way, then steps into the window display area.

"Has anybody handled or moved anything since the body was discovered?"

"Nobody, detective inspector," Gould says from the passageway. "As soon as I realised what had happened, the door to the window area was locked and one of my men was sent post haste over to Scotland Yard to fetch you. I'm completely baffled as to why somebody would want to kill themselves in my shop window."

"Oh? You think it was suicide?"

"I do. There's a carving knife in his left hand, inspector. You can see it clearly from the street."

"Ah ... so there is. Perhaps you could tell my colleague exactly what happened, to the best of your knowledge while I make an examination of the body. Then I'd like everyone who works here to take a look at the man. Maybe the victim is known to one of your staff.

"After that I'd like you to set up an interview room somewhere quiet so that we can talk to the staff and find out exactly where they were, and who they were with last night. You are, of course, welcome to attend each interview."

"Will I be able to open the shop after you've finished?" Gould asks tentatively. "This was supposed to be our first day trading. I have several reporters from the London newspapers due at eleven."

Once again Stride marvels at the resilience of the human spirit. A man dies a horrific death, but the show, or in this case the buying and selling must go on.

"I'm sorry, your department store is now a crime scene and will remain closed until I have satisfied myself that nobody on the premises is involved in any way. I'll let you know when you can reopen," he says shortly.

As Jack Cully shepherds off a disgruntled Gould and the still-whimpering dresser, Stride gets out his notebook and sets about his grisly task. He spends some time observing the scene, noting the exact position of the dead man, the way he lies on the table, one arm outstretched, the other bent under his head.

He checks the floor area for any boot marks or bloodstains leading to or from the table. Finally, he approaches the body and looks for any indications of a violent struggle, such as might indicate that the death of the poor unfortunate was homicide rather than suicide.

Stride observes that the man's head is positioned at an awkward angle, facing inward. It lies in a pool of blood, some of which has clotted the hair. A deep gash, like a red grin, stretches from just below his ear to under his chin. It is clear that this is the cause of his death. And there in his hand is the weapon that inflicted the death wound.

And yet.

Stride stares down at the man. Something is not quite right. He knows that suicidal wounds generally follow the natural movement of the arm from left to right or reverse, if the person is left-handed. Here, the wound clearly indicates a right-handed individual. Yet the knife is gripped in the man's left hand.

So, somebody clearly wanted the death to look like suicide. But all the initial evidence in front of Stride indicates that this man died not at his own hand, but at the hand of another. He continues making notes until he is joined by Cully.

"I've got the staff lined up ready to view the body, and Mr Gould is letting us use his office for the interviews."

Stride nods.

"Take a look at him, will you, Jack. Tell me what you observe."

Detective Sergeant Jack Cully has worked with Stride long enough to recognise that tone of voice. Without responding, he takes a couple of steps into the room then focuses his full attention upon the prone figure.

"The knife is in the wrong hand, isn't it?"

"Ah. You noticed. Keep looking."

"It's clearly the knife from the carver set at the head of the table. But there's no blood or anything on the blade."

"Indeed. Keep looking."

"Actually, there isn't a lot of blood anywhere else either, is there?"

"Continue."

"If someone had cut his throat in here, he'd have fought back and there'd be pools of blood and signs of a struggle, wouldn't there? Plates smashed, that sort of thing. Maybe footprints leading away from the murder scene."

"Go on. There's more."

"But if his throat was cut *before* his death and he was brought here *afterwards,* there'd be a trail of blood leading from the shop floor to the window. You couldn't miss it. And we haven't spotted any blood anywhere other than on the table itself."

"Well done," Stride says quietly. "My thoughts exactly."

"So, what are we presuming?"

Detective Inspector Stride shuts up his notebook and replaces it in an inside pocket.

"Right now, Jack, I don't know. It's a puzzler. I think we will have to wait until our good police surgeon has examined the body. There are several aspects of the case that do not make sense. Hopefully they will after the post-mortem report. In the meantime, let's see if anybody can shed some light on who he might be. Or was."

Stride positions himself and his notebook on the opposite side of the 'room'. From here he can see every person's face as they enter, and study their initial reaction as they view the corpse for the first time.

As each member of staff files into the window space, he watches them carefully. Some shake their head. Some look horrified. A couple vomit into their pocket handkerchiefs. A young woman has to be supported out by a colleague. After all the staff have passed through, observed, and been observed in turn, Stride rejoins Cully.

"The men are here to collect the body," Cully tells him.

"I think we can let them remove it. None of the staff seemed to recognise him. Shame. Would have saved us some time. Now we're going to have to send death notifications round to all the police offices. I'll head back and set things in motion our end. You get on with interviewing the staff. Begin with Mr Gould ~ and impress on him that nobody is to speak of this matter to the press. Make sure that he understands that *very* clearly."

Stride makes his way to the back of the store and thence out of the staff entrance. He pauses to examine the door, the handle and the area on either side. He walks slowly up the narrow alleyway, keeping his eyes fixed on the ground until he emerges into the watery sunshine of Oxford Street.

The crowd are still gathered outside the department store, engaging in London's traditional pastime of hanging around to see what might happen next. A few stalls have magically appeared, along with some sandwich-board men advertising the charms of other emporia.

Further down the street, cabs and carriages are drawn up along the curb, horse to rear axle, waiting for people to emerge from various other stores, their purchases parcelled up and carried by one of the sales assistants.

Stride has never got the hang of this department store mania. Why spend your money buying stuff you didn't need before you saw it and probably won't even like two weeks after you've bought it? The concept is lost on him, though Mrs Stride keeps trying to persuade him to take her 'shopping Up West.'

Also waiting, though not so prominently, are the usual quota of beggars, cripples, freaks, barefoot street children, Italian musicians, crossing sweepers, ragged girls selling lucifer matches, and the rest of the human detritus that spends its short life on the streets, unnoticed and uncared for.

Stride marvels that a city boasting it is the richest in the world contains people whose only crime is to have no money, no friends, no clothes and no place of refuge, thus reducing them to living and dying on doorsteps, in gutters, under dark arches, in ditches and along the lees of walls.

He knows exactly what lies in the lanes which open off Oxford Street, just a few footsteps behind the opulent gold and plate glass world of John Gould. Here are sooty ill-constructed old houses, the ancient walls crumbling, door posts and window frames loose and rotten. Here are stifling courts and alleys thick with human sewage, and troops of pale children crouching on filthy staircases, heads hanging, shaking with cold.

Stride returns to Scotland Yard to discover a group of the force's least favourite London inhabitants camped outside. The news of the dead man in Gould's window has already legged it round to Fleet Street. He lowers his head, turns up his collar and gets ready to shove his way through to the front step.

"Oi Stride, watch what you're doing!" protests the familiar voice of Richard Dandy, chief reporter on *The Inquirer*.

"What I am 'doing', *Mr* Dandy, is trying to go about my lawful business, which is investigating crime. You are currently preventing me from doing so by blocking the doorway," Stride responds tartly.

"Read our lunchtime headlines yet?"

Dandy waves a copy of *The Inquirer* in the air. Stride can just make out the words:

Gruesome Discovery! Mystery of Unknown Man's Body Found in Oxford Street Shop Window! How Did He Get There?

"First to break the story. As per," Dandy says smugly, looking round his fellow hacks and grinning.

"Only coz we don't print a midday edition," a fellow penny-a-liner growls.

By the judicious use of his elbows, Stride has now reached the entrance.

"So, Stride, you got any idea who he was?"

"Detective Inspector Stride. And if by 'he' you mean the unfortunate man referred to in your newspaper ~ then no, not yet," Stride says without turning round.

"Any of you hacks want to lay a wager I'll have the name by the end of the day?" Dandy grins.

Now Stride turns, his face dark with fury.

"I'm sorry you find the death of a fellow human being a source of amusement, Mr Dandy," he says, icicles hanging from every syllable, "Perhaps your editor might take a different view. I shall write and ask him."

Detective Inspector Stride barrels into the outer office, his thoughts verging upon the unprintable.

"If I had my way, every blasted member of the popular press would be arrested for crimes against honesty," he growls at the desk sergeant. "Find a broom, would you sergeant, and then go and clear the riffraff off our steps."

The desk sergeant, well aware of Stride's views, furtively stuffs the lunchtime copy of *The Inquirer* under his desk to read later, before heading for the door to carry out his superior officer's orders.

***

Meanwhile, in the parlour of a fine stuccoed four-storey townhouse, in the exclusive enclave of a Georgian square, elucidation is also being sought. Though of a different kind. Sir Hugh Wynward is seated by his wife's side, the communication and the lock of hair on the round table in front of them.

"That it should arrive today of all days," Lady Meriel murmurs, mopping her eyes. "Oh, it is too cruel."

Wynward picks up the envelope.

"Posted yesterday. Doesn't say where it's come from."

"But the hair ..."

"Yes. Indeed."

Lady Meriel turns her helpless face to her husband.

"So, what are we going to do?" she quavers.

Wynward rises, walks to the window and stands before it, hands behind his back. When he turns to face his wife, his expression is set and grim.

"I tell you what we're not going to do, and that's employ another of those private detectives. I'm not forking out good money to be told I'm left-handed, own a pair of shooting boots, sometimes smoke Indian cigars and carry a silver cigar case and a blunt penknife in my pocket. Not this time."

"But we ..."

"And no more séances and table-rapping and mumbo-jumbo and that's my last word on the matter. I forbid it. Do you understand?"

"But I ..."

"We are going to have to bite the bullet and call in the police. Whatever the consequences."

Lady Meriel bites her lower lip, twisting her handkerchief.

"Are you sure?" she quavers.

Sir Hugh waves her doubts away.

"I shall retire to my study and compose a suitable communication which I will dispatch at once to Scotland Yard. There is no point discussing the matter further. Now pull yourself together. You must not let the servants see you in this state."

He reaches for the bell. When the parlour maid enters, Wynward orders her abruptly to fetch some tea for her mistress. Then he picks up the note, the lock of hair and the envelope and carries them all out of the room without another word being spoken.

***

Stride frets his way through the morning. He writes up the death notice for the murdered man, and arranges for it to be printed and sent round to the other police offices in the vicinity. He deals with the top strata of paperwork, reading reports, and moving stuff from one side of the desk to the other, until eventually one of the young constables brings him a cup of steaming coffee.

After hunting around for a clear spot, and failing to find one, the constable places the cup cautiously on a newly emerged report, yellowing, covered with dust and labelled *'Urgent'*.

Stride picks up the cup and gulps down the bitter black brew.

"Right," he mutters grimly. "Time to see what Robertson has to say about our mysterious corpse."

The police mortuary at Scotland Yard is a plain whitewashed room located off the main building. Windowless, its wooden shelves contain bottles and cork-stoppered jars. Medical instruments are laid out on the counter. The air smells of cold and chemicals and finality.

In the centre is the scrubbed table with its drainage outlets, the saws, drills and knives, the body laid out on a slab like in an old-fashioned butcher's shop. A stark reminder of what so-called civilised man is underneath. Meat for worms.

Robertson the police surgeon, a raised eyebrow in human form, greets Stride with his usual air of dry detachment, honed over many years of observing the inner workings of humanity, generally via an assortment of small glass dishes.

"Good morning, detective inspector. I wondered when you'd drop by. Alas I have very little to tell you at this stage, having only just commenced examining the gentleman in question."

"What can you tell me?" Stride says.

He folds his arms and fixes his gaze firmly on a point slightly above the body lying on the mortuary slab. The police surgeon notices and smiles.

"Ah, inspector, I see once again you display your customary distaste for the fascinating autopsy process. What a shame. Just think ~ one day, this might be you."

"Thankfully I won't be here when it is."

The police surgeon gives a dry little chuckle.

"Possibly not. Possibly not."

He gestures towards the body.

"Well-fed. Prime of life. Expensive clothing. Silk shirt. His shoes are fine leather and hand-stitched."

"We don't think he died at his own hand. The wound to his throat did not match the hand holding the knife," Stride says.

The police surgeon regards him speculatively.

"Ah. So, your presumption therefore is that this man was slain by another hand? Most unfortunate."

Life is unfortunate, Stride thinks. Why should death be any different?

"He could hardly cut his own throat, then calmly sit down and transfer the knife to his other hand, could he?"

A gleam of triumph appears in the police surgeon's eye.

"Ah now that, inspector, is where you might just be mistaken."

Stride braces himself. This particular expression is always the precursor to some lecture on forensic medicine.

"Let me refer you back to September 1833," the surgeon begins happily, rocking slightly on his feet. "A man walking down Oxford Street cuts his throat with a razor, dividing the carotid artery, the jugular vein on one side and the trachea, *and yet* he was still able to run four yards before dropping dead on the pavement. Now, what do you make of that?"

"Well, I ..."

"In similar vein (if you will pardon the expression), I cite the case of a certain army officer, found dead in his room a few years later in September 1838. In this instance, the head was nearly severed from his body. There was no doubt in anybody's mind at the time that the act was suicidal, yet the razor had been put on the man's dressing-table."

"So, you think ..."

"Inspector, you know my methods by now. I do not 'think' or 'speculate', or 'make assumptions' based upon superficial evidence. I deal in facts. As yet, I have very few of them to go on, but I know that conclusions based upon appearance are often deceptive. Oh ~ and I found this envelope in the gentleman's waistcoat pocket."

He hands over a small crumpled envelope. On it is written the single word *To*. Stride looks inside. There is a piece of letter paper. *Numbers 32.23.*

He frowns.

"To whom? And what's numbers 32 and 23 ~ some sort of gambling?"

The police surgeon rolls his eyes.

"I think, detective inspector, you would do better to search for the answer in the bible. The book of Numbers, chapter 32, verse 23: *'Be sure your sin will find you out'*. And now, if you'll permit me, I should like to proceed with my examination. You will receive my report in due course."

Stride returns to the main building, where the day sergeant behind the desk is dealing with a small queue of Indignant Citizens with Legitimate Grievances.

"Got a bible on you?" Stride inquires as he passes.

The sergeant shakes his head.

"Know where I can lay my hands on one?"

Another head-shake.

Stride clicks his teeth disapprovingly.

"You'd have thought everybody would carry a bible in their pocket."

"I'm sure one of the men will have a bible in their locker," the sergeant says. "If you give me a minute, I'll go and inquire."

Stride returns to his office where he spends some time staring at the wall and thinking. A man who may or may not have taken his own life. An unsigned note containing a verse from the bible about sin and punishment. Investigating any murder was hard enough. Throw in the Deity and it became nigh on impossible.

As yet, Stride does not understand much of what has been going on, but he is pretty sure, from previous experience, that it is only going to continue, and will probably get worse.

***

London. Sprawling, brawling. Immense and immeasurable. Once it was possible to walk through every street. No longer. Nobody can now know the whole of the city thoroughly. It grows, and spreads; it has its secret places. It can be mapped, but never imagined. It must be taken on faith, not upon reason.

The great rebuilding spree has destroyed old gabled shops and tenements, the quaint inns with their galleried courtyards where coaches came rattling in to discharge passengers. They have been replaced by rows of new houses in brilliant limestone or burnished brick and terracotta.

New buildings appear on the surface, railways burrow beneath. Old London is being obliterated by another strange city that seems to rise up through it, like a phantom in a mist. The urge to drive huge thoroughfares from one side to another, to erect great monuments, is creating a chaos of demolition and reconstruction.

The city is changing its inhabitants for better or worse. Crushing them under the sheer magnitude of the place. London is now so large that any opinion, any vice or virtue could be held. There is energy and zeal and inventiveness. But the city is also monstrous, full of the bitter tears of those it has displaced and cast out.

**

Luckily few bitter tears are being shed at Sally's Chop House, a dark, low-ceilinged place off Fleet Street where the food arrives hot and covered in enough thick brown gravy to disguise its possible provenance and quality.

It is Detective Inspector Stride's favourite hangout, and in the absence of Detective Sergeant Jack Cully, who is conducting interviews at John Gould's, he has turned up for a bite to eat and a cogitate.

Stride always sits on his own in the same back booth, where he is currently being watched by the eponymous Sally, a huge man who wears a food-stained apron and a rather puzzled expression. The former is the mark of his profession. The latter has been provoked by what Stride is reading.

Sally clears his throat and edges closer.

"Everything to your satisfaction, Mr Stride?"

"Yes, no complaints, Sally," Stride says without looking up.

He licks a finger and turns a page.

"I see as how you are reading the Good Book," Sally says, assuming an air of pious reflection.

"Borrowed it."

"Ah. Explains it. I thought to myself: Mr Stride normally comes in here and reads the noospaper. Loudly. Bit of a shock to see you reading the bible ~ not that I'm saying there's anything wrong with it, this being a Christian country an' all."

Is it? Stride thinks grimly. The longer he works at Scotland Yard, the more he doubts in the gospel of the innate goodness of man. In Stride's experience, there is practically nothing people won't do, given either the opportunity or the offer of financial reward.

He eyes Sally thoughtfully.

"*Make me to know mine end, and the measure of my days, what it is, that I may know how frail I am,*" he says.

"I'm very sorry to hear that, Mr Stride," Sally says, shaking his head. "Sorry indeed. Though I have to say, you've been looking a bit peaky for a while."

"Don't worry, Sally, I intend to be with you for quite a while yet."

Sally adopts the blank facial expression that he finds usually works best with this particular customer.

"That's good then, innit. Nother pot of ale? Bit more gravy to go with your reading?"

Stride pushes back his plate.

"No thank you. Must be on my way. Paperwork to sort. Always paperwork. Sometimes wish I had your job."

Sally doubts this. He is not sure Stride would have the patience to deal with some of his more demanding customers ~ present company generally excepted.

"Oi, Mr Stride," he calls after the departing figure, "You left your bible on the table."

But his words fall upon empty air. Stride has pushed open the chop house door and departed.

Sally carries Stride's half-eaten plate over to the counter. When he returns to wipe the table, the bible has departed also.

***

Detective Inspector Stride returns to Scotland Yard. As Cully is still not back from John Gould's department store, he spends some time trying to achieve the paperless office by hiding documents in a cupboard until one of the station sergeants appears in the doorway, carrying an envelope.

"What is it now?" Stride snaps.

"Sir Hugh Wynward has sent his footman over with a letter."

Stride raises his eyebrows. Members of the aristocracy rarely communicated with members of the constabulary unless they had something to complain about. Which they usually did at length, using big words written in fancy slanting writing.

"Really? What does he want, I wonder? Hand it over then."

He breaks the seal on the letter and reads:

I request the presence of a senior police detective here at my home as soon as possible. Something of a very strange and untoward nature has just occurred.
Hugh Wynward

As this isn't the usual sort of communication he generally receives, Stride reads the letter through a couple more times. Then he gets up. He might as well go and pay this Sir Hugh Wynward a visit. It is either that or get on with the paperwork. And he loathes paperwork even more than he dislikes the aristocracy.

A short while later, Detective Inspector Stride finds himself standing outside an imposing black painted door with a shiny brass knocker in the shape of a lion's head. Above the door is an intricate tracery fanlight. The black and white tiles he stands upon are so pristine and sparkling that he could eat his dinner off them, though he guesses it unlikely the owner of the house would permit him to do so.

Stride knocks.

The door is answered by a tall broad-shouldered butler in afternoon attire. He looks down his nose disapprovingly. Stride hands his official card.

"Detective Inspector Leo Stride, Scotland Yard. Your master requested a visit," he says briskly.

The butler stands aside to allow him to enter the dark hallway, then nods silently towards one of the straight-backed hall chairs. Stride makes himself as comfortable as the situation allows. The man stalks off, carrying the card gingerly between thumb and forefinger as if it were a piece of unpleasant detritus blown in by the wind.

Time passes.

Stride studies the heap of visiting cards on the hall table by his elbow. They all seem to be from people with fancy names. Many of the cards bear crests at the top.

Rich women with irritating voices and men who look down their noses at anybody without a title.

Nobody comes to fetch him.

He gets up and turns his attention to the paintings that hang on both walls and extend up the staircase. Most of them seem to be hunting scenes depicting stags being ripped apart by packs of hounds. There are also various classical statues on wooden plinths. The sort of *objets* acquired by rich collectors.

The grandfather clock ticks loudly.

A housemaid appears, regards him curiously, and then vanishes into the depths of the house. Stride checks the time. He has been waiting for twenty minutes. Long enough. He decides to leave. Whatever is bothering Sir Hugh Wynward, it is clearly not important enough to call him away from his current business.

He opens the front door and stands on the top step, taking a deep breath. So much for the aristocracy and their time-wasting behaviour. Almost at once he becomes aware of movement behind him. He turns. A man stands in the hallway, arms folded, observing him curiously.

Thin to the point of emaciation, and dressed in mourning attire with a spotless white cravat tied round his neck, the man's pale high-cheekboned face is framed by dark hair streaked with grey. He has steel grey eyes under hooded lids. He reminds Stride of one of the vultures in the Zoological Gardens.

"Detective Inspector ~ leaving already?" The voice is chilly, clipping every syllable precisely. There is an unblinking quality to it.

"I presumed that you had changed your mind," Stride says.

Sir Hugh Wynward turns and gestures towards the interior of the house.

"Pray enter," he says.

Stride follows Sir Hugh back into the house, down the long corridor and into a large sitting room. A fire flickers coldly in the black marble fireplace. On either side is a gas jet, hissing gently in globes of pink and white. Dark red paper covers the walls. Gilt-framed portraits of family members stare out disdainfully. More statues perch on wooden plinths.

"I was engaged upon important business. Alas, it could not be put off," Wynward says. He pulls out a chair. "Please sit down, detective inspector and let me explain why I have summoned you here."

Stride sits. Wynward takes an envelope from the mantelpiece and hands it to him.

"Please appraise yourself of the contents of this communication."

Stride opens the envelope and draws out a lock of dark hair, tied in a red ribbon, and a small piece of paper, torn and crumpled at the edges. On the paper, written in a round schoolgirlish hand, are two words:

Remember me

He looks up.

"It came by the first morning post," Wynward says.

"I see," Stride says, not seeing.

"Our daughter Sybella ~ whose hair and ribbon that is, and whose handwriting my wife says she recognises, died a year ago in a train accident. She lies buried in the family plot in Highgate Cemetery. Had she lived, today would have been her eighteenth birthday."

Wynward looks straight ahead, his expression remote.

"My wife has never accepted that Sybella is dead. She believes that she has been given certain 'signs' over the year that the girl is still alive. Now this letter arrives. My wife is of a nervous disposition, and has reacted strongly to the communication. I should like the *truth* of the matter to be ascertained, once and for all. That is why I have called you in."

"You think your daughter may be alive somewhere?"

Cold grey eyes stare into his.

"I think that somebody may be trying to convince us of this. I am not a gullible man, inspector. But neither am I one to be made a fool of. Seek out the person, or persons behind this letter. Then let me know what you have found. I will deal with the matter from thence forward."

***

Highgate Cemetery, London's most fashionable necropolis, perches on a hill overlooking the smoke and filth of the city, not that the inhabitants are in need of clean air and green-groved surroundings. Here is the final resting place of many celebrated individuals, including George Wombwell, menagerie owner, and F.W. Lillywhite, the cricketer who invented round-arm bowling.

Here too, lies Lizzie Siddal, wife and muse of the poet Dante Gabriel Rossetti. She is buried with a manuscript of her grief-stricken husband's poems. At some time in the near future, he will have second thoughts about his decision, and have her dug up so that he can get the manuscript back.

Grief affects people in a variety of different ways.

Detective Inspector Stride stands by the burial place of a girl who can communicate beyond the grave. Or so it seems. A white marble angel guards the final resting place of Sybella Wynward. Her headstone reads:

Sybella Marianna Wynward, 1846-1863

Beloved and only daughter of Sir Hugh and Lady Meriel Wynward.
'Taken too soon'

Stride watches small grey rain clouds massing in the distance and thinks about the events leading up to the young woman's death: Sybella was travelling to Brighton to visit a former school friend, with the intention of accompanying the family to Italy for the summer.

She was very excited at the prospect, and had begged her parents to allow her to take the train, rather than endure the long and uncomfortable journey in the family carriage.

Against his better judgement, Wynward agreed, reserving a seat for her and for one of the maids in a first-class carriage. He accompanied them both to London Bridge Station, saw them both safely installed with picnic hamper, then he'd waved his daughter good-bye and set off back home.

That was the last time he and his wife had seen Sybella alive.

The first inkling that something was wrong, came in the form of a newsboy's shout. There had been a train smash on the Brighton line. Wynward heard it on his way back from his city broker firm, but strode on by barely registering the news. He reached his home to discover the whole house in turmoil.

A telegram had arrived from the friend's father informing him that Sybella and the train she was travelling on had not arrived at Brighton. Now seriously alarmed, and with the words of the newsboy ringing in his ears, Wynward had hastened to London Bridge Station, where he was informed that there had indeed been a terrible rail accident just outside Brighton.

Two trains, a passenger train and a goods train had collided head on and at speed. Further questions elicited the terrible disclosure that one of the trains had been Sybella's. Wynward hastened to Brighton. By the time he got there, the railway police, with help from the fire brigade and local volunteers, had completed the gruesome task of removing bodies from the wreck of the two trains, and from the surrounding area, where many had been thrown upon impact.

Wynward visited the city morgue. There he'd discovered the remains of his seventeen-year-old daughter. Her body was horribly burned and unrecognisable, but he was able to identify it as Sybella's from fragments of her red shawl. The body of the maidservant had never been recovered from the burned-out carriage.

And now, like Lazarus, the young woman had come forth. Apparently. So where is the elusive Miss Sybella Wynward, Stride thinks? On earth or in Heaven? For sure as eggs are eggs, she could not be in both places simultaneously.

***

Leaving Stride to contemplate the mortal/immortal paradigm, let us head for the pleasant and reasonably respectable environs of Hampstead. Alighting from the omnibus, we cross the road and make our way to Flask Walk, one of the small side streets running off the populous High Street.

There we find the Lily Lounge, a fashionable tea-room. It is currently full of customers enjoying pots of tea and a selection of the scones and excellent cakes that are all baked on the premises. Waitresses carrying laden trays rush to and fro, while the owner of the teashop, Mrs

Lilith Marks, surveys the busy scene from behind the wooden counter.

Lilith Marks is an imposing woman, her black silk dress enhancing her full figure, her dark hair pinned and coiled round her head. Few of the customers, mainly ladies who have been shopping, and gentleman hosting pretty female companions who are probably not their wives, would guess at her former profession.

Lilith writes out the bill for table four, and hands it to one of the waitresses. In the old days, her 'customers' would have left their money on the nightstand before making their way out into the night-time street. Now she owns four tea-shops, and has just successfully secured a concession to supply cakes and pastries to a newly opened West End department store.

Suddenly the tea-room door is thrust violently open and a distressed young woman clutching a small bag hurries inside. Head down, she makes her way to the counter, where she bursts into tears. The noisy chatter of light conversation ceases abruptly, as every eye swivels round to see what is amiss.

"Why Violet, what on earth is the matter?" Lilith asks, hurriedly shepherding the sobbing one into a back room and thus out of sight of the customers.

"Oh ma'am, you'll never guess what's happened," the young woman wails.

Lilith sits the hapless Violet down, pours her a cup of tea, then sits down herself.

"Drink this while it is hot. Then pull yourself together and tell me why you have turned up now and in such a state."

Alternating sobs with sips, Violet finishes the tea, rubs her eyes on her coat sleeve, sniffs, and takes a deep breath.

"It's like this ma'am: I arrived at the new place nice and early, just as you asked, ready to help set everything out for morning coffee. Then, just as I was cutting up the bread, one of the managers came and said I had to come with him at once, as there'd been a terrible accident and two detectives had arrived from Scotland Yard.

"I followed him down to the ground floor. All the staff were lined up by one of the big display windows and they were going through one by one. When it came to my turn ~ oh ma'am ~ there was a dead man sitting with his head on the table. His throat was cut and he was holding a knife covered in blood."

Lilith lays a comforting hand on the young woman's arm.

"How dreadful for you! No wonder you were upset."

"That's not the worst of it, ma'am. You see, I recognised him! It was that man who comes in here from time to time ~ the one you said we all had to be careful of and if there was any trouble, to come and tell you at once."

The colour drains from Lilith's face and her eyes harden into darkness. She sucks in her breath sharply.

"What did you say to the police? Did you tell them you recognised him? Think, Violet!"

Violet shakes her head.

"I meant to say something, but I felt I was going to be sick, so I ran out as fast as I could. Then, when the manager said the store wouldn't open today, I tidied everything up and decided to come and tell you. Did I do the right thing?"

"Yes, you did Violet. Exactly the right thing. And now I suggest when you feel better, that you get along home and have a good rest. You've been through a very bad experience."

She gets up, patting Violet on the shoulder.

"Stay here as long as you like. Then go. I'll let you know when you are needed again."

Grim-faced, Lilith buttons up her long velvet coat and pins on her fashionably trimmed hat. She gives the waitresses careful instructions. Then she sets off at a brisk pace. It has started to rain heavily but she barely notices. She walks on through the whispering wet streets, her mind ablaze with possibilities.

***

Rain patters off roof tiles, gurgles along gutters, splashes into soakaways. On a night like this respectable people hurry by, umbrellas held high, faces turned down. On a night like this, the sensible ones stay indoors, nursing teething toddlers, or admiring streaky paint work.

But this is London, the glittering glamorous centre of the universe, so despite the rain, the West End streets are full of crowds ogling shop windows full of tempting goods. Gin palaces, dance halls, supper rooms, music halls and penny gaffs spill light onto pavements, as they welcome their pleasure-seeking customers for another night of revelry.

Away from the brightly-lit attractions however, the devil finds routes for idle feet. Look more closely. Here in an ill-lit backstreet, a sharp-faced young man with incipient ginger sideburns, a spindly moustache and a thin overcoat raps three times at a door. Then repeats the process. Rain drips off his cheap top hat and into his cheap boots.

His name is Eugenius Strictly. By day he is a minor and overlooked clerk in an insurance business, but when the sun goes down upon his labours, he is transmuted into an apprentice alchemist.

The door opens a crack.

"Who be thee who knocks so hard on such a vile night?" a quavering voice whispers into the darkness.

There is a pause while Strictly runs through a couple of possible responses.

"I'm ... er, I am one who seeketh after knowledge," he says finally.

The door is opened wider.

"Then thou art welcome, seeker. Enter and let thy quest for gnosis begin."

Strictly follows the speaker up a flight of dark creaky stairs, through a half-open wooden door, and enters the candlelit attic room, which has been fitted up as a chemical laboratory.

A double row of glass-stoppered bottles line the shelf opposite the door. Small saucers, tripods and beakers of strange coloured liquids are piled in the butler sink and on the wooden draining boards on either side. In one corner stand two large glass carboys in wicker baskets.

An open flame burns merrily under a beaker filled with a bubbling yellow substance.

Two other apprentices stand round watching the beaker closely, their eyes eager, but runny with the fumes.

"Temper the flame, Master Finister," Dee instructs one of the apprentices. "We must keep the metall perpetually molten, such that it quickens and is pliant."

He speaks in a strange high-pitched voice, supposedly resembling that of his Elizabethan alter-ego. Bovis Finister ambles up to the table and turns down the flame under the beaker. He is a rotund, clumsy-fingered young man, with a big smiling face that means well.

"You're late," hisses Jasper Thorogood at the newly arrived apprentice.

"I had stuff to finish, alright? But I'm here now, an't I. What are we working on?"

"Who knows? At least you missed the lecture."

"What was it tonight?"

A shrug.

"Wasn't really paying attention. Ask Fatty ~ he'll probably be able to give you chapter and verse. Laps it all up like a cat in a cream shop, he does. Can't think why. Load of old tosh most of it. *Emerald Tablets* and *The Five Books of Mystery* or something ... all *we* want to know is how to make gold, lots and lots of lovely gold."

Strictly winks at his fellow apprentice.

"Indeed, we do."

He turns his face towards the table and assumes a respectful expression.

"Tell me, oh great Master Dee, what are we doing?"

Dee straightens up, blinking the smoke out of his eyes. He fiddles with his ruff, then addresses his student in the same queer high-pitched voice as before.

"We have embarked upon the next stage of the Great Work, Master Strictly. Tonight we will transmute iron into copper by the method of dissolving the ore in sulphuric acid. When we have the sulphate, we shall add iron to condense the solution by cementation. I invite you to step closer and see the process for yourself."

The two apprentices join their companion at the table. Dee rubs his hands together in an *Elizabethan* sort of way.

"As soon as we have fixated the copper, we will then go on to studie and consider in depth the nature of the higher metals, such as silver and gold. Master Finister, temper the flame once more and make sure no part of the spirit be emitted, we doe not want the body of the metal to be hard and churlish, do we?"

Dee peers at the bubbling liquid in silence. Then he spins round to face the two apprentices. His dark eyes glisten.

"So. While good Master Finister attends the triall, let us turn to other important matters: Have you brought with you the requisite funds, young masters? For without the monies to purchase such compounds as are necessary for the transmutation of metall, we cannot procede any further in our venture.

"This would be a shame as we are now so near to the production of gold, and with it the Stone itself, that will turn a hundred or a thousand times as much lead into pure gold."

Strictly fumbles in his pocket and lays two small coins down on the table.

"This is all I can spare for now. I will bring more next week."

Thorogood opens his purse and adds a further coin.

Dee claws up the money, which disappears into the depths of his black robe.

"You will be well rewarded. My magnum opus is nearing fruition. The alkahest is almost within my grasp. Just a few more weeks and we shall astound the world, young masters ~ yay, verily and forsooth, we shall astound the world!"

It is early next morning when the three apprentices finally quit the attic laboratory of Felix Lightowler aka John Dee, and stagger out into the street. Coughing and wheezing, they lean against a couple of lamp posts and mop their streaming eyes while they fill their lungs with the post-rain air.

"I need a drink of something," Strictly gasps. "That was quite a night."

His eyes blurry, Bovis Finister stares down at something he is carrying. It is wrapped in a cloth.

"Do you think this really is copper?"

The other two apprentices exchange a swift meaningful glance. The glance says that Dee may have chosen to hand the fruit of the night's work over to Finister, but it was not their intention that it should remain with him for long.

"Looks like copper. Hand it over, fat boy, I'll get it tested," Thorogood says, holding out his hand.

Bovis Finister demurs.

"Maybe I should keep it. It was given to me after all. Besides, my mum would like to see some real copper."

"You mum boils her washing and her puddings in a 'real copper'," Strictly sneers. "Hand it over, lump of lard, or it'll be the worse for you. There are two of us, remember ..."

He lets the words hang in the air, tightening his hands into fists.

Sighing resignedly, Finister gives him the lump of copper.

"See you in three days' time," Strictly says. "C'mon Jasper, let's go and get some coffee."

Laughing, the two apprentices head out into the darkness, leaving their erstwhile companion looking glumly at his empty hands.

"He did give it to me though," he murmurs sadly.

But his words fall on empty air. Bovis Finister gives a sad shrug, adjusts his cap and sets off for the small terrace house where he, his widowed mother, several lodgers and his younger sister eke out a perilous living together.

Meanwhile, Strictly and Thorogood seek out a coffee stall. Ignoring the whores hanging around it, they purchase mugs of black bitter coffee and take themselves over to a quiet doorway for a quiet chat.

"Did you take close notes of what the old fool did tonight?" Strictly inquires, blowing on his drink to cool it.

"Got it right here," the other replies, patting his coat pocket. "Everything is down in black and white. Chemicals, amounts, procedures, the lot."

"What's the plan?" Strictly's eyes gleam in the half-light.

"As soon as I've got the press, we will start making coins. Then we will make more copper, and more coins."

"And we'll kiss good-bye to late nights, and boring lectures, and mad old men forever!" Strictly adds gleefully.

"Indeed, my friend. In time. Remember, first we need to know how to make silver, and then more importantly, gold. I don't need to remind you that has always been the plan, and the plan will be carried out to completion."

Thorogood lifts his mug and tips the contents down his throat. The he wipes his finger round the inside, and sucks it.

"And now I shall bid you goodnight, young master," he says, imitating Dee's affected voice.

Strictly grins.

"He is completely mad, in't he?"

"Probably. But if he's the route to riches untold, he can be however he likes. To the future," Thorogood says, chinking his empty cup against Strictly's. "To *our* future, and may our paths be paved with gold."

***

Night wears on. In her nicely appointed bedroom in a very pleasant neighbourhood where the likes of Thorogood and Strictly would never be allowed to enter, a young woman sits at her window, gazing up at the moon.

Miss Constantia Mortram is eighteen. She has plump white shoulders, a small rosebud mouth, large blue eyes and chestnut ringlets. You have seen young girls resembling her on contemporary portraits or fashion plates. She typifies the ideal beauty of the age.

Earlier, Miss Mortram has returned from a party where she wore her brand-new blue silk dress, and bronze slippers. She was the cynosure of all eyes.

Especially all male eyes. Not that she is interested in all male eyes any more ~ for she is about to become engaged to one of the most eligible bachelors in town.

Now, wrapped in a becoming white peignoir and draped in a soft cashmere shawl, she is thinking romantic thoughts, dreaming of young love, and wishing upon one of the bright twinkly stars. As young girls do on nights such as this.

Suddenly, she is aware of a slight movement in the street below. She bends forward, narrowing her eyes. She can just make out the shape of a dark hooded figure, standing in the shadows thrown on the pavement by a street-lamp.

Constantia Mortram gasps. Her throat dries. A thrill runs down her spine. This is exactly like the scene in *Lady Caroline's Clandestine Lovers,* where dark-eyed Byronic hero Captain Francis Stainforth stands beneath the heroine's window, silently worshipping the Beloved before leaving for France and the French Wars, from which, older, wiser and scarred for ever, he will return to claim her for his own.

She is just contemplating what she should do next, when the figure suddenly steps into the flickering gaslight and glances up at her window. The hood falls back slightly, revealing a triangle of chalk-white face. Their eyes meet. Only for a second, but it is enough to freeze her young blood.

Then, just as suddenly as it appeared, the figure disappears, melting into the shadowy dark, but leaving Constantia Mortram breathless, bewildered and shaken. She does not believe in ghosts, she tells herself firmly. But if that is true, what has she just seen?

***

Detective Sergeant Jack Cully is walking to work. It is a wet cold morning, the air raw with the smoke from a million chimneys. The damp feels like a second skin, and his eyelids are swollen and sore, as if they have been stuck together with glue. Cully stifles a yawn. He did not realise that cutting teeth went on for so long. And so loudly.

At one point in the night, he could have sworn that he woke up to see his beloved wife Emily standing bolt upright against the bedroom door, fast asleep on her feet with young Violet Cully propped on her shoulder, sucking her fist and gurgling. Though maybe it was just the result of acute sleep deprivation making him hallucinate.

Yawning, Cully enters Scotland Yard. He is just about to head for Stride's office when he hears his name being called. He turns. A fashionably dressed lady rises from the Anxious Bench ~ the place where families and individuals wait for news of their loved ones.

"Detective Sergeant Cully, a minute of your time please, if you can spare it."

Cully recognises her instantly.

"Mrs Marks! What brings you here so early? Has something happened to you?"

"Perhaps," Lilith says obliquely. "Though not in the way you mean. You have a dead man on your premises, sergeant. I believe he was found yesterday in the window of a West End department store with his throat cut. Am I right?"

Cully's eyes widen. He nods.

"I may know who he is."

He stares at her, eyebrows raised.

"Really? What on earth makes you think that?"

Unperturbed, Lilith meets his gaze.

"May I please see the body?" she pauses, "That is, unless you are one of those men who believe we women are too delicate to view such things."

Cully smiles. Once, he certainly was a member of that group. Marriage to Emily has transferred him out of it for ever.

"I shall ask one of our men to inquire of the police surgeon when it would be convenient to visit the morgue. If you are able to wait?" he adds.

"Oh, I can wait," Lilith says grimly, settling herself back on the bench.

Half an hour later, Cully escorts Lilith Marks over to the police mortuary. The dead man's body lies on the slab, covered for decency's sake by a black cloth. The police surgeon regards Lilith impassively.

"You are sure you wish to perform this task, madam?"

Lilith ignores him. She steps up to the table and pulls back the cloth. There is a swift indrawing of breath, followed by a long silence. Finally, she turns. Her face is ashen, but her dark eyes are lit by a strange inner fire.

"Yes gentlemen, I recognise this man. His name is Montague Foxx. The Honourable Montague Foxx ~ though there was nothing honourable about him in life."

She takes a step back, swaying unsteadily on her feet. Cully reaches out an arm to steady her.

"You are quite sure, Mrs Marks? There is no possibility that you might have mistaken him for somebody else."

Lilith gathers herself together with an effort of will. She turns to face him.

"I am quite sure, detective sergeant. Even after all this time, I think I can still recognise my own husband."

***

Lilith Marks had been fifteen when Montague Foxx, dapper, debonair, debauched young man about town, had first crossed her path. In those days, she'd been Lil Malkovitch, living in Bethnal Green and working in her father's tailoring business.

They'd met by chance. She was delivering a suit to a client's house in the pleasant district of Knightsbridge. He was leaving his bachelor flat for a morning's idleness. As she sauntered past, her dark hair and robin-bright brown eyes, her pliant figure with its delicious curves, stopped him in his tracks.

He followed her and they struck up a bantering conversation in the street. Lilith had a quick wit, even at such a young age, and Foxx's handsome chiselled face, grey eyes and fair wavy hair was a contrast to the heavily bearded, serious young males she'd encountered in her tightly-knit Jewish community.

They didn't even look her in the face, let alone speak to her. She was a woman. *Tref.* Forbidden. It was as if she was invisible. Foxx's eyes appraised her figure in a way that made her blush, and feel hot and shivery inside. He flattered her, made her feel special. No surprise then that she agreed to see him again.

Over the next few months, Montague Foxx clandestinely courted Lily Malkovitch with food, flattery, presents, flowers, and finally coaxed her into his bed. It was Lilith's first experience of sex, terrifying and exciting. She then waited expectantly for Foxx to propose marriage. He did not.

It took time and ingenuity and the withdrawal of further favours, but eventually he agreed to marry her. Her parents were horrified. They beat her, threatened her, locked her up, called on the rabbi, but Lilith was in love and determined. So one day, she packed her box and walked away from her home, her family and her community for ever.

Foxx obtained a licence, then took her to a house where a man in long black robes who said he was a minister of the church of England, performed the ceremony. Lilith did not query why they hadn't been married in one of the big intimidating churches that peppered the city. She presumed this was how things were done in the 'Christian' world she had now entered.

Foxx took the lease on a small house in Putney. He told her his parents had gone to live abroad, but would be back some day, when they would welcome her into the family. She believed him. Why would she not? Anyway, she had other things to focus upon ~ soon after the wedding she discovered she was pregnant.

"It was a difficult time," Lilith told Cully. They were sitting on either side of a table in one of the bleak interview rooms. "I was seventeen, and all alone in the world. I tried to get back in touch with my family, but I found out that after I'd left, my parents had gone back to the rabbi, and on his advice, they'd held a funeral service, torn their clothes and sat shiva, the mourning ritual in my community for somebody who had died. As far as they were concerned I no longer existed.

"Carrying a child did not suit me. For many months, I felt so ill and wretched that I stopped taking care of myself, and as a consequence, my husband began spending more and more time away from our home. Days, and then days and nights would go by with no sight of him.

"I began to see the hopelessness of my position: I had tied myself to a man I barely knew, on the strength of attraction alone. Once my looks had faded, and my belly started to swell, he no longer wanted me. And I had no family to take me in and care for me.

"My daughter Essie, named for my lost older sister, was born at home. I was on my own at the time, but luckily one of my neighbours heard my cries and sent for a local woman who knew about these things. Essie was a beautiful baby ~ dark eyed, with a mop of curly black hair. I took one look at her and fell in love ~ for real this time."

If she had hoped the birth of their child would effect a reconciliation between them, Lilith was soon to be disillusioned. Foxx continued to treat the house like a hotel, coming and going as he pleased, leaving her to clean, cook and look after the baby. Gradually Lilith's exhaustion started to be replaced by a growing anger.

It was this anger and its outcome that ended the relationship. One night Foxx swaggered in late, drunk and loud and woke the baby. At the end of her tether, Lilith screamed abuse at him, throwing at him all her pent-up frustration, together with his untouched dinner plate.

Five minutes later, she found herself thrust out into the street, the door locked behind her. No yelling and screaming and beating on the door with her fists availed. On the contrary, she then found herself arrested for breach of the peace by a passing night constable, and was carted off to a police station.

In the time it took for Lilith to explain what had happened, and to be released without charge, Foxx had cleared off, taking Essie with him. Lilith returned to an empty house and a landlord demanding unpaid back rent. She was left with nothing but the clothes she stood up in, unable to comprehend the catastrophe that had so swiftly overtaken her.

Lilith searched for Foxx and her child for months and months, but they had gone, swallowed up in the vast teeming population of the great city. Day and night, she scoured the streets, hoping to catch a glimpse of them. To no avail. It took a very long while before she could accept that she would probably never see either of them again.

The day Essie disappeared from her life was the day Lilith died inside. From then on, it didn't really matter what happened to her body. It was just a shell, harbouring the ashes of a broken heart. She changed her name and moved to another part of London.

In the years following Essie's removal, silence became part of her. She hid inside it. There she could make herself invisible, or she could be whoever she chose to be. It was at that time Lilith became a woman who sold her body. She had no other options. She did it with a detachment born out of total despair.

"And then one night, I saw him again," Lilith said. "I was with a gentleman, having dinner in a West End supper room. And there he was at another table, in the company of a much younger woman ~ almost a girl. My blood turned to ice and then to fire. I got up, walked straight over to him and demanded to see my Essie."

"What did he say?" Cully asked.

"At first, he pretended he didn't know me. Then, when he saw I did not mean to go without an answer, and that my presence was drawing unwelcome attention to him, he told me the news I had dreaded to hear ever since the day I lost her: Essie had died of diphtheria before her first birthday."

Lilith pauses, wiping her eyes. Cully sits in silence, politely averting his gaze. He waits until she has got back enough control to continue.

"After that, I don't remember much of my life," she says, shaking her head. "I just did what I had to do to feed myself and survive. Until the day I met the man who released me from the prison I'd locked myself into."

"Mr Herbert King?" Cully says.

"Yes, Herbert. He saw something more in me than just a body to take pleasure from. But that relationship wasn't to be either ~ and you know how the story ended, for you were part of it: he was murdered by that terrible woman. My lovely man."

She stares straight ahead, her eyes dark pools of pain.

"But he left me some jewels in his will, and that was how I was able to leave my former occupation behind and buy the tea-room. Even so, I was not entirely free of Foxx ~ for he came into the tea-room a couple of times. Always with a very young girl on his arm. I took care to stay in the background so he did not recognise me. And now he is dead and gone, and good riddance."

Lilith stands up.

"I have taken up too much of your time, sergeant. I must get back to the tea-room. It will be the lunchtime rush soon, and the girls will need supervising."

She adjusts her bonnet.

Cully rises.

"Before you go, I have to ask you: when did you last see your husband?"

"Eight months ago ~ and he isn't my husband. He never was ~ the marriage licence and the priest were false. I found that out after he'd left me."

"And last night?"

She smiles thinly.

"I was visiting a good friend. I have no doubt that she will vouch for me."

"So, you have no idea whether he had any enemies?"

Lilith pauses at the door.

"Apart from me? Clearly he had ~ for somebody hated him enough to kill him, but it was not me, Sergeant Cully, though God knows I have wished it so many, many times. If and when you find them, shake their hand from me, and tell them they have rid the world of a vile and evil man and it is a better place for his absence."

Lilith leaves Scotland Yard. She is shattered by what she has seen on the mortuary slab, and marvels at the power Foxx has to affect her, even after his death. As she walks back, she thinks of the things she didn't tell: the nights when love making turned to brutal love taking, leaving her bruised and bleeding and sobbing.

Then there was the discovery that her husband had left her with an unwelcome reminder of his former presence, resulting in a stay in a Foul Ward, where a degrading examination also elicited the news that the damage he had done to her internally meant she would never be able to bear another child.

The news had broken Lilith. She had wept so hard she thought the seams of her face would split open. Slowly she'd descended into an abyss, where the air was thin and her heart bounced around her ribcage. Her sanity became as frail as water tension. Each day was a constant battle.

She remembered lying in the hospital bed, wondering whether she was going to spend the rest of her life looking over her shoulder, measuring out her days by their distance from the same fixed point in the past when she returned to find an empty house and a missing baby.

Her return to the tea-room takes her past *John Gould & Company*, where she observes that the shutters are still down, the lights out, and there is no sign of business being enacted. Lilith pauses in front of the big display window. On the other side of that glass was where the man who'd ruined her life had spent his final hours.

Part of her wishes she'd been there to witness his final agonies. Suddenly Lilith is overcome by such fury for all she has lost, all the damage he did to her life. She bunches her gloved hand into a fist and slams it against the wooden shutters. Then, recalling where she is, she snatches it back and walks quickly away.

She is a business-woman, she tells herself sternly. People rely on her. She cannot allow herself to give in to her emotions. She must stay in control. Lilith takes a couple of deep, steadying breaths, before she steps over to the kerb and flags down a passing cab.

***

"You let her go?" Stride exclaims. "For God's sake why?"

"I had no reason to detain her," Cully says. "She clearly wasn't involved in the murder."

Stride rolls his eyes up to the ceiling.

"Oh, was she not? Do you have *proof*, Jack? She might have been. She clearly had motive, not to say opportunity."

"She also had an alibi for the night Foxx was murdered."

"I'm sure she *says* she has ..." Stride pauses, letting the words hang in the air.

Cully decides to walk past them without acknowledging their presence.

"Robinson asked you to call in to the mortuary. He says he has something he wishes to show you."

Stride winces.

"Ah. Not sure I want to see it, especially if it's floating in a jar. You'd better come with me, given you are also part of the investigation."

The police surgeon is at his desk writing up notes when Stride and Cully enter the bleak mortuary. He glances up, giving Stride a wide enthusiastic smile, and beckons him closer.

"Ah, detective inspector ... just in time. I was in the process of finishing my autopsy report on the interesting gentleman who was brought in yesterday."

"Is he?"

"Oh, yes. Exceedingly so," the police surgeon nods, signing his name at the bottom of the page with a flourish. "So, gentlemen, if you would care to accompany me to the table, I shall share my findings with you both."

Grimacing, Stride follows him. Robinson goes to the head of the mortuary slab and picks up a small glass dish.

"Now then, what do you make of these?" he says, leaning across the sheet-covered body.

"Beads. Carved jet beads?" Stride says.

"Where did they come from?" Cully asks.

The police surgeon rolls the small black objects around in the dish.

"Seeds, not beads, detectives. Seeds from the Datura plant, an herbaceous perennial grown in greenhouses and conservatories throughout the length and breadth of the country, and poisonous if ingested. Which our victim appears to have done. I found these in his stomach, along with some partially digested ones."

"He didn't die from a throat wound after all?" Cully exclaims.

"So it would appear. Though it may have contributed to his demise. As might the stab wound in his lower back."

"Then what killed him?"

"A combination of those factors I have just mentioned to you."

"And when did he die?" Stride asks, instantly regretting the question.

"Sadly, that is a point upon which I cannot enlighten you. The effects of rigor mortis could have set in early on, and dissipated by the time the body was found. On the other hand, rigidity can be delayed for several days. Indeed, in a case I have been reading about recently, it did not set in for nearly a week. Mind, the victim was also decapitated."

"What about the Datura seeds?" Cully asks gingerly, as the surgeon places the little dish back on the dissecting table.

"The effects would be fairly rapid and would involve fever and delirium, an inability to distinguish between reality and fantasy and ultimately, heart failure. My suspicion that it may have been the Datura that ultimately killed him is also based upon the extreme dilation I observed in the pupils."

"Let me get this straight," Stride says. "Someone poisoned him with these seeds, stabbed him in the back, then transported him to the shop window, where they cut his throat and staged his death so that it looked like suicide?"

"That is for you to ascertain, detective inspector," the police surgeon says drily. "I am, as you know, a mere medical authority. I deal in facts. These are the facts. The field of speculation I leave to your good selves and to your colleagues. I would also add that some Datura plants are employed for their known aphrodisiac qualities ~ but alas, I cannot say for certain whether this was the case here."

He reaches for a fearsome looking cranial saw.

"If you would both excuse me, detectives, I need to begin the examination of my next cadaver. So many bodies, so little time."

As they walk back to the main building, Stride says, "I have never come across anything like this in the whole of my career, have you?"

"It does seem a little bizarre," Cully frowns.

"Bizarre isn't the word I'd use, Jack. This smacks of revenge. Cold-blooded and carefully planned revenge. And I know of only one individual who fits that category. So I'd definitely like you to pay Mrs Marks a visit. Ask her for a detailed account of her movements over the past week."

"You can't possibly think she played any part in her former husband's death? Why would she come and identify him if she did? She'd lie low and keep quiet. I know I would."

"Ah well, that's where you are wrong. It's exactly the tactics a clever woman like her would adopt. We believe her sob story, and eliminate her from the investigation, while all the time she is there, right in front of us, hiding in plain sight.

"Go and interview her, Jack. Preferably at her home, where you could casually stroll into her conservatory and see what plants she grows. Yes. Why don't you hurry straight along to that tea shop she owns and arrange it? And don't let her beguile you with ham sandwiches, as she did last time."

"Last time she was completely innocent, merely the subject of nasty gossip."

Stride taps the side of his nose with an index finger.

"Mrs Marks keeps turning up regularly, doesn't she? Like a bad penny. I don't like bad pennies, and quite frankly, I'm starting to have my suspicions about her. You know what they say: *'Hell hath no fury'*. Yes. I shouldn't be surprised if our lady tea-room owner isn't at the bottom of this after all. A woman scorned and abandoned. And let us not forget she has access to knives on a daily basis, doesn't she?"

***

Leaving Cully to make his reluctant way to Hampstead, Stride heads for his office, where a selection of the morning papers have been placed on his desk. Many of the front pages have chosen to run with the body in the shop window, attaching the usual slew of lurid headlines to a variety of gruesome illustrations.

Several others, however, have taken up the current fracas over a plan by the Society for Affording Nightly Shelter to the Houseless to open an asylum for the poor and indigent, which would offer shelter and assistance during the oncoming inclement winter season.

Unfortunately, the building that the hapless society has chosen is within spitting distance of some of the grand town houses in Bloomsbury, and the grand inhabitants are spitting bile, fury and protest at the prospect.

More so after they have learned that the place will be open day and night to receive the poor and destitute, who will be offered bread, a warm shelter and in cases of extreme debility, soup, brandy and medicine. Outrageous!

The press is adding fuel to the fire by printing off various official statistics and commissioners' reports that prove there was no need for *any* destitution in the city, as there were workhouses, outdoor relief, indoor relief, hospitals and casual wards in abundance.

As he reads, Stride rolls his eyes in disbelief. Apparently there is also employment for all who want to work. Thus, those who are houseless and hungry must *ipso facto* be idle and dissolute. Or as *The Inquirer* puts it in its own inimitable way:

Destitution? It's all Gammon & Humbug!

Today's front page is devoted to the premise that most of the street beggars encountered by its readers are in fact impostors. '*That fellow in rags with the imitation paralysis who goes staggering along will have veal for supper tonight*' it states.

The article, penned by his nemesis Dandy Dick, goes on to inform its readers that the derelict woman begging in a doorway has probably hired, for fourpence a day, the two puny children who cling to her ragged skirts and goes home at night to turkey, sausages, hot punch and roaring songs. It was all complete rubbish, but rubbish served on a daily basis rapidly becomes acceptable fare to a resentful public.

Stride wonders what Sir Hugh Wynward makes of the matter. After all, the shelter is just around the corner from where he lives. Where his daughter once lived. He digs out Sybella Wynward's letter from under the pile of newspapers and studies it intently. London postmark. He decides that the handwriting on the envelope does not match the handwriting of the note; it is more masculine.

So, two people are involved. A couple? But why? And what is their motive? Blackmail? Some sort of private vendetta? It is a mystery. Stride reminds himself that in his time as a detective, he has come across several investigations that are similar to the Wynward girl. Multiply them by the number of unreported incidents, and there could be hundreds of individuals who simply went out one day and never came back, crossing over into some other life.

That might possibly be the case here. But Stride's thoughts keep returning to the burned body, the fragments of red shawl. If, by some miracle, she escaped the inferno of the blazing train wreck, why has Sybella Wynward chosen this particular moment to advertise her existence?

At his request, Wynward has furnished him with a list of his daughter's closest friends. Stride now starts rearranging the list into some sort of order dependent upon location and closeness of the relationship.

Over the next few days he intends to speak to each of the young women in turn. Even if they haven't got a clue where Sybella is, or even if Sybella is, the news of her possible reappearance might shock one of them enough into coming up with somebody who has. Stride decides he is going to tug at a few threads, and see what unravels as a result.

***

We move location to a London street. It is the sort of street where people stand upon their dignity, having very little else to stand on. Nothing behind the front door worth stealing, but they all have their pride, which is priceless. Here, in a terraced house with blackened brickwork but a doorstep so pristine that it defies description, Bovis Finister's mother is using a goffering iron on a large white starched ruff that looks vaguely Elizabethan and rather familiar. Its owner is even now refilling the book bulks in front of his shop.

An exchange of services has led to Bovis being accepted as one of the alchemist's apprentices, though his mother is under the impression that he is being privately educated in reading and writing, and the finer arts of being a gentleman for when the social elevation of the Finister family finally arrives.

Lines of drying washing hang across the kitchen. Petticoats and vests, gentlemen's woollen combinations and socks drip and dangle. A row of headless white shirts hang by their shoulders just above where Bovis and his sister are eating their midday meal at the small scrubbed deal table.

"There now," Mrs Finister says, testing the goffering iron's blades by spitting on them, before gathering and goffering two cuffs. "Once I've sewn these back in place, you can take the coat to Mr Lightowler as payment for your next lesson."

Bovis nods and continues shovelling sticky dumpling into his mouth with a bent spoon. His sharp-faced little sister Liza-Lou scrapes round her plate with a grubby finger, then sucks it noisily.

"Manners, Liza-Lou," their mother reproves.

"Ain't got none," Liz-Lou replies, wiping her mouth on the back of her hand. "Don't want none. Ain't gonna be gentry like wot Bovis is."

"Still no reason to be rude. We may be poor, but we've got standards."

Squinting into the light, Mrs Finister threads a needle, then takes a black velvet coat out of a wicker basket by the fire that is busy creating its own internal fog, as it encounters the damp grey wall plaster.

"If you've both finished your dinners, I need you to do some little jobs. Bovis, you deliver the last lot of washing for me. You know the 'ouses. And try to remember to go round the back or down the area. People don't like the whole street to see their washing delivered."

"Yes Ma."

"Liza-Lou, you can help me with the mangling."

"Aww Ma ..."

"And when you're done with that, you can go round to Mother Emmet's and get me some more of her embrocation. My chest's that tight at night I can hardly breathe."

Bovis takes his plate to the sink and clatters it down. His mother winces.

"Shall I empty the washing boiler before I go?" he inquires.

She shakes her head.

"No, leave it, son. We don't want to waste the hot water. I can use it to boil the dumplings for the lodgers' suppers."

Bovis Finister puts on his cap, slips his arms into his thin jacket and hoists the big basket of clean washing onto his shoulder.

"You got the addresses?"

He nods.

"Round the back, remember?"

He nods.

"Make sure they pay you. And come straight home. No stopping off to watch them I-talian street singers or that performing monkey. And keep the money in a safe place. Gawd knows I works hard enough to earn it."

Bovis shuffles out of the kitchen.

"When my bruvver's a gen't'l'm'n, will we still have to live here and take in washing?" Liza-Lou asks.

"I hope not. When that day comes, we'll all move to a nice little house with a garden."

"And I shall have a blue silk dress and ride around London in a carriage, won't I?" Liza-Lou announces triumphantly. "And eat my dinner with a silver spoon off of a gold plate."

Her mother smiles indulgently at her.

"You will, my duck. And all the handsome young gentl'men will want to court you for their wife."

"But I sha'n't have any of them, coz I'm not stupid, and I ain't never getting married to no man to work my fingers to the bone for 'im."

Mrs Finister gives her a tight-lipped look. Then she sighs, putting her hand to the small of her back.

"You get on washing them pots while I set up the mangle. We've got a way to go before that day arrives."

***

A clumsy youth in ill-fitting boots and carrying a basket of washing is hardly going to attract the notice of passers-by, especially when the passer-by is Detective Inspector Stride, who is currently on his way to talk to one of Sybella Wynward's closest friends, a young lady called Constantia Mortram, at her parents' house in Hyde Park Gardens.

Another 'elegant residence' Stride thinks gloomily, as the footman announces him, and he enters another parlour that is all red plush and embroidered chair backs. Two women await his arrival, seated together on a crimson velvet sofa. One is young and blooming, with ringlets and rosy cheeks; the other is an older version with more outlying wither. A small pug dog is stretched out in front of the fire. It runs over to Stride, yipping.

"Pugsley! Bad dog ~ leave the nice policeman alone," the young woman laughs.

Mother and daughter survey Stride with the haughty, detached upper-class air that he has, over the years, come to recognise and loathe.

"We received your note, detective inspector, but we confess to being puzzled as to *why* you should wish to call," Mrs Mortram drawls languidly. "Are we not, Con?"

"I'm *most* intrigued, Mama. I cannot think of a single crime I might have committed recently, though perhaps the inspector's visit goes back to the occasion when I stole a pencil off Mademoiselle Atelier's desk. I was a naughty child in those days you see, inspector," Constantia smiles slyly.

There is a silver coffee pot on a low table at her elbow, a jug of cream and two porcelain cups. A maid pours coffee, passes one cup to Constantia, one to her mistress. They sip, eyeing him amusedly over the rim.

"Indeed, ladies, I can quite understand your perturbation," Stride says drily. "I am here on behalf of Sir Hugh Wynward ~ I gather he is an acquaintance of the family."

At his mention of Sir Hugh's name, Stride sees that the pretty witty young miss suddenly stiffens, her fingers tightening compulsively round her coffee cup. All the merriment leaks from her face, leaving it pale and serious. She sets down the cup, then stares at her lap, refusing to meet his eye.

"Sir Hugh has recently received an unexpected communication which led him to call in Scotland Yard," Stride says, choosing his words carefully.

"What sort of unexpected communication? Who was it from?" Constantia demands in a low eager voice.

"I am not at liberty to say, miss. The matter is confidential. But I would be grateful for anything you could tell me about your friendship with his daughter Sybella."

Now she glances up, her face blank, eyes void of any expression.

"Sybella is dead," she replies woodenly.

"Tell me about her when she was alive."

A pause.

"We were best friends. We were at school together. When we left school, we wrote and called upon each other practically every day. We were planning to come out together this summer. And then she .... then ... she ..." Constantia Mortram's voice falters. Her eyes brim with tears.

Mrs Mortram puts her arm round her daughter's shoulders.

"You do not need to speak of it, my love. I am sure the police officer understands."

"Madam, I am trying to understand what Miss Sybella Wynward was like as a person. It might help my investigation."

"What does it matter?" Mrs Mortram exclaims fiercely, "She is dead and buried now, and your visit is upsetting my daughter. I'm afraid I must ask you to leave. Constantia was very close to Sybella ~ they were like sisters, and her sudden death upset her terribly. She is still badly affected, as you can see. She has nothing more to say to you. Nor do I. Please leave my house."

She signals to the parlour maid, who walks to the door and opens it. Standing on the threshold, the maid folds her arms and waits for Stride to rise and follow her out. The pug barks and makes a rush for his trouser leg.

Stride shakes it off, getting in a good kick that sends it yelping back to the hearth rug. He collects his hat from the small table by the front door, and steps out into the halting light peculiar to London in October.

In the parlour, Constantia Mortram sits with her face in her hands, her shoulders shaking with sobs. The effect is quite startling. Eventually, she lifts her head.

"I think I shall go up to my room for a while, Mama. I am very upset."

"Of course you are, my pet. What a horrid little man! How dare he come here asking his nasty impertinent questions! I shall give orders to the servants that he is never to be let in again."

Constantia leaves the parlour and hurries up the stairs to her bedroom, where she locks the door behind her. For a few seconds she stands by the door, ears straining. Mama is known to pay unexpected visits.

When no heavy footsteps sound on the landing, she goes to her little rosewood writing desk. Drawing out a piece of writing paper from a leather writing case, Constantia finds a pen, and a new nib. Then she dips the pen into an ink bottle, and starts scribbling furiously.

Half an hour later, and now wearing her best bonnet and fur trimmed cape, Constantia Mortram slips quietly out of the elegant cream-stucco house, and walks briskly in the direction of the nearest post box, a letter in her gloved hand.

***

Meanwhile, matters are proceeding apace at *John Gould & Company*. Now that all the staff have been interviewed and the police have departed, the store has finally been permitted to start trading.

John Gould is at first mightily relieved. Then amazed and delighted. It seems that the circumstances surrounding the fatal non-opening have spread far and wide. Crowds are flocking in. Everybody wants to see the famous window (or infamous depending upon which side of it you are standing). And then they want to purchase the same cutlery, the identical dinner set, and exactly the same pattern of table linen that featured in the original window display.

Never has Gould seen so much business being enacted in all his years in shop keeping. Dishes and door-scrapers are flying off the shelves. Cheeses and coffee are being weighed and bagged up as fast as his assistants can manage it.

If he read the works of the great French philosopher Voltaire, as opposed to the Grocer's Monthly, Gould might well have agreed that '*Tout va pour le mieux dans le meilleur des mondes.*'

The tills are ringing, his heart is singing, and to make the afternoon complete, he has just finished giving an exclusive interview to a London reporter, who has promised to mention his newly opened store on the front page of tomorrow's newspaper.

Gould stands on the ground floor under the vaulted glass ceiling, which is at the epicentre of his empire. His thumbs are tucked into his waistcoat pockets. He is a man at peace with the world. A man at the zenith of his profession.

Which is more, he reflects, than can be said for the detective police, who have not yet discovered how a complete stranger was spirited into his store, under cover of darkness, when all the doors were firmly locked and bolted, and then brutally slain in one of his display windows. He told the friendly reporter as much earlier.

Plus a few other comments. Strictly 'off the record', of course.

***

While Gould is mentally reckoning up the day's takings, Jack Cully is making his way back to Scotland Yard. In his coat pocket is the list of everybody Lilith Marks visited in the past week, or everybody who has visited her. It is not a long list. Actually, there is only one name on it. And astonishingly, it is a name he recognises from the recent past.

If he were a suspicious man, Cully might conclude that Mrs Marks has erred on the side of economy. He is pretty sure that is what Stride would think. But Cully has learned to trust his instincts, especially where the fairer sex are concerned. Marriage to Emily has taught him far more than all his years in the detective division.

Cully prides himself that he can pick out dissembling at fifty paces. Mrs Marks, while slightly taken aback at finding herself the focus of police attention, agreed without a murmur to supply him with what he asked.

Cully watched her face closely as he questioned her. There was no indication that she was telling anything but the honest truth. And no, in answer to his inquiry, she didn't have a conservatory. Nor the time to cultivate plants of any sort, even if she wanted to. Which she did not.

Most of Mrs Marks' days were spent visiting one of her several businesses, or making the delicious cakes and scones that were getting her a reputation for fine baking. As proof, Cully has been sent on his way with half a seed cake in a cardboard confectionary box. A parting gift.

He is sure Stride will not approve. He would probably see it as a bribe to buy compliance, but Emily loves seed cake, and is far too busy with a fretful toddler, or running up children's clothes for an ever-growing list of clients, to bake cakes.

Cully's feet ache. The cold wind is nipping at his fingers. Lunch is a distant memory and his stomach has reached long past hungry. All he craves now is his warm hearth, his sweet wife and his adored little daughter. He decides that he will smuggle the seed cake into the station, and after leaving a brief report on Stride's desk, he will smuggle it out again.

***

Night-time. The West End swells have all gone home to dinner. The gin palaces and public houses turn out. Streets dwindle, their glory fading as the evening closes in. Traffic diminishes by the hour, until the only sound is the clump of the night constables' boots.

London is a trackless desert at night, when the great tide of human life stands still. In the interval between the death of the previous day and the birth of the next, the city is empty, unborn. The watchman's footsteps sound on the pavement, followed some while later by the lamplighter, who leaves behind a little track of smoke mixed with glowing fragments of his red link, and faint traces of sulphuric acid in his wake.

It is the dead time, when the city changes from metropolis to necropolis. The liminal zone between sleeping and waking. Look more closely. Two figures, muffled up against the cold, hurry along a shabby street.

They have dined cheaply at a chop house, lingering as long as possible over their meagre meal, before seeking equally cheap entertainment elsewhere. This involved alcoholic beverages, consumed at the sort of hostelries whose existence depended upon other hostelries being full.

Now they are returning homewards in a line less straight than the one they set out in. The area they are approaching is one where dwellings are accessed by a network of forlorn, muddy and barely-lit courts and alleys. None of the courts have proper pavements.

Here, there is a frowsty blight on the window-panes and gas-lamps, and the whole neighbourhood is pervaded with a miasma of stale fish, old clothes, rank tobacco and noxious chemicals from a nearby factory.

The two finally reach a paint-peeling lodging house with dirty window curtains, whereupon one of them draws a key from his pocket and opens the front door. This is the lodging of Jasper Thorogood, maker of false eyes and, as his dining companion is about to discover, false currency also.

"Come in," he says, beckoning to his companion.

"Is it here?" the other asks.

In answer, Thorogood leads the way up to the small back bedroom and flings wide the door.

"Behold," he says gesturing towards a rickety table, upon which stands a metal press with a large rotating screw handle at the top.

Eugenius Strictly stares at it, open-mouthed with admiration.

"Cor ... where did you come by it again?"

"One of our customers. He used to make medals and such, until he lost an eye from a piece of hot metal. Couldn't see to do the fine engraving, so he wanted to get rid of his stock. I made him an offer he couldn't refuse, and here it is. Our very own coin press, all ready to use."

Strictly rubs his hands together.

"When do we start making money on it?"

"We already have. Take a look at these."

Thorogood goes to the mantelpiece and sweeps a little heap of copper coins into his palm. He holds them out.

"What do you think?"

Strictly weighs them in his hand.

"They look alright, only they feel a bit ... different."

"Of course they do ... right size, but made from melted down spoons, plated with that copper we took off Bovis. So what we do is mix them up with proper money. People don't check if you hand them a lot of small change. Here," he tosses him an apple. "I used some of them earlier to buy this fruit off a coster. Never noticed a thing."

"You are a marvel, Jasper. You really are a marvel."

Thorogood smiles modestly.

"But this is nothing, my friend. We need to be able to make gold. Then we can produce guineas and sovereigns. So for now, let us continue to be the good attentive students Master Dee thinks we are. We observe, we make notes and we bide our time. Then, as soon as we are ready, we pounce."

"Huzzah to the pouncing!"

Strictly throws his cap into the air and catches it. Then as the hour is so late it is almost next day, and he has seen what he came to see, he bids his fellow apprentice farewell, and makes his way out into the darkly noxious street and from thence back to his own lodgings.

***

Night wears on. In her small townhouse in Maida Vale, Lilith Marks wakes suddenly. Moonlight drips round the window blind, not getting far. She sits upright, ears straining. In her mind she hears it quite clearly: a soft rustling in the dark.

Before she can stop herself, remind herself that it is the dream again, Lilith is out of bed and reaching down into a cradle that isn't there. Her arms seeking for the warm, sweet baby. That isn't there either.

Time stretches and slows.

Essie.

She speaks the name into the darkness. As if saying it will bring her back. Lilith passes the back of her hand across her forehead. The pain is vast. Her grief is endless and hidden and long. Her bones ache with the agony of it. She is overwhelmed by it, out of her depths in it. She shudders with the effort of gathering herself together. Breathe. Breathe. Count to ten. Count to a hundred. A thousand.

And so it goes. And goes and goes.

***

Dawn arrives, remaking the city anew. Fog rests in the morning streets. It renders everything limp, like the belly of a dead fish, slippery and wet. Roofs have a silver sheen. Cobbles are slick and sticky underfoot. Dampness pervades everything; the grey walls of buildings consuming light, birthing rot. Lines of mildew run green tracks along everything.

Early dawn, and the streets are full of groaning market carts. Creak-axled and cabbage-laden, they toil slowly towards Covent Garden, their drivers trudging alongside. They bring with them the mud of farms, the fruits of the earth and the dialects of country lanes.

Here is the vegetable world in all its glory: apples, carrots, shades of green in watercresses, shallots, the familiar fronds of the cabbage, onions with shining faces, beetroot and parsnips with long sensitive roots. Later, the carts will return, piled high with manure for the market gardens that ring the city.

It grows lighter. The coffee stall at Hyde Park vanishes like a hobgoblin at the approach of day. It has served its rope-tasting brew to the early city workers. Now shop girls and clerks pass along the thoroughfare, to be followed by the later starting clerks in gaudy waistcoats, and finally, the suited civil servants, who eye up the shop girls as they dress the windows.

Ten o'clock, and vice and virtue rub shoulders in the thronged street, saunter in the park, or take a turn in the Burlington Arcade. Look more closely. An elegant brougham has just drawn up at one end of the arcade. A middle-aged woman, expensively dressed, alights, carefully adjusting her veil and bonnet.

There is something fragile about her, as if she might shatter into little pieces at any moment. She positions herself in a doorway and waits, glancing frequently to left and then right. Her expression is warily eager.

Here comes another lady ~ her attire also proclaiming her to be one of the gilded rich. As she approaches, nose in air, ignoring the importunate street people who cluster at corners, their hands outstretched, Lady Meriel Wynward steps out of the doorway and greets her with formal fondness. A moment passes, then two become three, as they are joined by Mrs Mortram, her high-coloured face hidden also under a veil.

Three upper class ladies make their way to Fortnum's, where they order Indian tea and no cakes. While they wait to be served, they go through the formal social rituals: inquiring after absent family members, commenting on the marital prospects of offspring, complaining about the servants.

Tea is brought and poured. Lady Meriel plays with her fingers, clears her throat. The other two pause, teacups held aloft, little fingers daintily crooked. Their expressions are politely attentive.

"I have asked you both to meet me here because I am very troubled. Something has occurred and I wish to ask you both, as friends and confidantes for your advice," she says.

"Is it to do with a certain communication?" Mrs Mortram says, lowering her voice. "We had a most unpleasant detective round t'other afternoon. Poor Con got very upset."

"It is to do with that, yes. We have had a letter from Sybella. At least ..." she falters, "A letter with a lock of Sybella's hair and the words: *Remember me*. I am now thinking of consulting Mrs Kitty Fisher. My husband has forbidden me to talk to the spirits, but I cannot rest until I know whether it is some sort of vile trick, or whether my daughter is trying to communicate with me, either in this world or the next. What is your view?"

Lady Parthenope De'Ath's expression could have been chiselled from granite.

"It is a serious matter, Meriel. Should you not take care? Better to leave the matter in the hands of your husband I think, rather than consult quacks and fakirs."

Lady Meriel's mouth folds in on itself and sets in an obstinate line.

"Hugh has put it into the hands of the detective police. And how long will they be? I simply cannot sit idly twiddling my thumbs while we wait for them to reach their conclusions. It may be months. They may not even reach a conclusion. So I have booked a sitting with Mrs Fisher for midday. I'd like you both to accompany me. Whatever pain I must suffer, it will not, *cannot* be worse than the past year."

She stands, clutching the edge of the table.

"Of course I quite understand if you do not wish to support me, Parthenope. You, after all, have never suffered the loss of a child."

Lady Parthenope rolls her eyes in a not-this-again way.

"I would accompany you, Meriel, but alas, I have a fitting with my dressmaker. Had you *told* me you wished for moral support, of course I should have given it to you. Whatever my personal reservations."

Lady Meriel turns to Mrs Mortram.

"And you, Grace? My oldest friend ~ will you also desert me in my hour of need?" her voice quavers.

"Oh Meriel, must you be so ... naturally I shall come with you, if that is what you want," Grace Mortram sighs.

"It is what I want."

Bidding their critical friend a frosty farewell, Lady Meriel and Mrs Mortram quit the restaurant. They retrace their steps, until they arrive outside a green painted door on the upper landing of the Arcade. A sign proclaims:

Mrs K Fisher
Clairvoyant and Medium
Cards, Divination & Crystal Ball
Spiritual phenomena forthcoming from
11 am. - 3 pm. & from 4 pm. - 6 pm. daily
Séances by arrangement

Lady Meriel knocks timorously. The door is opened by a sullen young girl with a squint and a runny nose.

"Ow ~ have you come for a reading?" she says.

"Indeed. I am Lady Meriel Wynward. I believe I am expected."

The young girl wipes her nose on her sleeve and waves them into the anteroom.

"I'll go and tell her."

Lady Meriel collapses onto one of the luridly yellow and pink striped sofas and fans herself. The room is stuffy, the air stale. The dark crimson walls are adorned with photos of Mrs Fisher in a variety of occult poses, some involving plinths, others with what looks like white silk scarves coming out of her mouth.

Mrs Mortram folds her arms. She does not believe in all this mumbo-jumbo. Not for one credulous minute. But she is trying her best to put herself in her friend's shoes. If she had lost Constantia, who knows how grief might affect her, and to what lunatic depths she might sink?

"My heart is beating so fast," Lady Meriel whispers tremulously. "I am sure the spirits have something to impart. I feel their presence keenly."

Mrs Mortram purses her lips. She hopes Sir Hugh does not find out that his wife has disobeyed his wishes. There will be repercussions. Rumours abound that he beats her in private. She has met him several times socially, and she wouldn't be surprised. A cold man. Something of the night about him.

At last the grubby red curtain at the far end of the room is drawn aside, and a hand beckons. Lady Meriel gets to her feet, swaying as if buffeted by an invisible breeze.

"You will wait here for me, won't you?" she asks.

Mrs Mortram nods.

"I shall be here. Now go," she says.

Lady Meriel slips beyond the curtain, entering the small, dark stifling back room where the spirits dwell. There is a round table covered with a bobble-fringed cloth. Upon it is a lit candle, a crystal ball and a pack of cards.

Behind the table sits Mrs Kitty Fisher. She has a hooked nose, a greasy black curled wig, and a bright spot of colour on each cheekbone. She wears an assortment of flowing garments with sigils and stars embroidered on them.

"Sit yourself down, my lovely lady," she says. "I knew you were coming to see me before even I got your letter. The spirits told me."

Lady Meriel sinks into a bentwood chair and clasps her hands together in her lap.

"Now, shall we cut cards?" the medium says.

She pushes the pack of playing cards across the table.

"Three times, my lady, if you would be so kind. Use your left hand ~ the one closest to your heart, and let us see what Fate has in store for you."

Obediently, Lady Meriel makes three cuts into the pack.

Mrs Fisher turns over the top card on each pile: an upside down ten of clubs, the queen of hearts and a three of spades. She spends some time staring at the cards, mystically nodding and sighing to herself. Then she glances across the table at her client, who is almost collapsing in anticipation.

"Ah, my lady. What an interesting set of cards you have given me today. Now, are you ready for what Fate wants you to know?"

"Yes," Lady Meriel whispers, clenching her gloved hands so tightly that the seams are in danger of splitting. "Yes I am. Tell me what you see."

Ten minutes later, Lady Meriel Wynward parts the curtain and rejoins her friend Mrs Mortram, who is still waiting patiently in the anteroom. Lady Meriel's expression is flushed and hectic, her fingers fiddle with the ropes of pearls round her neck.

"She is alive, Grace! I sensed it, and the cards have confirmed it. It was as if they knew everything. My life has been all upside down since she went, but now my heart's desire is coming towards me. Our family will return to what it was before Sybella was taken from us. We have been two; we will be three once again."

She clasps her hands to her bosom and smiles radiantly. Mrs Mortram adjusts her facial expression to as close to delight as her scepticism will allow.

"Are you going to tell Sir Hugh?" she inquires, "or the detective police?"

A shadow passes across the sunshine of Lady Meriel's face.

"I dare not. He will be angry with me ~ he has forbidden me to seek solace from those who have passed over. But at least I know now, and knowing is all. Mrs Fisher says it explains why she never received any direct message for me from the other side. She was not there, you see. Sybella. She was in this world all the time."

Mrs Mortram almost opens her mouth to ask tartly if that is so, then who is buried in Highgate Cemetery ~ but decides against posing the question. Her friend's face is so joyous, so full of hope. It would be like kicking a small puppy.

"I am so glad you are happy at last," she says instead.

"Oh I am, dear Grace. I couldn't be happier. Now, let us sally forth into the glorious autumn sunshine. I have a lot of shopping to do."

"You have?"

"Of course. Clothes must be ordered for Sybella's return. I must buy her a new bonnet, a warm shawl and some gloves. Come, let us make our way straight to Swan and Edgar's; there is not a moment to lose."

The two ladies return to Piccadilly, where the roadway is crowded with fine equipages, the barouche of rank and the brougham of beauty rubbing shoulders (metaphorically) with the mail-phaeton, the hansom, the curricle and the cab.

They enter the portals of Swan and Edgar, emerging some time later accompanied by two shop assistants, their arms piled high with boxes. Lady Meriel bids a fond farewell to her companion before being helped into the brougham by the Wynward footman. She gives him instructions, and is borne swiftly away in the direction of Oxford Street.

***

Another part of London, another group meeting of society's female elite. This time, the cadet branch. Constantia Mortram's hastily scribbled letter has summoned her two closest girl friends to a powwow in her bedroom.

Twins Dorinda and Veracia Davenport, clad in identical arsenical green frocks with matching hair accessories, are squished together on the Italian chaise-longue. Constantia has taken the dressing table chair, as befits her status as caller-of-meeting.

The bedroom door is closed. The servants have been given strict orders not to disturb them. Constantia clears her throat daintily and sits a little more upright. The twins lean forward expectantly.

"So, has the little police detective been round asking about Syb?"

The twins nod in perfect synchronicity.

"Such a funny man. He had a walrus moustache and he wore *brown* boots," Veracia says.

"They had been mended too," Dorinda adds scornfully.

"Did he mention some sort of 'communication'?"

The twins agree that the word 'communication' was used at the aforesaid meeting.

"Did he say what was in it?"

Two heads are shaken vehemently.

"He did not have much of a chance to impart anything much. Mama was rather ... Mama-like," Dorinda says.

"Mine also," Constantia sighs.

"Mamas are all very well in their way," Dorinda drawls.

"But not when they are in *our* way," Constantia says firmly. "So we none of us know what the communication was, except that whatever it was, Syb's mother and father are taking it very seriously. My mama had a letter from Lady Meriel yesterday and has gone to meet her in town this morning."

"You might find out what's going on when she returns?"

"If I do, I shall write to you both at once."

Dorinda purses her mouth.

"It is still strange though, isn't it, Con? Each of us think we might have seen Syb ~ only we can't be sure it *was* Syb, because one bonnet looks very much like another on a crowded street when you are driving past in the rain."

"Or taking tea at Fortnum's and watching the passers-by," Veracia adds. "Or looking out of one's window late at night," she adds nodding at their hostess. She pauses, then adds in a lowered voice, "I cannot help being reminded of that story we read at school. About the girl who secretly entered a nunnery to escape a terrible curse, and how her family was haunted and followed by her evil spirit-double, until the curse was lifted?"

A gasp of horror, followed by a shiver of delight.

"Oh yes! I remember that story! It kept me awake for whole nights on end, and I was forever looking over my shoulder for ages after to see if my evil spirit-double was following me," Dorinda says. "So it might have been Syb's ghost come back from the dead to wreak revenge upon her family? Oh, how very ... Syb. Though we couldn't possibly tell the little police detective man that, could we?" she adds disappointedly, her face falling.

"No, we certainly could not," Veracia agrees.

"I would never tell anything to a man who wears brown boots, anyway," Constantia says loftily. "So that, my dearest friends, is an end of the matter. What we saw, or *think* we saw, must remain our secret."

"We shall take it to the grave," Veracia says, her eyes sparkling.

"Besides, nobody would believe us," Dorinda adds.

"Exactly," Constantia agrees. "And now we are all agreed upon the matter, let us go downstairs and have some tea and cake."

***

Meanwhile, Detective Sergeant Jack Cully, whose boots are a respectable black, and polished every night by his loving wife, is checking out Mrs Lilith Marks' alibi. He is accompanied by Inspector Lachlan Greig, who has newly arrived at Scotland Yard from Bow Street, and is under Cully's helpful wing until he settles in.

Their journey has brought them to a smart new office building just off City Road, where they are waiting to interview the owner of the business on the top floor, who is currently in a meeting.

To Cully's surprise, the outer office is staffed by a young female clerk in a white blouse and navy skirt. She sits at one of the high wooden desks, a quill pen in her hand, an open ledger in front of her. He is just getting over the shock of this, when the door to the inner office opens.

Two people emerge: a thin male clerk with straw coloured hair, carrying a large brass bound ledger under his arm, and a slender young woman with a determined expression and a halo of unruly red hair that is barely controlled by a net and pins. Her face lights up when she sees Cully.

"Detective Sergeant Cully. This is a pleasant surprise. At least, I hope it is."

Cully has not seen Miss Josephine King for some time. Their paths last crossed when he and Stride were called in to investigate the murder of her uncle. She has not changed much, he thinks. Still the frank, straight-in-your-face expression, and the bright, untamed mass of hair.

"I hope so too, Miss King," he says, introducing his companion. "I called in at the old place, and they kindly directed me to your new premises. I hope it is a sign that the business is prospering."

"Yes, J. King & Co. is already making a name for itself in the city. Even though the owner of the company is not *quite* what the city expects."

She smiles drily. "But you haven't come here to discuss business with me, have you?"

She turns and walks back into the inner office. The two men follow her. Bidding the clerk to fetch three cups of coffee, Josephine King settles herself behind an impressive desk and props her chin on her cupped hands.

"Now gentlemen, I presume you are in pursuit of an investigation? Yes, I see it in your faces. So, you had better tell me what it is about, and how I can be of service. Naturally, I will help you to the best of my ability."

Some time later the two officers leave, shown out to the street by Josephine's trusty clerk Trafalgar Moggs.

"That was a very unusual young woman," Inspector Greig remarks.

"She is indeed," Cully replies. "Detective Inspector Stride is terrified of her! She ran rings round him last time they met. As soon as he heard who we were intending to interview, he suddenly discovered some paperwork that urgently needed his attention, and volunteered you to accompany me instead."

"That scared, eh?" Greig smiles. "Mind, I can see why. You'd struggle to put much past the lassie. She had a glint in her eye, did she not?"

"Oh, she does not tolerate fools gladly," Cully agrees.

The two men start walking back to Scotland Yard at a steady thinking pace, passing shops and small businesses as they go. While they proceed in companionable silence, Cully reflects upon what Josephine King has told them.

She has confirmed that Lilith Marks was with her on the night in question. He knew that she would. He also knows Stride will not believe it. For some reason, he has decided that Mrs Marks is involved in the death of Montague Foxx.

Motive and opportunity, Stride will say. She had the one, so logically she may well have the other. Cully, however, is sure she is innocent. The trouble is, until he finds out who murdered Foxx and placed him in a west end department store window for the whole of fashionable London to gawp at, he cannot prove otherwise.

Inspector Lachlan Greig is also thinking about the meeting that has just taken place. But his thoughts are running on very different lines. Greig started his career in the Leith Police as a newly qualified officer, moving quickly up the ranks, before making the decision to leave his home town and come south.

Initially, he found the immensity of London difficult to come to terms with, and though he is settling into his new job well, and beginning to find his feet, he is often lonely. He recalls the young lady's crisp air of authority, her open frank manner, her bright eyes, slender figure and coronet of flaming red hair.

Greig thinks that he might rather like to encounter her again one day in the not too distant future. Perhaps this time in slightly less formal circumstances.

***

While Cully, Greig and their respective thoughts are returning to Scotland Yard, the object of their cogitations is giving careful instructions to her chief clerk. After which she fetches down her bonnet from its peg, and hurries out of the offices of J. King & Co.

Hailing a passing cab, she gives the driver her desired destination, and a while later, she is set down in Hampstead High Street. Josephine makes her way to the Lily Lounge, where the lunch time rush has dribbled away to a few late stragglers.

Lilith is in the back room, sorting out the lunchtime takings. Her expression betrays no surprise whatsoever at Josephine's unexpected appearance. She merely pulls out a chair and orders one of the waitresses to rustle up a beef sandwich for her.

While she eats, Josephine studies her friend. It seems to her that Lilith has aged since they last met. The lines from her nose to the corners of her handsome mouth are more pronounced. Her shoulders droop, and every now and then, she utters a sigh that seems to come from somewhere deep within.

At length, when she has placed the takings in a cloth bag ready for the bank, Lilith turns to face her.

"I can guess why you are here," she says. "You have had a visit from Detective Sergeant Cully, and you are come to ask why?"

Josephine nods.

"What did he tell you?"

"Nothing. He merely asked me to confirm whether I spent last Wednesday evening in your company. Which I did, and so I told him. But you are suspected of having done something, that is clear, and so I have come to ask you what it is, and to offer my help in any way that I can.

"You have been my friend, my confidant, and a wise advisor to me over the years. You rescued William and me from the clutches of that evil Romanian Countess. If you are now in difficulties yourself, then I am by your side. Whatever the matter may be."

Lilith regards her steadily, but with troubled eyes. Josephine meets her gaze and holds it for a few seconds. Then she reaches out a hand, and lays it softly on the older woman's arm.

"Please tell me everything," she says.

So Lilith does. And when she has done, Josephine brushes away the tears and says, "Whatever you need me to do to clear your name and remove any suspicion that you were involved in the death of this evil man, I will do."

Lilith permits herself a faint smile.

"Brave child. But you cannot accompany me on the journey I must make. Nobody can. I am shortly to return to a life I left behind many years ago. Not to participate, but to discover the truth. If I can rely on your discretion, that will give me great encouragement."

"You have it. And William will be on hand should you require a man's presence ~ if he can tear himself away from his current ladylove, that is."

Lilith laughs.

"He certainly has come a long way from the scruffy street sweeper you took in out of charity."

"He is now the senior groom at a large livery stable," Josephine says proudly. "And so grown that he is head and shoulders taller than both of us. Mind, he eats like one of the horses he tends: Mrs Hudson has had to double the grocery order."

She rises, pushing her empty plate away.

"I will leave you now. Please send me word if ever you need me. And know that I shall be there in an instant."

Lilith takes her hand and holds it between her own.

"Are you sure? I am about to go hunting monsters, and monsters, even dead ones, can take you into some very dark places."

"No darker than we have been to before," Josephine reminds her. "And we all came out of that encounter safe and sound, remember?"

Lilith smiles her agreement, then accompanies her friend to the tea-room door, where she waves her off cheerily, hoping Josephine will not perceive that it is an act. Behind the bravado, she feels vulnerable and if she thinks about it, which she is trying not to do, slightly afraid.

The world was full of examples of what fate might befall the curious. Bluebeard's wife and cats came to mind. But she has chosen to open the door on her past, and set her foot on the shadowy path that leads back in time, so now there is no turning back.

***

Stride stirs a cup of black coffee with a pencil. Sometimes he wonders whether there are ever any long straws in this job. It has been a tedious day. There has been a lot of paperwork. There is always a lot of paperwork. Currently top of the paperwork pile is the report from the coroner's court.

The inquest jury assembled to pronounce upon the death of Montague Foxx have, in the absence of any clues, motive or witnesses, returned a verdict of wilful murder against person/persons unknown. The body has been released to a distant member of the family for burial.

He reads some more reports, then crumples up one of them and throws it across the room, uttering the sort of noise Mr F. W. Lillywhite (defunct) made when delivering a fast round arm ball to a hapless opponent.

Stride thinks about his earlier interviews with Miss Veracia and Miss Dorinda Davenport, young ladies of exceptional beauty with a mama of implacable hostility. What was it about these people? They treated the detective division like petty tradesmen: there when needed, dismissed when no longer wanted. And when asked to assist in an enquiry, they erected a wall of silence, behind which they squatted, cold-eyed and uncooperative.

Stride is sure he would progress better with Sybella's friends were it not for the presence of their mamas, leaping to protect their offspring whenever they felt their emotional welfare was being threatened.

At the first trickling tear from Miss Veracia, and the second stifled sob from her sister, their gimlet-eyed mother stopped his interview immediately, informing him icily that he was overstepping his duty. He was then turned out of the Belgravia townhouse without another word being said.

Stride was angry, and as he walked back to Scotland Yard, he got angrier, and then to make matters worse he was stopped in his tracks by the headline in the lunchtime edition of *The Inquirer*, which read:

Body in Shop Window: Police Investigation 'A Total Farce!' says Shop Owner

He stood in front of the news stand skimming the article, because he refused to waste money on actually buying a copy of the newspaper. Grimly, he noted the by-line. Then he diverted via Oxford Street, pushed his way past the doorman at the entrance to *John Gould & Company,* and insisted upon being taken straight to Mr Gould's office.

Once he'd been admitted to the inner sanctum, Stride had explained very slowly and carefully in a speaking-to-the-hard-of-understanding voice, why talking to the press was A Very Bad Idea, and why talking to *this* particular member of the press was An Even Worse One. Gould had listened in total silence. Finally, having extracted a promise that as far as the press was concerned, Gould's lips would henceforth be sealed, Stride left.

Now he sits at his desk and gloomily sucks the end of the pencil, wishing pencils came in tobacco flavour. He doesn't smoke any more, his wife has forbidden it, but he frequently thinks he might take it up again anyway. Smoking is good for dealing with problems.

Stride's problem is that he is outside his area of expertise. He is used to dealing with ordinary people. The sort that bluster, and look sideways, and deny everything to begin with, but subjected to enough pressure, eventually give in and confess that they did it.

His thoughts drift to Sir High Wynward and his circle. The upper classes are terra incognita. A closed book. He is sure the young women he interviewed earlier have information that would be useful, but how is he to find out when he can't question and browbeat them?

Stride has promised to keep Sir Hugh Wynward abreast of any developments. There have been no developments, but he will cobble something together in the next half an hour to keep him satisfied. Because at the end of the day, he is a professional detective, and that is how it works. And as far as the body in the window of *John Gould & Company* is concerned, he simply cannot allow scum like Richard Dandy to be proven right.

***

It is a fine clear night. The sort of night when a young man of a romantic inclination might hang around outside his current girlfriend's house, on the off chance that she could sneak away from her duties for a few minutes' courtship. Sadly the man on this occasion, William Smith (formerly of the gutter), is out of luck. His ladylove is busy upstairs serving the fish course.

For Mrs Mortram and her husband are hosting a dinner party. The other guests consist of the Davenports, some business contacts of Mortram, the Davenport twin girls, and a few eligible young men, friends of Constantia's older brother, who have been whistled up for the occasion.

Diamonds and coloured feathers adorn elaborately curled hair. Light from crystal chandeliers shines down upon bare polished white shoulders and arms. Light reflects off cut glass, shiny silver cutlery and plated serving platters.

The turbot is distributed, the silky white wine poured and the servants depart temporarily to assemble the meat course, leaving the men to tuck in and the women to push the food around on their plates ~ for a lady must never be seen to be eating with relish.

The older women chat politely to their dinner partners, check on the behaviour of the young people at the end of the table, and exchange glances across the table. Wait until we are alone, the glances say. We have much to talk over.

The three young ladies toy with the fish and the young men. They sip their wine, flutter their lashes, and eye each other with an air of expectancy that has nothing to do with the food or the proximity of masculine company.

Eventually, the roast beef gives way to apple pie and raspberry pudding. Then cheese. The ladies dip their fingers into the rose-scented finger bowls. Mrs Mortram coughs discreetly and rises from her place.

"Now ladies, shall we leave the gentlemen to their debates and their cigars?" she says airily, rustling to the door.

Mrs Davenport follows her. The three girls link slender arms and tag along behind. The older women head straight for the small parlour, where coffee is waiting on a tray.

"Well, Grace, what are we going to do about this Meriel business?" Mrs Davenport inquires, when she has been furnished with a small cup of the fragrant brew. "Surely to goodness there cannot be any truth in it?"

"Of course not," Mrs Mortram says, waving a dismissive hand. "We read the reports in the newspaper. We were all there at the funeral. It is some trick ~ one of those mediums she is always consulting. They have decided to send Meriel a lock of hair. Presumably an attempt to get her to give them more money to 'contact' poor Sybella, or some such idiocy. You know how gullible Meriel is? Always has been."

"But shouldn't we have a word with Hugh?"

Mrs Mortram shudders.

"Not I. The man gives me the willies. Whenever I meet him, I always feel as if someone has walked over my grave."

"He seems to be taking the letter seriously though."

"So I should hope. It is a serious matter being the subject of fraud and blackmail. His reputation is at stake. No, let the police do their work. It is not for us to interfere. Besides, who knows what kind of person is at the back of this? We have our girls to think of, and their futures. I have high hopes that young Mr Hanchard might be about to propose to Constantia. He has been very attentive during the Season."

"Really?" Mrs Davenport pulls her chair a little closer. "Do tell ..."

Meanwhile 'our girls' have taken refuge in the conservatory, where they are currently sitting close together in a huddle of wicker chairs and spread skirts.

"So, Con," Dorinda says, glancing furtively over her shoulder, even though they have shut the door firmly behind them, "tell us everything you know."

"Well ... Mama says Lady M got a letter in the post from Sybella ~ that was the famous 'communication'. The envelope wasn't in her handwriting, but apparently the note was."

"What did the note say?" Veracia asks.

"'*Remember me*'. And there was a lock of Syb's hair, tied in a red ribbon."

"Ghost hair? But that's impossible," Dorinda cries.

"Yes, it is. But you know Lady M. Mama said she had to accompany her at once to some little fortune-telling woman, who told her that Syb was alive, and coming back to her."

Veracia rolls her eyes.

"She didn't come back the last time she ran off, did she? When that hired detective found her, they had to virtually drag her home in a locked carriage."

"But we were at school then. It was different." Constantia reminds her.

"Maybe she is still alive ... could it be possible?"

Constantia Mortram shakes her head.

"Even if she had, by some miracle, survived the train crash, do you honestly think she'd want to return? Would you, in her shoes?"

Dorinda smiles acidly.

"WE are not in her shoes though. Our Mamas do not make us go to strange spiritual gatherings. Our papas do not browbeat us and lock us in our rooms for refusing to marry our mad relatives."

"Shh, Dorry, you mustn't say things like that," Veracia chides.

Her sister tosses her feathered head.

"Why must I not? Everybody knows it to be the truth."

There is a long meditative pause.

"I do miss Syb," Veracia sighs. "London hasn't been the same since she went. Con, Dorry, Vee and Syb: the four Musketeers."

"One for All, and All against Miss Barbara Pristle," Constantia says, naming the draconian head mistress of the Select Ladies' Seminary they'd attended.

"Do you think we ought to mention ... you know ... what we think we saw, to our Mamas?" Veracia asks hesitantly.

"Absolutely not. They won't believe us. And if it gets out, people will laugh at us. We will be the talk of the town and not in a good way. Besides I think Harry may be about to propose ~ he's been dropping hints. I'm not going to sacrifice my chance of making a good marriage upon some impossible whim."

Constantia meets each eye, holds it without blinking, then lays her hand, palm down, upon the small occasional table.

"Are we all agreed, Musketeers?"

The twins place their hands upon hers.

Constantia withdraws hers from the bottom of the pile, and nods her head decisively.

"Then it shall be so. And now, we must join our Mamas for coffee. If questioned, let us agree that we were talking about our new winter bonnets."

***

London is wide awake at midnight, and sinks into fitful slumber at two a.m. Now it is four o'clock and a cold wind is blowing. The dead hour. The bells of St Paul's have sounded, followed by Bow bells and the bells of St Clement Danes. The river Thames, that liquid coin that runs through the heart of the great city, flows intractably on to the sea.

At this dead time of night, the river is blacker than black under a starless sky. Slicker and darker and more impossible than the wind. It has nothing to say. The great warehouses that line its banks are closed. The moist wharves that teem with crates of china and tubs of aromatic oranges and figs, muscovado and molasses are gated and barred up. They too have nothing to say.

The long wall of the Custom House is a dead thing, full of half-blind windows. The blackened coal barges and lighters rock to and fro, pulling on their anchor chains. The moored wherries and river steam boats, and the swift galleys of the Thames Police wait patiently by landing stages. and slimy river steps.

On bridge after bridge, the long rows of gas lamps mirror themselves in the dark waters below, looking for all the world as if they were being held up by the spirits of those who plunged into the dark waters, whose only epitaph now is a placard on the wall of the Police Station: 'Dead body found'.

Four gives way to five, and now the bells mark the first hour of the working day. The first workpeople appear, the first fires are lit under street-corner breakfast sellers. and the long and broad streets of London yawn and stretch, and get ready to fill with life once more.

***

And exactly one hour later, at 6 am, Mary Mullins, who is employed by the Mortrams as a lowly housemaid, descends the uncarpeted back stairs from her unheated attic bedroom and begins her day. She cleans out the grates and sweeps the rooms. By seven, she has washed her filthy hands, and is ready to take the jugs of hot water upstairs to her master, mistress and Miss Constantia.

Mary Mullins is a pretty girl. Sixteen years of age, well-made with a neat waist, shiny brown hair and a bright complexion. Her face glows from a plentiful supply of soap, for her mistress has a 'thing' about cleanliness.

Mary does not mind. Where she came from, the local orphanage, soap was a non-existent commodity. So were names. There she was known as girl number 56. She likes the soap and she likes her new name, even though she gathers that it is the same as her predecessor ~ all the housemaids have been Mary Mullinses. It makes life easier for the mistress. Mrs Mortram is a busy woman and hasn't got time to remember different servant names.

Mary Mullins the fourth changes from her dirty gown to a clean cotton one, adding a white apron and small cap, and opens the curtains of the breakfast room. She lays the white cloth on the breakfast table, and arranges the cups and saucers on either side of Mrs Mortram's place at the end of the table.

Then she places the teapot, sugar basin and milk ewer just behind, recalling that when she first arrived from the orphanage, she didn't know how to set a table, let alone wait on company. Last night, she and a hired waiter served a four-course dinner, and she didn't drop a thing. She is coming on nicely.

As the family descend the stairs ready for their breakfasts, Mary Mullins hurries down to the kitchen, where the cook has placed the rack of toast, a stand of eggs, bread and butter and a plate of rashers on a tray, ready to be taken up to the family.

As soon as her serving duties upstairs are done, she goes back to the kitchen where her own breakfast of porridge and bread and butter is waiting. She is sharp set, and consumes it with relish before beginning her morning chores.

The household work plan for the comfort of the family and the dispatch of jobs has been written out in Mrs Mortram's firm hand on a sheet of paper, and pasted to the kitchen wall.

The paper has been varnished and given a small ornamental border to make it look slightly more pleasing, and definitely more permanent. Here is enumerated the order of work for each day, and the rules for the coming and going of the servants.

Mary Mullins puts a large white holland housework apron over her answering the door apron, and gets ready to make the beds and tidy the rooms. She is fetched from her work a short while later by a ring at the doorbell. It won't be the first disturbance, but it is the one that will have the most far-reaching consequences.

Removing the holland apron, she trips downstairs. On the doorstep is the old clothes merchant, 'Ole Clo'. He is expected. Ordering him to go and wait by the area entrance, she hastens into the scullery, where Mrs Mortram has left a bundle of cast-off garments, together with a note saying what she will accept in payment. Mary Mullins picks up the bundle and ascends to street level.

The man opens the bundle and examines the goods. While he is busy, Mary peeks over his shoulder at the pile of second hand garments lying in the small pony trap. They are strewn in a casual profusion of rainbow colours. The man notices her interest. He walks to the cart, setting down the bundle, and picks up a dark blue dress almost the colour of her eyes.

"You vants to see something nice? Take a look at this luvverly dress. Almost new. One careful owner. See, hold it up against yerself. I reckon it'd be a good fit. That blue suits. Vat you think?"

Mary's hungry gaze feasts on the pretty frock. She has a new lace collar, and a blue neck ribbon almost the exact match. She also has some money saved from her wages and the tips she gets from visitors to the house. Is it enough for a new dress?

The man reads her expression.

"Look, I'll make yer a deal. Here's the money for the bundle, and I'll throw in the blue dress for a shillin' just because I likes yer pretty face. How about that?"

Mary darts down the area steps. Luckily the cook is upstairs discussing menus. She runs up the back stairs to her attic room, and takes her little purse from under her pillow. Carefully counting out twelve pennies, she returns to the street and hands them over, getting the blue dress in return.

The old clothes man nods his thanks. Then he slaps the tired pony's reins to get him moving, and a jubilant Mary Mullins carries the blue dress inside. She has a rare evening off tonight and her current sweetheart is coming to take her out. She was wondering what to wear to increase his admiration for her even further. Problem solved.

***

Lilith has spent another bad night. Once again, her rest was troubled by disturbing dreams. This time she found herself standing on the pavement watching a funeral procession, with herself following the hearse, and it seemed to her that the coffin being borne along was her coffin and that the solitary mourner was her own ghost.

In the dream, a little wind was driving the fallen leaves along the pavement and for a terrifying second, fear took hold of her with a cold hand, and the whispering of the dead leaves seemed to be warning her that one day soon, like them, she would be swept into the gutter and nobody would ask where she had gone.

She had awoken at the crack of dawn with a craving that there should be at least one person to whom her disappearance would be a calamity, and that she would not end her days alone and unmourned.

Now, after readying her waitresses and preparing the food for the lunch time rush, Lilith has slipped on her bonnet and left the Lily Lounge for a destination far less salubrious than Hampstead. She is on her way to visit Mrs Frost.

Everyone in 'the business' ~ and if you didn't know what 'the business' was, then you weren't in 'the business', knew Mrs Frost and what she did. Mrs Frost ran what some called a House of Ill Repute, though there were just as many who spoke quite highly of it.

Very early on in her unfortunate marriage, Lilith discovered Mrs Frost's calling card in her husband's coat pocket. It was the first indication that there was another less salubrious side to Montague Foxx.

Reaching Whitechapel, Lilith makes her way to Spicer Street, where Mrs Frost has her notorious establishment. Ironically, given what goes on behind closed doors, the houses in Spicer Street are amongst the cleanest in the district. The windows have neat green blinds and there are smart brass plates on the door.

Lilith raps on the door. It is opened by a young hall-boy in a bright blue silk suit. He eyes her curiously.

"Is Mrs Frost at home?" Lilith asks, placing her foot firmly in the doorway.

The boy considers her question carefully.

"She might be," he concedes eventually. "Who's callin'?"

Lilith steps over the threshold, straight into a front room full of grubby chaise-longues, silk hangings and photographs of opulently-bosomed ladies, some wearing gowns, some not. She plonks herself down upon the nearest chaise-longue and peels off her gloves.

"I'm an old acquaintance. Tell her it is 'Mrs Foxx'. She'll know what it's about."

The boy disappears.

A short while later he is back, followed by a deep throaty cough which turns into a small shuffling elderly woman with a yellow shipwreck of a face and dark suspicious eyes. Dressed in a bright bottle-green gown, she wears a red wig, slightly askew, and a lorgnette, which she lifts and places upon her bony nose.

"Well, I'll be Cedric's maiden aunt!" she wheezes. "Long time no see, as the sailor said to the boiled lobster."

Mrs Athene Frost levers herself onto an adjacent sofa, emitting a strong odour of cheap gin and armpits.

"He ain't here."

Lilith folds here arms and stares her out.

"He wasn't here larst time neither. So what d'you want?"

"You know what I want," Lilith replies coldly. "Information."

"Oho! Information is it? But information is currency, as they say."

She holds out a taloned hand, palm up. Her beady sunken eyes peer at Lilith greedily.

"In my business, we don't ask for payment until after the customer has finished."

Mrs Frost laughs rustily.

"Yes, I heard you had moved out of whoring and into catering. Same thing, opposite ends, as you might say."

Lilith remains silent.

"I've moved on meself. As you prob'ly saw when you come in. Driven out by circumstances beyond my control, as they say. First it was the Christian do-gooders handing out pamphlets and trying to draw the girls away

~ you wouldn't credit the allure of tea and buns to a hungry youngster.

"Then it was the writers accosting them and asking what it was like being a 'prostitute', coz they were writing a book about London life. Prostitute indeed! Independent working girls, they were. Had their own clothes ~ none of that rent-a-frock stuff.

"It got so bad round here that the girls couldn't chat up a client without someone with a notebook and pencil butting in, or a man in a dog-collar handing out tracts. Business started to go downhill rapidly. Got out two years come October."

She sucks her gums.

"Now I lets rooms to theatricals. Good money, especially during panto season. I have Fifi and her performing felines staying, and Miss Vesta Swann, she's a shantooze ~ that's French for singer. Oh, and the Tiny Tumblers are in the first floor back ~ they're a family of dwarves. Eight of them. I'd charge them half the rent, but the little buggers eat like bloody race horses."

She pauses, eying Lilith narrowly.

"So ... you 'eard the news about Monty then. Nasty business."

Lilith agrees.

"Surprised you showed up. Would of thought you'd be hanging out the flags and having a party to celebrate."

"Do you know who did it?"

Mrs Frost considers, head on one side, a move that sets her wig at an even more rakish angle.

"How long have you got? I could give you a whole list of people who'd not be shedding a single tear over that man's end. Top o' the list would be you."

"But I didn't kill him."

"So you sez."

Lilith decides to move the conversation into safer waters.

"When did you last see him?"

Mrs Frost scratches under her wig with a long dirty fingernail.

"Lemme think. Last time I saw Monty, he was in the Rooster and Gherkin talking to one of my lodgers. Signorina Mimi Casabianca, mystic and medium, she called herself. They were quite friendly, though not in the way you think I mean."

"Where is she now? Can I speak with her?"

Mrs Frost shakes her head. Another risky manoeuvre.

"She ain't here no more. Packed up and flitted a while back. Owed me a week's rent, little bitch. If I ever get my hands on her, I'll mystic her, an' no mistake."

Lilith pulls on her gloves.

"Thank you. I won't trouble you further."

"Oh it ain't no trouble. If I could tell you anything, I would. B'lieve me. He's dead and gone, and I don't owe him shit."

She leans forward.

"You want to go down to the King's Head, that new place in Holborn. He was keeping company with one of the barmaids. Ask her. She may know who done him in. Tho' why you wants to find out is beyond me. I thought you'd be out dancing on his grave."

Lilith takes her leave. She would indeed like to dance on Montague Foxx's grave. But preferably as a free and unsuspected-of-causing-him-to-be-in-it-in-the-first-place woman.

***

As Lilith is returning back to the tea-room on one side of the city, over on the other side of the city Detective Inspector Stride is on his way to a less congenial location. He has a meeting with Sir Hugh Wynward to report on the progress of his investigation.

95

Stride reflects bitterly that every time he has to deal with rich people, he ends up doing exactly this. Wasting time on pointless meetings at which he is made to feel that he isn't doing his job adequately.

He infinitely prefers to send round a written report. Words were good. You could hide behind words. But the upper classes liked you to turn up regularly, so that they could berate you face to face.

Stride bangs the lion's head knocker as loud as he can, and is shown into the hallway by the snooty butler. The rich have a way of looking at you, he thinks. It is as if you were something they brought in on the soles of their shoes. And their servants are cut from the same cloth too.

Over the past few days, he has spent a lot of time in the company of very rich people and their various offspring. They all kept telling him how happy Sybella Wynward was, and what a wonderful life she had. How much she was loved. How much she is missed. But every now and then, Stride got the feeling that they were not quite telling him the whole story.

A quick cautionary glance, a slight hesitation, a discreet finger applied to the lips when someone thought he wasn't looking. There is more to this case than he is being led to believe. Though he is being led to believe a lot of unlikely stuff. And he doesn't believe it. Not for one minute.

Stride follows the broad-shouldered butler along a darkly lit corridor, and is shown into an equally darkly lit study, with mahogany bookshelves full of dark leather-bound books with gold lettering on the spine. Sir Hugh Wynward rises from a chair, tossing a copy of *The Times* onto a side table.

"Ah, detective inspector, please sit."

Stride perches himself uneasily on the edge of a hard chair. Sir Hugh regards him silently and with a slight air of disapproval. Stride cannot help the sensation that he is being judged and found wanting.

"Well now, have you anything to tell me regarding the communication we received?"

Stride does a rapid mental assemblage of suitably anodyne waffle.

"My men are making diligent inquiries. All avenues are being explored. I expect positive results will be forthcoming in the not too distant future," he says, his eyes fixed upon a portrait of Sir Hugh that hung above the fireplace. It regards him with the same stern, disbelieving expression.

"Maybe they will be. However. I have thought long and hard about the matter since we last met, and now I have come to the conclusion that whoever posted that letter intended it as a cruel joke. To pursue it further might be playing into their hands. Also, I am not wholly convinced that I want my private life and that of my family to become the source of gossip and speculation."

Stride blinks.

"I'm not sure I understand you. Are you are asking me to drop my inquiries?"

"I think that might be the best thing to do in the circumstances I have described to you, yes."

"But surely you want to get to the bottom of this?"

Sir Hugh is about to reply when the study door is suddenly thrust open, and a distraught looking middle-aged woman in an assortment of ill-matched garments rushes in. Sir Hugh rises quickly and grasps her shoulders, but she shrugs him off with a peremptory gesture.

"No, please!" she cries, her hands fluttering to her breast, where they catch amongst the ropes of pearls hung around her neck. "No! I beg you! You shall not give up. She is alive, I know she is. You must find her. I beg you!"

"Meriel ~ you forget yourself."

The voice cracks like a whip.

The woman flinches, as if she has been struck a blow. She takes a step back. Her face seems to crumple into itself. Sir Hugh Wynward seizes her roughly by the elbow and half escorts, half frog-marches her to the door.

"You will not enter this room unannounced again, do you understand?" he hisses in a low undertone which Stride, seasoned by years of listening to people speaking in low undertones in the hope that he won't hear them, hears perfectly.

Lady Meriel bites her lip, like a child that has been scolded.

"I only thought ..." she whimpers.

"No, you did NOT think. We have discussed this. Sybella is dead. She. Is. Dead. And that is the end of it. Now go to your room and wait. I shall be up to see you as soon as the detective has left."

Lady Meriel gives a strangled sob, and rushes from the room. There is the sound of pattering footsteps stumbling into the distance, then a door slams somewhere overhead.

Calmly, Sir Hugh Wynward positions himself in front of the fireplace, directly underneath the portrait. Two sets of predator eyes now regard Stride coldly.

"Of course you will forget what you have just witnessed, detective inspector. My wife is afflicted with hysteria. At times, it affects her badly. She has never been a strong woman and she has suffered greatly since that letter arrived. Another reason to ignore it. And now I must now go and deal with her. James will show you out."

He rings the bell.

"But you haven't ..." Stride begins.

Sir Hugh Wynward picks up the copy of the *Times* and begins to turn the pages. The door opens.

"The detective inspector is leaving," Sir Hugh says, from behind the pages of the newspaper.

Stride follows the stiff-backed butler back to the front door. As he reaches the gate, something makes him turn and glance up. Lady Meriel, her face white and drawn, is staring out of a first-floor window. When she sees him, she raises a hand and presses the palm to the glass. Her mouth opens wide in what might be a farewell, or might equally be a scream.

Stride walks away, puzzling over what has just taken place. He is not convinced by what he has heard. Not from Sir Hugh, nor from any of the people in his social circle. He is clearly being lied to and he doesn't like it.

And another thing, he thinks angrily, as he turns the corner of the square: why has the wife of Sir Hugh Wynward got bars on her bedroom window?

***

Felix Lightowler is also puzzled about bars, though in his case the bars are made of gold. Or possibly of gold. Well, they will be once he has managed to put together the correct combination of Materialls that will turn molten base metals into pure gold.

Lightowler sits at the back of his bookshop in the dying light of the autumn afternoon, copying out some pages headed: '*Opinions uponne the Makynge of Golde*' by an obscure sixteenth century alchemist (or Alchymist) called Johannes Philadelphus.

He discovered the pages bound in an antique Book of Hours, which has been left with him for rebinding by an acquaintance who works at the British Museum. He wants it back.

Gold hath these natures, he writes down. *Greatnesse of weight, closenesse of parts, fixation, softnesse, pliantnesse, colour or tincture of yellow.*

He pauses, enjoying his immersion in a time when spelling was arbitrary and involved a lot of esses. In the fullnesse of time, Lightowler intends to bring out his own book (or boke) on the 'workyng of metalls'. Thus he is scribbling down as much as he can before he has to part with this one, on the basis that the more he can borrow from other works, the easier it will be to create his own.

As he copies the spindly handwriting, he ponders upon the absolute simplicity of the basic alchemic premise: if gold contains these properties, and one makes a substance that has the same properties, then that substance must be gold.

It is so simple. So logical.

All he has to do, is combine the substances in the right quantities and heat them to the correct degree, for the requisite amount of time. He has recently bought, for this purpose, a new and better furnace and a rather odd piece of glassware known as a pelican.

Lightowler has not thought further than the actual processes. The lure of riches untold has little appeal: it is the actual making of the thing ~ the achievement of gnosis, that is his ultimate goal.

Not that this is true for his trio of students. Masters Thorogood and Strictly are only interested in getting and spending, like most foolish young men of their type. He has seen them exchanging sly looks and scribbling notes when they think he hasn't noticed. Oh yes.

Base Metals, the pair of them.

They will spend a lot more before they get anything out of him, Lightowler reflects darkly. The shop barely pays its way. Their contributions are currently keeping him in chemicals and equipment. Once he has corrected the errors and impostures associated with the making of Gold; once he has cured the leprosies and impurities of Metalls, he will shuck them off like the rotten fruit peels they are.

As for Master Finister, he might not be the sharpest knife in the drawer, indeed in cutlery terms he is probably more of a spoon, but an alchemist needs his laundry done and his ruffs and cuffs nicely goffered. Authenticity has to be maintained at all costs, and if the cost is to have Bovis Finister as junior apprentice and furnace blower, then so be it.

Lightowler finishes his copying, closes the book and prepares to put up the shop shutters for the day. A hot meat supper awaits him at the Lamb and Flag. And after supper, he will make a 'triall' of the work of Johannes Philadelphus and see what can be achieved.

***

William Smith, orphan and street arab, has come a long long way since his street-sweeping days on Westminster Bridge. He has left the gutter behind him, along with his battered broom, ragged clothes and intermittent meals. Now, he has a well-paid job at Bob Miller's Livery Stables caring for the carriage horses and riding ponies of the rich and indolent.

He has a proper name too ~ no more just 'Oi' shouted across a crowded street by prospective clients. Best of all, he has a home in St John's Wood, and a family in Josephine King, who has taken him in and cared for him.

Most people meeting them assume they are brother and sister. There is a slight resemblance. But their relationship is deeper than that. When you are in trouble, and your back is up against the wall (literally in his case), you soon learn who your friends are. And that they might not be members of your actual birth family.

Here is William now, whistling a merry tune as he saunters back home after a night out with his sweetheart. Victuals have been consumed, small beer drunk and a good time had by both parties culminating in a squeeze of a trim waist and a snatched kiss on the doorstep before parting.

William lets himself into the house. The light is on in the drawing room, so he makes his way there and discovers Josephine staring meditatively into the dying embers of the fire, her slippered feet on the fender and a cup of hot chocolate by her side.

William drops into the companion chair.

"What's up?" he asks.

She sighs.

"I am worried about Lilith, dear William. This murder of her former husband has stirred up a lot of bad memories for her. And it doesn't help that she feels she is suspected of causing his death in some way. I wish I could help her, but I can't."

"She ain't no murderer, I know that!" William declares stoutly.

"Indeed she is not. But unless she can prove it, she fears she may be arrested and have to stand trial for something she did not do. And that would be the end of her business, and perhaps of her life."

"Then we have to prove her innocent," William says.

"Believe me, I am cudgelling my brains to work out a way of doing just that."

She turns to face him.

"But enough of my worries. How was your night out with the lovely Mary?"

"She's a great gal, no mistake. Got the looks, good com'pny..." he frowns.

"But?" she prompts.

"No, nothing. Not Mary at any rate. It's summat else. A strange thing. I've been trying to make sense of it all the way home. Mary was wearing a new blue dress ~ new to her, she said. But it wasn't new to me. Last time I saw the blue dress, it was being worn by my Ellen, who died in that Brighton rail smash last year, along with the young lady she was accompanying. Now then, how do you explain that?"

Josephine shakes her head.

"I can't explain it. Maybe you were mistaken? I imagine one blue dress might look very much like another."

"Maybe I was, but then again, maybe I wasn't. My Ellen was given a blue dress by her young lady, the one who died. She had to let the dress out at the sides, on account of she was a bit bigger. This dress was let out at the sides, exactly the same. And Ellen didn't have enough white thread to sew back all the buttons, so she used whatever she could find in her workbox and this dress had buttons sewn on in diff'rent colours. And I gave Ellen a little glass headed pin as a going away present. Guess what was pinned to the collar?"

"Did you ask Mary where she got the dress from?"

Will makes a wry mouth.

"Well no, I didn't. Bit awkward, innit. On account of, if I did, I'd have to say why I was asking, and it might upset her. Wearing a dead girl's dress ~ that's unlucky. Wearing the same dress as your sweetheart's last sweetheart? That's more than unlucky, specially for me."

Josephine thinks back to a year ago.

"I thought they never found Ellen."

Will sighs.

"She died alright. Nobody could survive that accident. Her young lady, Miss Sybella died and my Ellen would never have left her side. She was like that. I remember going round to the house a few days later to pay my respects," he pauses. "Huh. They told me to shove off. The butler said he'd horsewhip me if I ever showed up again. Not nice people ~ except for the young lady. Ellen always spoke well of her."

There is a pause. William studies the glowing embers in the fireplace, his eyes remote.

"What I don't understand is how my Ellen's dress got back to London without a single mark on it," he says slowly. "And with my little pin still on the collar, exactly as it was the night I said good-bye to her. It's a complete mystery."

"It is a mystery, William. You are right."

"Well, I don't like mysteries. Never have since that business wiv the Countess. So tomorrow, I'm going to go round to the house and this time, I won't take no for an answer. Ellen was my first love. I owe it to her to find out what's going on."

***

Detective Inspector Stride is walking briskly to work, relishing the relative peace and quiet, the lack of paperwork, and absence of random individuals demanding he sets their world to rights NOW. The only sounds in his little oasis of calm are the snap of twigs, and susurration of fallen leaves under his feet.

Turning out of the small side road, he hears the thud of hooves, the creak of leather and jingle of steel, as a troop of horse guards pass by on their way to the park. He pauses to contemplate the magnificent procession before walking on.

Over the years Stride has worked out various routes to work, depending upon the time of year and his level of irritation. This one is top of his therapeutic list. The interview with Sir Hugh Wynward, and the desperate and strange behaviour of Sir Hugh's wife, are gnawing away at him like a rotten tooth.

Stride has been told to abandon an inquiry. One that he has thrown a lot of time and energy into solving. Not that he has got any nearer to solving it, but in the course of trying to, he has been blanked and shown the door by a lot of unpleasant people who think that having fine houses and money in the bank makes them better than him.

Now, at the whim of one of the most unpleasant men he has ever had to deal with, he has been given his marching orders. And he still doesn't understand why. If it were his child, he'd move heaven and earth to find out what was going on.

And then, as he turns into Craig's Court, Stride runs slap bang into the one member of London's great citizenry he definitely does NOT want to encounter in his current mood.

Rancid Cretney scurries up to him with an air of aggrieved righteousness.

"There you are! Well, I told you, din't I?"

"Mr Cretney! What a surprise seeing you here," Stride says with forced enthusiasm. "How may I assist you on this fine autumn morning?"

As Rancid Cretney's diet has always been entirely irony-free, he fails to recognise the sarcastic tone.

"I said them people next door was Up to Something No Good! And now I know they are Up to Something No Good."

He leans closer. Stride tries not to breathe too deeply as *essence de Cretney* starts filling the space between them.

"Last night I was minding my own business as usual, having just finished my supper, when I heard a huge bang coming from the other side of the wall ~ like someone had lit up a firework. So I went to my window and looked out, and I saw a whole lot of yellow smoke coming from the window next door.

"Next thing, I heard footsteps on the stairs and someone disappeared round the back with a bucket ~ the nearest pump's in Leggat Alley. Then they came back with the bucket full of water and went into the house again. Now then, what d'you make of that?"

"Not much, Mr Cretney."

"So you're not going to investigate it?"

"Did anyone die, Mr Cretney? Was anyone removed from the property on a stretcher, dripping blood or with a limb or limbs missing? No? Are you sure? Is the property still standing? Is your property still standing? Yes? Then perhaps it was just some jolly prank that misfired. As you suggest, a firework."

"But ..."

"A firework, Mr Cretney. And if my men had to investigate every firework that got let off accidentally or deliberately, we wouldn't be able to go after the real criminals in this city, would we? Now if you'll excuse me, I have important matters to deal with, so I shall bid you good day."

Stride makes a run for the front entrance of Scotland Yard, Cretney trailing in his wake like a small lugubrious tugboat.

"You ain't getting rid of me that easy, inspector. I know my rights. I can ~"

The remainder of his words are muted by the slam of the main door.

"If that man comes inside this building, he is not under any circumstances to be shown to my office," Stride instructs the desk constable crisply.

He disappears into the back of the building. Even the hell of paperwork is preferable to the inane ramblings of a nosy parker like Rancid Cretney. And to think he took the scenic route to work to calm himself down ...

***

A few hours later, Mrs Gertie Thursday, aka Madame Lazonga, clairvoyant and medium, finishes her lunch, wipes her mouth on a large man's handkerchief and removes the dishes from the parlour table, stashing them under the sofa. She covers the table with a bobbly black cloth and closes the curtains.

She then takes a wooden board out of a fancy velvet-lined case and puts it on the table, placing a small teacup at the centre. Candles are lit and placed around the room. Madame is preparing for one of her regular afternoon séances.

Madame Lazonga sits exclusively for the upper classes, who derive much comfort from her messages from the 'other side' and value the opportunity she provides for emotional release and an opportunity to sob, or express similar inappropriate or indiscreet emotions in a relatively private environment.

Today, she is expecting her usual ladies ~ her clients are mainly female, though sometimes the odd man attends one of the gatherings. These women are the cream of London society, rich, well-educated. One would think they were above such dubious pastimes as spiritualism. One would be wrong. Tragedy does not distinguish rich from poor.

While the clients assemble in the anteroom, where refreshments are served by her little maid, Madame Lazonga makes her final preparations. At her signal, the maid shows the ladies into her inner sanctum. They enter with an air of barely suppressed excitement, and take their places round the table. The lights are turned out. Madame Lazonga waits patiently for all to settle down.

"Ladies, I greet you on behalf of the spirits. Welcome, thrice welcome once again to our little gathering. I hope all have come with open minds and willing hearts," she intones in a fluty voice.

Everyone nods. They have.

"Then let us join hands in this world, and extend our mental hands to welcome those who have passed over into the world of light. The spirits have indicated they have much to communicate this afternoon."

She closes her eyes. Her breathing becomes loud and stertorous. She raises her face and begins to intone in a loud dramatic tone,

"Oh Akhnaten, God of all the Pharoahs, Ruler of All You Survey, Powerful in All You Do, Spirit Guide to this poor Wandering Soul on the Path to True Enlightenment, I summon You here. Please indicate Your presence by knocking twice on the table."

Silence. Two knocks sound. There is a swift and communal indrawing of breath.

"Oh Akhnaten, I repeat, let me know that You are here and waiting to communicate with us from the other side."

Two more knocks.

"Let us now place our fingers upon the teacup and see who wants to communicate with us from that bourne from whence no traveller may return."

Fingers are extended and laid tentatively on the edge of the upturned cup.

"Speak, oh spirits, speak. We are listening."

The cup begins to move. Slowly, it spells out the word *Bernard*. There is a cry from one of the women.

"My son ~ is it you?"

The teacup spells out the words: *Yes mother it is I*.

"Oh my darling, my boy. How are you?"

Laboriously, the teacup spells out: *I am well mother do not weep*.

The recipient, who is dressed in black from head to toe, drops her head and weeps. The cup spells out: *I said do not weep mother*, before flying violently up into the air and off the board.

Time passes. There is a lot more of this stuff, with messages flying to and fro between the attendees and the spirit world, some bringing comfort, others warning of impending doom and disaster. All are received with great solemnity.

Between messages, the spirits encourage the participants to sing spontaneously and at random, as it helps the messages to pass through the ether. Towards the end of the session, in what might be called the *grande finale*, Madame Lazonga takes two slates and hands them to one of the participants to hold.

She asks another to choose a stick of chalk from a bag. She then proceeds to bind the slates together with twine, having first inserted the chalk between the boards.

"I want you to concentrate hard upon somebody you wish to contact," she says to the slate holder, in a low voice. "And let us all join in. The spirits tell me they have a message of hope to bring you."

Everybody closes their eyes. Some begin to sway from side to side. The selected lady clutches the boards, her face screwed up in concentration.

Suddenly there is a series of creaking sounds. Madame Lazonga claps her hands.

"I felt something happening!" she exclaims. "Tell me the name of the one who is dear to you."

"Her name is Sybella."

"Unwrap the boards! See what the spirits say to you."

Lady Meriel Wynward, for it is she, unties the twine, her hands visible shaking. Madame Lazonga takes the slates from her, separates them and holds them up. There is a gasp from the assembled company as they all see the name *Sybella*, written clearly in yellow chalk on one of the boards.

Lady Meriel covers her face with her hands and starts sobbing uncontrollably, and as she is comforted by the ladies on either side of her, Madame Lazonga announces that the session is over. The spirits have delivered their final message. The little maid escorts the participants out, making sure that each lady leaves a generous contribution in the bowl strategically placed by the door.

Meanwhile, Madame Lazonga dismantles the table, and stows away the various props and bits of equipment. The session has been a great success. Obviously it helps that a listening tube has been cunningly built into the dividing wall with the anteroom, so that every word spoken by the waiting participants is clearly audible to her. Even so, she took a bit of a gamble on the spelling of Sybella.

***

As Lady Meriel Wynward is being carried back home across London after the startling revelations of the séance, with her heart beating far too fast and her mind whirling with possibilities, her cook is playing host to a very personable young man, who has made considerable inroads into the freshly baked fruit cake she was planning to serve up for her employers' afternoon tea later.

William Smith sits in the Windsor chair at the head of the table, a mug and plate before him.

"'Nother slice, Mr Smith?" the cook inquires, knife poised.

"Well, Mrs Sedley, h'if you insist. I has to say, Mrs Hudson our cook, is a great one for roasting and biling, but she'd be hard put to make a cake like this. Succulent, that's the only word for it. Succ-u-lent."

Mrs Sedley cuts him a second generous slice.

"Fancy you turning up that time and being threatened by James," she says. "The very idea! We none of us knew about it, believe me. And I shall be speaking my mind to him when you has gone. Ho yus!"

"I nivver thought you did know. Ellen was allus very 'preciative of you, Mrs Sedley. She said you went out of your way to welcome her when she started here. It was her first post."

"Pore little mite," Mrs Sedley says, her double chin quivering. "Fourteen years old and straight out of the workkus, she was. Thin as a rake and as nervous as an unbroken colt. And the master such a cold fish and the mistress scarcely in her right mind most of the time."

"You made her feel welcome, and you fed her up," William says, stirring sugar into his mug of tea.

"And di'n't she grow up lovely? Them big brown eyes and such a rosy colour in her cheeks." She rolls her eyes and heaves a great sigh. "Still can't believe what happened. Her and Miss Sybella, both taken together. Two young lives snuffed out ~ just like that. And then suddenly out of the blue ..." she pauses, her eyes narrowing.

"Out of the blue ...?" William prompts.

The cook purses her mouth.

"A couple of weeks ago, a letter came. Miss Sybella's writing and a lock of her hair inside the envelope. Put the mistress into a terrible state, almost like she was when they told her Miss Sybella was dead. The master was furious. Said it was someone blackmailing them for money.

"He called in the detective police, but then t'other day he suddenly changed his mind. My Lord, the fun and games when that happened! Both of them screaming and shouting like they was being boiled in oil. And the mistress locked in her room and the doctor sent for."

"Why did he change his mind?"

"Who knows? That's the hairystocracy for you, innit. She's dead, he says, I saw her body and that's an end to it. And the mistress threatening all sorts if he doesn't change his mind. But he won't. Cold as ice and hard as steel, he is."

William runs a wetted finger thoughtfully round his plate.

"What if I was to tell you something, Mrs Sedley?" he says quietly. "Only it's a bit of a puzzler and I shouldn't want it getting out beyond these four walls, if you follow me."

The cook folds her arms.

"Go on, Mr Smith. I'm good at puzzles. And keeping secrets. Kept enough of them since I started working here, Gawd knows."

So William Smith tells the Wynward's cook about Mary Mullins, the blue dress and the little glass-headed pin. And when he's done, the cook nods her head a couple of times and says,

"I know the Mortram's cook ~ not int'mate like, but we meet in the fishmongers and poulterers and such. How about if I ask, casual like, who buys their old clothes ... I could say my mistress is looking to get rid of some dresses. That'd be alright, wouldn't it?"

"That'd be more than alright, Mrs Sedley."

"Then you leave it with me, Mr Smith. Stop by in a couple of days and I'll tell you how I got on. As you say, it is a puzzler and no mistake."

William Smith smiles his thanks, downs the last of his tea, and mounts the area steps. He has just turned the corner when a light-coloured brougham pulls up at the kerb and a pale wild-eyed woman descends clumsily, fumbling in her bag for the front door key.

Lady Meriel Wynward stumbles across the threshold, only to come face to face with the butler.

"My Lady?" he inquires.

"Oh. James. Umm. Yes. Please tell cook I shall take tea in my room," she says, sliding out of her coat and unpinning her bonnet with trembling fingers.

"As you wish, my Lady. Excuse me for inquiring, but is my Lady feeling alright?"

Lady Meriel rolls her eyes and gives him a vacuous smile before heading for the stairs. The butler watches her uneven progress. Then he goes, as instructed, to alert Sir Hugh that his wife has returned. From somewhere. Looking rather dishevelled. Again.

***

As Jack Cully heads towards his destination, the gold and russet trees that grow in the city's open spaces are being slowly enwrapped in blue evening mist, leaving their branches spangled with the lights of the street-lamps.

Cully has learned over the years that successful detection comes from a random combination of solid backbreaking slog, sudden flashes of blinding intuition and things that just turn up unexpectedly.

In this latter category is the note that arrived this morning from Mrs Lilith Marks. It read: *You might like to talk to Aggie Crabbe, barmaid at the King's Head, in Holborn.* And so here he is now, standing outside the public house wherein Aggie Crabbe is employed.

The King's Head is one of the new style of public houses springing up all over London, built to appeal to the aesthetic as well as the alcoholic. Warm lights spill enticingly out into the darkening street. Candles glow their welcome in the window.

Cully pushes open the gold and glass panelled door and enters. Inside, there are clusters of lighted globes hanging from the ceiling, ornate mahogany and cut-glass screens, and a long polished bar, with pewter tankards arranged decoratively in rows behind it.

Also behind the bar, are a couple of very attractive barmaids, who are busy pulling pints for a group of young men. They are joshing each other and the barmaids in loud well-bred voices. It is the kind of group that, after a few more drinks, will suddenly turn aggressive and disputatious and have to be ejected onto the street.

Cully orders a small drink, then leans casually across the bar.

"I'm looking for a Miss Aggie Crabbe. Do you know where I might find her?"

The slightly older of the two barmaids smiles knowingly. She has fair hair neatly tied in side bunches, a small mouth, dimples and dancing eyes.

"You're lookin' straight at her, mister. An' I know who you are, and why you are here."

She glances round.

"Why don't you take your drink into the snug over there: it's quiet and I'll join you when I've served these gentlemen."

Cully follows her directions, seating himself in a small partitioned booth. A short while later the barmaid joins him, a glass of cream gin in one hand.

"I'm due a break; we've been non-stop at it since midmorning."

She sips her drink, closing her eyes.

"Now that slips down nice and easy like silk."

Cully waits for the drink to have its effect. The barmaid takes a few more sips. There is a loud crash from the other end of bar, followed by raised voices. She shakes her head.

"Not my business. Let the gaffer sort it out. Now Mr P'liceman ... Mrs Marks said you was investigating the death of the late and not very lamented Mr Monty Foxx. Is that right?"

Cully nods.

"Well, sorry to say, I don't know who did the deed, but if I did, I'd blow him a kiss and thank him from the bottom of my heart, straight up. Monty was a nasty piece of work, and it was a bad day for me when he breezed into this pub."

Cully makes a please-do-continue gesture with one hand.

"There was always some dodge going on with him," Aggie says. "Some scam he was running. I never knew what he was up to half the time. Either he was flush and throwing money about like water, or you'd not see him for weeks coz he was lying low somewhere to avoid his creditors. I got fed up of people coming in and threatening me. Like I'd know where he was?

"The only thing I can tell you is that the night he was murdered, he came in for a quick drink. Said he was going to meet a friend about *'a nice bit of business'*. That was all he said, and that was the last time I saw him. I didn't ask the name of the friend, coz to tell you the truth, I didn't care." She laughs bitterly. "Funny thing, Monty always boasted that when he died, he'd like to go out with a big splash and everybody knowing about it. And they did, didn't they? Throat cut and the death splashed all over the newspapers."

It is late by the time Cully reaches home, and he has walked many miles to reach it. He slips off his boots and leaves them by the front door. Tiptoeing into the bedroom, he pauses by his daughter's wooden cot and gazes down at her. Violet lies on her back in a hot sprawl, her tiny mouth partly open, pulling in the night air with small hissing sounds, as she travels the labyrinth of sleep.

Wisps of wet hair scatter like cuttings around her face. Her eyes are tight shut, as if she is concentrating very hard upon something important. She is so perfect. Cully leans down, almost touching her. Then, his heart bursting with love, he gently inhales the sweet innocence of her baby breath.

***

Meanwhile, in an attic room that smells of charred wood and burned chemicals, and now has crunchy bits underfoot, a bearded figure in black robes and a big ruff is poring over *Opinions uponne the Makynge of Golde* by Johannes Philadelphus.

Felix Lightowler has gone so far as to remove the precious book from his shop, so that he can go through it meticulously line by line. He makes notes about certain words and phrases that have been jotted in the age-spotted margins. The candle sputters and drips.

Lightowler is trying to understand what went wrong with last night's Worke. He performed the experiment exactly as it was written down in the alchemist's spindly writing. The Small Furnace was fine tempered, the Metall remained molten at all times. He endeavoured to keep the Parts Close and Smooth.

And then unexpectedly, the whole thing had suddenly blown up, causing him to dive under the table for safety. Luckily, some sixth alchemical sense warned him just before it happened, so he has managed to emerge from the disaster unscathed.

Not so the three apprentices, who did not possess his foresight or turn of speed. One suffered burns to his hands and arms, and the other two got a few scratches from flying glass. All were left with scorched clothing.

Not for the first time in his life, Lightowler wishes that he could actually converse face to face with these mysterious figures from the past. He gets the feeling that some process, vital to the success of the venture, is always being deliberately kept back. As if an ancient thumb has been applied to an equally ancient nose.

He sighs, glancing across the room to the wreck of his table, now covered with a cloth. All that money spent on new equipment. Wasted. All that hope. Destroyed. Just splinters of glass and bits of burned wood left.

Lightowler massages his aching forehead with his index fingers. The flickering candlelight, and the residual smell of chemicals, has given him a headache. He rises despondently and goes over to the table. He lifts up the cloth.

Then he stands very still, scarcely believing the evidence of his own eyes.

***

Lady Meriel Wynward, wrapped in a pale cashmere shawl, sits in front of her dressing-table mirror, while the ladies' maid, whose name she cannot remember, brushes her hair with smooth strokes. She has always liked having her hair brushed, right from childhood.

As the brush moves up and down her hair, Lady Meriel's mind roams through her childhood. She remembers past lovers, little notes on pressed paper, the scent of violets, dance cards with red tasselled pencils.

She remembers that she was sixteen when she was introduced to Hugh. Eighteen when they married. She barely knew him, had never spent much time alone with him. He was her father's choice. She was a sensitive girl, prone to strange fancies and outbursts of hysterics. It was thought marriage at an early age would 'settle' her.

After the honeymoon, spent on the Riviera, she had haltingly asked her friends whether 'it' was always like that and when they told her it was, something inside her had wilted.

He started shouting at her early on in the marriage, which shocked her at first because she had never been shouted at before, but she soon learned to recognise the signs: the tightening of the hands, the indrawing breath, the little tic above the left eyebrow. She would smile, murmur something placatory, and slide quickly out of the room.

Sometimes she managed to make it up to her own room and lock the door before he caught her. If she didn't, he would beat her, screaming words that sounded as if they were embroidered with blood. He never beat her where it would show. For that she was grateful. The brush moves rhythmically up and down.

She remembers the cold white hospital where she went to recover from the birth of her daughter. It was so far from London, that when she finally returned, the baby looked at her with the eyes of a stranger.

But the wet nurse said this was often how they were after a long absence, and she worked hard to change its mind, so that soon, the little face would crinkle up into a smile when she peered into its crib.

Nothing lasted. The girl with the dance card. The baby with the smiling face. Her father and mother. Gone, all gone. Passed over to the other side. What was his name ~ the boy with the chestnut hair who took her riding in Hyde Park, that lovely hot summer?

The maid puts down the brush and begins to separate the thinning hair into bunches.

Lady Meriel feels a melancholy tug inside her, as if her body has its own tides and currents and can feel the pull of the moon. How epic her nights have become, she thinks, and how she longs for someone to lay their hand upon her brow, and tell her that all will be well in the end.

Heavy footsteps sound in the corridor. They pause outside her bedroom door. The maid stops her preparations, glancing apprehensively over her shoulder, then at Lady Meriel's face, the skin suddenly taut, eyes wary, pale lips parted in anticipation.

The footsteps move away. Lady Meriel draws breath, and indicates that the girl is to continue. She must look her best. Today might be the day her dear long-lost Sybella returns. The spirits have spoken, and unlike everybody else around her, the spirits do not lie.

***

Emily Cully doesn't have the luxury of a lady's maid to set out her clothes and brush her hair. She is also sadly deficient in the cashmere shawl, dressing table mirror and silver-backed brush department.

Emily Cully rises at the crack of dawn to get the kitchen ashes raked, the fire lit, the breakfast started, and Jack's shaving water on the go. When all this is done, and provided her daughter does not wake and loudly demand attention, she allows herself a brief sit-down and a well-earned cup of tea.

Hardly luxury, but to Emily that few moments' peace at the start of her day is worth all the money in the world. As she sips, she reads a few pages of whatever newspaper Jack brings home. It varies, depending upon which one his boss Mr Stride hasn't torn up in a rage.

This morning, Emily is reading the review of a melodrama called *The Body In The Shop Window*. It is loosely based on the case Jack is investigating. At least, she thinks it is. Though she is not sure how the 'Ballet of the Shopgirls' fits into the original scenario.

Emily takes the pan of hot water off the stove and pours some of it into a china bowl. She carries the bowl into the bedroom, where Jack Cully is already up and in his vest. Violet is still sleeping peacefully, her eyelashes two spiky crescents upon the pink moon of her face.

Emily places the bowl on the chest of drawers, then sits on the bed and watches her husband shave. The faces he pulls never cease to amuse her. It is at times like this that she appreciates not being born a man.

"I didn't wake you last night?" he asks.

"No dear," she says, because a good marriage is built upon small accommodations and harmless little lies.

Jack Cully smiles at her, because a good detective can spot a harmless little lie a mile off. He finishes shaving and dressing, then goes downstairs to mind the toast, leaving Emily to deal with young Violet, who is beginning to stir.

While he is busy in the back kitchen, there is a gentle knock at the front door. Opening it, Cully discovers a young woman carrying a basket. She wears a shabby black bonnet and mantle, her face is wax-pale, and there are dark shadows under her eyes.

"Delivery for Mrs Cully," she says dully, handing over the basket.

Cully guesses she must be one of Emily's outworkers.

"Would you care to come in, miss," he suggests. "My wife is attending to our little girl, but she will be down shortly."

The young woman follows him to the kitchen, where she sinks into a chair. Her eyes look hungrily round the cosy room, then come to rest on the brown teapot and the rack of hot toast and pat of butter.

Cully has a sudden flashback to the first time he met Emily, a half-starved needle-slave in a big department store. This young woman has exactly the same demeanour and pinched expression. He pours out a mug of tea, sugars it, and pushes it across the table, followed by a plate of toast.

The seamstress wolfs down the toast, then picks up the mug, cradling it between her hands. Cully notices that both index fingers are red and swollen.

"Thanks Mr Cully," she says. "Mrs Cully always speaks so nicely about you. I can see why she does now."

Cully places another slice of toast on her plate, as Emily herself, wrapped in a warm woollen shawl, enters the kitchen carrying Violet in her arms.

"Alice! How are you?" she asks, placing the toddler on the rag rug with a few toys.

"All the better for a cuppa and a bite to eat, thanks to your good man here," Alice says. "I was proper famishing and it's a cold morning. I sewed the bodices for you, and done the smocking, like you asked."

Emily lifts the lid of the basket and takes out the tiny garments.

"This is beautiful work, Alice. But you shouldn't have rushed to finish it. I said I could wait until you were sorted."

She glances quickly across at Jack, who is warming some milk for Violet's breakfast.

"Alice's husband worked on the docks."

Jack picks up on the past tense.

"I'm sorry. It must be a hard blow to have no work. What with winter coming on. Perhaps he'll be able to pick up another job somewhere else?"

Emily makes frantic signs behind the woman's back.

"He won't be looking for more work. He's dead, Mr Cully," Alice says flatly. "A crate they was lifting slipped and fell on him. Crushed to death, and the company say it isn't their fault and won't pay me for the work he did that morning."

"I am so sorry," Jack Cully says gently.

She looks away, biting her under-lip.

"He was my first and only. And now he's gone and I shall never see his dear face again in this world," she says, bending over her mug of tea to hide the tears.

"Well, let me pay you for your work at once," Emily says, reaching for her purse.

"Thanks, Mrs Cully. I won't say but that the money will come in handy. I had to sell a few bits and bobs to pay for the funeral."

Emily gives her the money.

"But this is too much, Mrs Cully," Alice exclaims.

"Then set it against the next order," Emily says firmly.

Tears come to the seamstress' eyes once more.

"You are very kind ~ both of you."

She rises.

"I'll be getting on my way now. You need to have your breakfast before you go to work on your cases, Mr Cully."

Jack Cully pulls a face.

"I wish I had something to 'work on', Alice ~ the case I'm in charge of seems to have run into the sand."

"Is it still the man in the department store window? Mrs Cully said you were investigating it. I keep hearing the newsboys calling the headlines."

I bet you do, Cully thinks ruefully. The press is having a field day with the story. The incompetence and lack of progress made by the police is being daily paraded before the public as if they were the criminals.

Alice pauses on the threshold.

"Did I say, Mrs Cully, that I'm friends with one of the girls who works at that department store?"

"No, you never mentioned it before," Emily says.

Jack Cully pauses in the act of buttering his toast.

"I don't know if it is important, but on the night it happened, we went out for a bite of supper together. I said good-bye to her and was just seeing how much money I had left in my purse, when three men came by. Two of them were kind of dragging the third man along between them, as if he was blind drunk.

"I pretended to look at the window, coz I didn't want any trouble ~ a woman out on her own at night can attract the wrong sort ~ you know what I mean. They passed me by, and then I went straight home."

Alice clasps her hands together.

"Do you think it is important, Mr Cully?"

Jack Cully regards her steadily.

"It may be very important indeed, Alice."

Alice's eyes widen.

"If I'd known, I'd have come by sooner, but what with Eddy's death ..." her voice trails into silence.

Cully crams the last of his toast into his mouth, then reaches for his coat, which is on the back of a chair.

"Can you remember the men?" he asks.

"I think so. Two were very tall, and the other, the man they were helping, he looked older but he was better dressed than they were."

"If you can spare the time, Alice, I'd like you to come with me to Scotland Yard. We have a police artist, and if you could describe the men, he might be able to make a picture of them that someone recognises."

Alice bites her lip hesitantly.

"I can come, if it won't take too long, Mr Cully, only I left the children with a neighbour to mind."

"I promise it will be done as quickly as possible."

"You both start off, and I'll get your next order ready," Emily says, passing a piece of sopped bread to Violet, who has been playing with some empty spools of cotton.

Emily takes the basket and goes to the dresser. She puts a pile of small cut out baby dresses into the basket. Then, as Jack and Alice wait in the hallway, she darts into the larder, quickly wraps up a meat pie and some potato cakes and places them under the work.

The thought of Alice's children going hungry wrings her tender heart. She knows Jack won't mind having bread and cheese for his supper. Emily waves her husband and Alice off. Then she returns to her warm kitchen and her small daughter, who is waiting impatiently for her own breakfast to arrive.

***

A short while later, Mr Absalom Eye of Hooke & Eye, Solicitors, is awaiting the arrival of his first client of the morning. The firm is an old and established one, having been in the legal business since the eighteenth century. It has built an enviable reputation and an extensive client list amongst the upper echelons of London society.

Hooke & Eye have occupied the same chambers in Lincoln's Inn from their foundation. The building reinforces the impression of old and established. The dust on the windowsill confirms it. The ancient lawyers' clerk with his wig and scratchy pen conveys it. The leather bound legal tomes, with faded gilt lettering on their spines, suggest that, on the balance of probability, it may indeed be the case.

Absalom Eye, who is technically the younger partner, though actually considerably senior in years to Daniel Hooke, the senior partner, now draws the client's folder towards him and opens it at the first page. He reads the letter of instruction he has recently received, nods a couple of times thoughtfully, and makes a few notes in the margin.

At ten precisely, the ancient lawyers' clerk knocks discreetly at the door, and announces the presence of the client. Absalom Eye rises, greets him with all the formality of an old established law firm, before he resumes his seat behind his desk.

The client sits in the leather chair diametrically opposite. A branch from one of the ancient elms taps rhythmically against the window. The wall clock ticks. Eye clears his throat carefully.

"I have received your instructions, Sir Hugh, and have prepared the necessary papers for you to sign."

The client's face betrays no emotion whatsoever. It could have been carved out of marble. Or wax.

"The monies from the trust fund that were due to your late daughter, Miss Sybella Wynward, upon reaching her eighteenth birthday, will now revert to her mother, Lady Meriel Wynward, to be overseen by yourself as you see fit and proper."

"And this is now legally binding?"

"Indeed."

"It cannot be revoked or challenged in any way?"

"Only in exceptional circumstances."

A flicker of interest, a slight incline of the head.

"Which, given the sad and tragic demise of the young lady, are not likely to occur."

"Just so. And should anything happen to my wife?"

"Then any monies remaining in the trust would revert to Lady Meriel's nearest kinsman ~ whom I believe to be her nephew Arthur."

A look of scorn crosses the client's face. His upper lip curls.

"Here is the document, if you would care to append your signature."

Eye presents the client with a couple of sheets of paper, covered in clerkish copperplate. The client reads through it carefully, nods his acceptance, picks up a quill pen and signs the document with a flourish. He blots the signature, and hands the document back to the lawyer.

"I will have my clerk make a fair copy for you and deliver it to your house by close of business today," Eye says.

The client rises.

"Good. I do not desire there to be any possibility, however slight, of misinterpretation or difficulties of any kind to arise in the future."

"You may rest assured that there will not be."

The client gives him a slight formal bow and is shown out.

Eye watches him go. An unpleasant cold man, he thinks. He tries momentarily to put himself in the client's shoes, and imagine what he would feel like if one of his children were to be tragically killed. It is impossible to achieve ~ he is after all a lawyer, but he is sure he would feel *something*.

Meanwhile, Sir Hugh Wynward, having completed things to his satisfaction, buttons up his overcoat, adjusts his muffler and sets off briskly in the direction of his club. A fortifying beverage is required before his next port of call.

***

Detective Inspector Stride is metaphorically twiddling his thumbs. He is doing this not at his desk, but upon a park bench, hunched up against the cold. A ham sandwich and a cup of bitter black coffee are his only companions.

Stride checks his watch, then leans back against the railings to contemplate some sparrows bathing in a puddle. The little birds shiver the water from their feathers and hop about in the pale sunshine. He throws them a few crumbs.

Stride's mind is sloshing backward and forwards like thin soup. He is too angry to think properly. A short while earlier, his decision to head for Sally's Chop House had been forestalled by the unexpected arrival at Scotland Yard of Sir Hugh Wynward.

He had come, he informed an astonished Stride, to apologise for the behaviour of his wife and to request him now to terminate his inquiries into the mysterious letter forthwith.

In the course of the ensuing interview, Sir Hugh had disclosed, in a voice that faltered every now and again, the mental distress of his wife, which was serious and ongoing. Listening to him, Stride had reached the conclusion that the man was either telling the truth, or the stage had missed out on a major talent.

By the time he left Stride's office, Wynward had managed to make it quite clear that *any* further intrusion into their lives by Stride, or another member of the force, might tip Lady Meriel over the edge. An edge to which she was already perilously close.

Stride had accompanied the man out, watching him walk to the waiting carriage and it seemed to him that with every step, Wynward's demeanour became less distraught. As the carriage drove off, he could have sworn there was something positively triumphant and gleeful about the expression on Sir Hugh's austere hawk-like features.

He could have been wrong. But Stride was a good judge of character, and he was pretty sure that he was not. However, the fact remained, that whatever his thoughts at the time, he now finds himself minus an investigation. And he is not happy about it.

Stride has tried to conduct a professional and methodical inquiry into the current whereabouts of Hugh Wynward's daughter, at the father's express request, but with precious little co-operation from any of the young woman's close friends or from the Wynward parents themselves.

A stray dog might show more concern for its offspring than Miss Sybella Wynward's cold sinister-eyed father, he thinks. As for the mother, there is something definitely awry ~ his mind drifts back to the wild eyes and the bars on the bedroom window.

He would have liked to get Lady Meriel on her own and talk to her. But that is not going to happen now. For reasons that he cannot fathom, the door is slammed shut, the drawbridge pulled up, and he has been denied admission. Whatever strange things have been taking place behind the respectable white-stuccoed facade, they are apparently no longer his concern.

Stride is a professional policeman to the core of his being. He hates walking away from a case. He hates even more being told to walk away. He throws the last of his crumbs to the birds and heads back to his office, trying to forget what has happened. But like a bruise, his mind keeps bumping up against the strangeness of it, and won't let it alone.

***

It is five o'clock in the afternoon, and the dealers in second-hand clothes, whose shops line both sides of Petticoat Lane and its surrounding streets, are thinking about shuttering up for the day. Business has been brisk since they first opened their doors to the public at half-past one, but now trade is slowing as the crowds thin.

Step inside one of the crammed shops.

Here in the dark, pungent recess are wardrobes bulging with old clothes. Old clothes rise to the roof, old clothes weigh down the shelves, old clothes hang from the walls and litter the floor.

The air is fragranced with the peculiar sour, mildewy smell of old clothes. Look around you: what stories could some of those mountains of bonnets, pyramids of hats, avenues of dresses, galleries of coats and chaos of shawls tell if they could speak?

That brocade might have been worn by a Duchess, now waiting to be purchased by a drab. The clothes that belonged yesterday to my Lord, were then worn by his lackey, are now here ready for their final owner.

Maybe the heavy looking overcoat, swinging in the breeze, once belonged to a Cabinet minister? Yesterday it travelled towards the Queen's palace. Tomorrow it may be journeying towards one of the Queen's prisons. Who can tell?

The clothes keep their secrets. Not so the clothes' sellers. Or so hopes the young man who has just entered the shop. He wears a decent wool coat, and brings with him a definite equine odour, though you'd be hard put to distinguish it from the other smells that linger in the air.

The shop owner, who is eating olives extracted from his waistcoat pocket, surveys him with a practised eye.

"Good day, young chentleman ~ how may I help you? A fine beaver hat, maybe? Or how about a nice striped silk weskit? Chust the thing to charm the young ladies."

William Smith pretends to admire the display of hats, then remarks casually, "I bet you some of these could tell a tale."

"Indeed they could. Now, vat may I show you?"

"It ain't so much the showing, as the telling, I'm int'rested in. If you gets my drift."

The shopkeeper shakes his head.

"I do not. Mebbe you explain this drift to me?"

"A blue dress. Let out at the sides. Wiv buttons on the back sewn in diff'rent colours. What might that dress have to say about the young lady wot sold it to you?" William asks thoughtfully.

"And vat is your interest in blue dresses, young man, if I may be so bold as to inquire?"

"Blue dress. One blue dress," William says. "You sold it to my sweetheart Mary. Wot I wants to know is: who sold it to you."

'Ole Clo' stares at him suspiciously.

"You from the ecipol? Cause I got nuffink to hide. Everything you see here is legit and paid for. I don't deal in stolen schmatta. Never have. I got a family to look after. You can ask anybody round here, they'll tell you the same. 'Ole Clo' is as honest as the day is long. And now, since you ain't int'rested in buying, I'm closing the shop. Good day."

"Wait a bit, wait a bit!" William says. "Hear me out, would yer? I ain't from the police. I'm trying to find someone ~ the girl wot sold you the blue dress."

"Vy?"

William Smith favours the old clothes man with his most open and sincere expression. The one that used to get him extra pennies when he wore rags and swept the filthy streets.

"That girl ~ the one who wore the blue dress first, and sold it to you, she was my sweetheart. Only we argued, and then she was sacked from her place of work, and I ain't heard nor seen her since. I'd just like to know she was doing alright. If she's down on her luck, I might be able to help her out ~ for old times' sake."

The thing about a good lie is that it always needs to contain a modicum of truth.

'Ole Clo' sucks his teeth.

"And the other girl is your sweetheart now?"

"She is."

"You lead a very ... busy life, young man, if I might say so."

"Don't I jist," William agrees happily, rolling his eyes.

"Vell, young man, I'll tell you vat I can recall. It ain't much, but it might help you."

A short while later, William Smith leaves the old clothes shop, the possessor of a startlingly bright striped waistcoat and some information. He heads back to the livery stables, mulling over what the old clothes man has told him.

William hoped the information he got would throw light upon the mystery surrounding Ellen and the blue dress. It seems he was mistaken. If anything, he is even more in the dark now than he was before.

***

William Smith is not the only person in London to find his way forward taking an unexpected and unwelcome sideways turn. The two would-be alchemists Jasper Thorogood and Eugenius Strictly have found their road to riches unexpectedly blocked by an absence of Dee.

Ever since the night of the Big Bang, they have waited to be summoned back for more lessons and lectures. When three days passed with no communication from Master Dee, they decided to take the initiative into their own hands, and arrived at the door of his house under cover of darkness.

But to their surprise, they found the house deserted. The curtains were drawn at the downstairs windows, and there was no small candle burning upstairs to indicate that the occupant was waiting for them. They stood at the door and knocked for some time, but lo, it was not opened unto them.

After knocking loud enough to awaken the dead, a first floor window was thrust up in the house next door, and an angry-looking man in a greasy cap shouted at them to bugger off or he'd call a constable. Discretion being the better part of valour, they took his advice and left.

The door was not opened unto them on the following night, the night following that, and the night after the other two nights. After six days of closed door, they went round to Bovis Finister's home, where a sharp-faced little girl in a grubby pinafore informed them that Bovis was 'hout' and then tried to sell them a box of lucifer matches.

It is all very frustrating. Thanks to Thorogood's notes, they are now able to produce copper ~ or rather, a copper-coloured substance that adheres to lead coins and makes them look coppery to the initially unsuspecting eye.

They have passed enough of the coins over various shop counters to know that the eye is deceived. They have not hung around long enough to ascertain what length of time is required for the deception to be discovered, because they also know that the same eye might send a message to the brain reminding it who handed the counterfeit copper coins over in the first place.

They need to up their game. So now here they are, on a gloomy Saturday morning, heading for the bookshop where they know Lightowler carries out his daily business.

"Maybe he's dead," Strictly observes. "Maybe he's been lying on the floor of that house, mortally wounded, and slowly starving with nobody hearing his cries and coming to his aid."

"Maybe you read too many sensational papers," Thorogood sneers. "He was perfectly fine when we left. Not like that fat fool Finister. Or me. Charred cuffs and I was lucky that glass splinter only grazed my cheek.

"Look, there's the shop. Let's go and see what he's been up to. I paid him good money for my lessons and I want my money's worth. Right now, I'm not getting it."

But even as they approach the shop, they can both sense that there is something amiss. No bulks of books extend onto the pavements. A few approaching tourists peer into the window, then walk away. When they get to the shop, they find it dark and shuttered. A hand-written notice pinned to the door reads: **Closed until further notice**.

Strictly and Thorogood, alchemist apprentices without a master, stare at the notice in dismay. They are young. They are greedy. They are used to getting what they want. This is not what they want. Thorogood gives the door a vicious kick.

"Old bastard!" he shouts. "Open up! I know you're in there."

"Y'know, I don't think he is," Strictly observes quietly.

Thorogood turns on him in fury.

"So where the hell is he? He ain't at home, he ain't at his place of work. Man next door hasn't seen him or heard him for days. People don't just bloody disappear without telling someone where they're going."

But clearly they do, and they have done.

To understand what has happened to Felix Lightowler let us return to where we left him on that fateful evening when, in the persona of John Dee, he lifts the cover upon the wreck of his latest experiment, and sees the gleam of gold winking up at him from the bottom of the shattered vessel.

After staring at it for some time in disbelief, Dee carefully scrapes out the Metall, and then subjects it to various tests to determine whether it is indeed gold. Having completed the tests to his satisfaction, he sits down at a table, rests his chin in his hands and tries to work out how he has managed to make it.

The following day, still barely crediting what has happened, Dee takes a sample of his gold to a reputable goldsmith of his acquaintance. The man weighs it, examines it with a loupe and pronounces it to be indeed the quintessence of that perfect Metall.

He makes a joke about discovering a gold mine. He offers to buy the sample. Dee agrees to sell it. The goldsmith suggests he would be willing to buy more, if Dee brings it to his workshop.

Dee uses the money to refresh his store of materials. He purchases more equipment. That same evening, he makes another Triall ~ taking careful precautions to keep the furnace temperate. He follows Philadelphus' instructions exactly, insofar as it is possible to do so.

This time there is no Big Bang. But next morning, upon waking, he finds gold in the vessel once again. Dee writes up his observations. He now sees that the Philosopher's Stone, that elusive substance that could transmute Metalls into gold, is in fact NOT an actual physical entity, but a set of procedures.

This would explain why all his predecessors over the centuries failed in their endeavours. It is clear as crystal now. Their Practices were full of Errors and Impostures. They were trying to make a real 'Stone', not realising that the stone was actually a code word for getting to the desired outcome.

The revelation stuns him. That he, a humble antiquarian bookseller and seeker after knowledge, should have grasped something that thousands of men had yearned and sought after. Men who were frequently tortured and persecuted for practising 'dark and occult arts'.

All died without ever seeing that glorious golden gleam that meant they had achieved their life's work. All but one man, to whom he owes an eternal debt of gratitude. Before returning the book to its owner, Lightowler carefully cuts out the pages containing Johannes Philadelphus' *'Opinions uponne the Makynge of Golde'*.

Thus having thus ensured that the secret remains secret, he closes the bookshop, packs his belongings, and disappears from London.

***

It is not so much a disappearance, as an appearance, that is baffling young William Smith. Even Mrs Hudson's delicious dinner of steak and kidney pudding, peas and boiled potato, cannot distract him from his quest.

Here he is, sharing supper with Josephine King, while describing his visit to 'Ole Clo'. William relates word for word what the second-hand clothes merchant said to him. Then adds,

"But I still don't understand how my Ellen's blue dress came to be sold by another girl."

Josephine has had a long hard day at the office. She is desperately worried about Lilith. She is trying to pay attention, because if it is important to William, then it is important to her.

"I knew it wasn't my Ellen as soon as the old Jew started describing her. My Ellen was my age, with dark brown hair and a good figure. The girl who sold him the dress had fair hair, and she was much older, he said."

"Did he remember where she lived?"

William shakes his head.

"He said if he remembered anything, he'd let me know. I thought I might go and take a walk around after dinner, though. Just in case."

"But if this girl isn't Ellen, what can you hope to gain by it?" Josephine asks.

"Dunno. I jist need to find out what happened. I can't get it out of my mind that Ellen might still be alive. They nivver found her body, did they? P'raps she was thrown clear of the train, and lost her memory."

Josephine has her doubts. In her experience, once people are declared dead, they tend to stay dead. But William's face is so bright, his eyes so eager, that she can't bear to dash his hopes to pieces.

"If this girl can tell me how she came by Ellen's blue dress, I might be nearer to discovering what happened to her," he says.

"Then of course you must go," she says warmly. "I shall wait up for you, and you can tell me all about it on your return."

So, his dinner finished, William Smith dons his warm outdoor coat and cap and sets off on his great mission. In a great city with millions upon millions of inhabitants, the chances of finding one single individual could be compared to the mythical haystack and accompanying needle.

But sometimes, Fate has been known to reach out and dangle a magnet.

***

A London fog is like no other fog anywhere else. Dense, muddy and sooty, it coats buildings and scarifies the air so that breathing becomes painful, even to the strongest lungs. People run against each other and shout. Cab men call out aloud upon the suspicion that something is coming the other way.

At night, familiar landmarks cannot be identified. People stumble about, going in circles. A few poor creatures lose their sense of direction completely, and end up under cab or dray wheels, or plunge into canals. Others abandon themselves to the narrow streets, relying on predestination to bring them, somehow or other, to the place they want, if they are ever to get there.

Small boys with red torches stand at the entrance to railway stations, offering to show the way for two pence. There is not a breath of fresh air to be had anywhere.

Even behind closed doors, the fog cannot be escaped, for it creeps under door sills and through letterboxes and round window blinds, until every room is filled with a light cloud and the family within takes on a semi-phantasmic appearance.

By early morning the fog has lifted slightly. Detective Inspector Stride makes his way through pinched, narrow streets and courts, the rows of houses sewn with dull greys and blacks from the smoke-filled air. The street lamps are still on, their pale light seeping through the bandages of fog.

Despondent is not a word that came easily to him. But here it is; it has arrived. He enters the building, grunts at the desk constable, and is just about to head for his office when a familiar voice hails him from the Anxious Bench.

"Mr Stride! Mr Stride!" Rancid Cretney calls out, rising and hurrying towards him.

Stride feels his heart sink. He adjusts his face to indifferent with a side order of mild annoyance.

"Mr Cretney ~ here you are. What is it now? Only I am a very busy man, as you can see."

Rancid Cretney spends a few minutes working a small piece of gristle out from between two teeth.

"It's them neighbours of mine again, Mr Stride."

"And what have they been up to now?"

Cretney pauses, scratches his head under his cap.

"That's just it, Mr Stride. They ain't been up to nothing. Nothing at all. Ain't heard them; ain't seen anybody coming or going for over a week. Now what you think of that?"

Stride feels his eyes rolling back in his head.

"Let me see if I understand, Mr Cretney," he says slowly. "First you complain about the noise you claim your neighbours make, now you are complaining about the noise your neighbours aren't making. Why Mr Cretney ~ WHY in the name of all that's holy are you bothering me with this?"

Rancid Cretney comes so close that Stride can appreciate at first-hand how he got his nickname.

"Be-coz, Mr Stride," he says lowering his voice to a throaty whisper, "I fink they may be dead. Stands to reason. Not a sound. Dead or weltering in their own gore," he continues with great relish.

"Maybe they are just going about their business a bit more quietly, so as not to annoy you, Mr Cretney?" Stride suggests, taking a step backwards.

Cretney pauses to let the idea settle, then beats it off with a mental stick.

"I know what I know," he says stubbornly. "And I am here to report a crime, as is my duty as a law-abiding citizen. And it's yours to investigate it."

"But what crime exactly, Mr Cretney?"

Rancid Cretney's sallow visage assumes an expression of mulish obstinacy.

"The crime what has been committed. The one I just reported."

Stride purses his lips.

"When you can furnish me with a few more details, I *might* instruct my officers to investigate, Mr Cretney. Until such time, I suggest you go home and enjoy the peace and quiet of your own fireside."

Stride folds his arms and adopts the 'filling-the-space-with-his-presence' stance to indicate that the encounter is over. Cretney stares at him sullenly.

"So you ain't going to do nothing?"

Stride winces at the double negative.

"Regrettably, I am unable to order my men to force their way into somebody's house at the request of a neighbour. It is called breaking and entering without permission, Mr Cretney. It is a crime, Mr Cretney. People have been sent to prison for doing it. Not my men. Is that clear to you, Mr Cretney?"

Cretney frowns as he processes Stride's words. His mouth moves rhythmically as his brain decodes what has been said.

"You ain't heard the end of the matter, Mr Stride," he says finally. "Summat is up. I know it and I shall be back here when I knows what it is."

"I have no doubt you will," Stride murmurs, as the self-designated local neighbourhood watch, bristling with indignation, marches out of the police station, leaving the lingering odour of his presence behind him.

Stride catches the amused desk sergeant's expression and rolls his eyes.

"As if we didn't have enough work dealing with real crimes, now we're being asked to deal with imaginary ones," he says disgustedly.

The night constables' reports have been placed on Stride's desk. He hangs up his hat and resignedly prepares to do battle with the usual random assortment of misspelling and erratic punctuation. The fog, Mr Cretney and now the semantic vagaries of his officers. The trajectory of his day is definitely lurching towards a downward spiral.

***

Across London, Lady Meriel Wynward has not left the sanctuary of her room for two days. She is suffering from a temporary inflammation of the lungs brought on by travelling through London in the fog. The family physician has been called, and prescribed bed-rest and a soothing medicinal syrup.

While she rests, Lady Meriel thinks about the recent séance she attended. It was held at the house of an acquaintance ~ a fellow believer, but not one of her own set of friends, who do not approve of her 'dabbling with the spirits' as Lady Parthenope scornfully refers to it.

The group sat around a dining-room table, the room in darkness except for two screened lights. The séance began with a reading from the Book of Ezekiel, in which a spirit appears before the Prophet.

Lady Meriel has the passage marked in her bedside Bible. She has turned to it often in the last two days of her incarceration. Now she sits up with a grunt of effort, then leans forward, a position that she finds helps her to breathe. She opens the Bible, and reads:

'Behold a whirlwind came out of the north, a great cloud, and a fire enfolding itself, and a brightness was about it, and out of the midst thereof as the colour of amber, out of the midst of fire. Also out of the midst thereof came the likeness of four living creatures. And this was their appearance; they had the likeness of a man.'

The medium, who was a lady of personable appearance, then started to groan and sigh; her breathing became stridulous; she appeared to be in some distress. Eventually, a small luminous cloud appeared behind her.

The cloud had hovered in the air, gradually taking the shape of a human form. It began to move round the group, finally coming to rest by Lady Meriel's side. Lady Meriel had barely time to register its presence, when she felt a sense of warmth, as if a shawl had been draped across her shoulders.

Then she had the sensation of a face very near her own, and of breathing. A gentle voice in the darkness whispered, *"I am so happy you are here,"* and she felt the touch of a hand, at first resting on her head, then stroking her cheek.

It was all too overwhelming. She had cried out, tried to turn her head to see the apparition ~ but in an instant, the spirit had gone and there was nothing there but darkness and empty air. The séance had continued, with loving messages passing between various participants, but Lady Meriel heard none of them. Her focus remained upon the spirit visitation, and the words, which she was sure had been spoken in Sybella's voice.

The séance ended with more messages being spelled out via the letters of the alphabet, arranged in a circle on the table. None of them were for her, though that didn't matter either. The deep craving of her soul was satisfied. She returned home in a state of rapturous ecstasy ~ and promptly fell ill with a chest infection.

Lady Meriel lies back on her pillow, a smile lighting up her wan features. Sybella has communicated, and soon she will return from that place where the dead go. She knows it. The spirits have confirmed it over and over.

To her surprise, Hugh is behaving reasonably towards her. He has not scolded her or snapped at her for days. Indeed he has been kindness itself, arranging for her maid to bring her beef tea and milk puddings ~ and this from the man who, in his rages, shouted that he wished her dead and out of his life forever.

A tear slides down her nose and plops onto the Bible. She closes it quickly and places the book on her bedside table. Her hands feel as if they are too heavy for her, as if they were great paddles, rather than fragile webs of bone and skin and knotted blue veins.

Lady Meriel closes her eyes. Her jaw goes slack. Her breathing becomes deep and regular. She floats away to a pleasant place where a little girl with dark ringlets smiles as she runs across a sunny lawn, her chubby arms outstretched.

A short while later, Sir Hugh will enter her bed chamber and stand by the bed for some time, staring down at her with a narrow-eyed calculating expression on his aquiline features, but she will not be aware of it.

***

Jack Cully has stopped off at his favourite coffee stall to fortify himself after another restless night with a teething toddler. He does not know how Emily manages on so little sleep. By mid-afternoon, it is as much as he can do to keep his eyes open and his head off his desk.

Now he enters Scotland Yard, carrying the cup carefully, and checks the Anxious Bench. It is empty. The desk sergeant glances up from his copy of *The Illustrated Police Gazette*. Cully notices the picture on the front page, under a headline that reads:

Detective Police Seek Men in Connection with Shop Murder!

The image shows two tall burly men dragging a third man past a department store that is clearly *John Gould's & Company*. Alice has done very well. The police artist has managed to capture the features of the two men, one wearing a dark jacket and muffler, the other in corduroy trousers and a peacoat. The third is unmistakably Montague Foxx, drawn from the original police Death Notice. He is wearing the suit in which he was found murdered.

Cully is just wondering whether some sort of reward might be offered, when Stride comes hurrying towards him.

"Jack, there you are! Can you step into my office for a minute?"

Stride closes the office door. Then he picks up a copy of the *Times*.

"Tell me about this picture."

It is the same picture. Cully has had it distributed it to most of the newspapers, as well as the main police offices. He explains to Stride about Alice, and what she saw on the night of the murder.

"I've been studying this picture, and one of these men is interesting," Stride says.

Cully raises an eyebrow.

"Interesting in what way?"

"He reminds me of somebody."

Cully waits.

Stride points to the man on the left.

"I can't be absolutely sure, of course. But *this* man reminds me of Sir Hugh Wynward's butler."

There is a pause. Both detectives stare silently at the drawing.

"Really?"

"I know. I confess I was surprised myself. But I've been staring at it for the past half hour, and the more I look at it, the more I see the resemblance."

"It might be an accident," Cully says. "One of those strange likenesses. Don't they say that everybody has a spitting image of themselves somewhere?"

"Possibly, possibly. But suppose it isn't?"

"So, what do you propose to do about it?"

"What I propose to do is write a note to Sir Hugh Wynward asking if we can call round at his earliest convenience. I will stress the urgency, but I won't mention why, at this stage. When we get there, we will question the man ~ I believe his name is James, as to his whereabouts on the night in question, and if we receive no satisfactory answer, we'll bring him in and see if Alice can identify him."

"We could go straight round now. Save time," Cully suggests.

Stride shakes his head.

"Not with people like that. You can't just turn up on their doorstep if you want their co-operation. Protocols, Jack. We have to obey the protocols. Sadly."

He reaches for his pen and a sheet of writing paper.

"I'll send one of the constables round with the letter. Get him to wait for a reply. With a bit of luck, we should be in possession of either the facts or the man by mid-afternoon."

***

Lady Meriel Wynward stirs. There is a moment sometimes upon waking, the in-between moment before she remembers about Sybella, when she feels almost normal. Then the past washes in like a floodtide and bears her away with it once more.

She turns back the coverlet and tries to rise. On the second attempt she manages to stand. The world swings, then settles. Her feet find her slippers and she shuffles across the room to the door, feeling like a child that has been sent to bed before it is properly dark.

Lady Meriel opens the door a crack and peers out. Somewhere beyond the safety of her window-barred room, she can hear angry voices. One of them is unmistakably that of her husband. A cold hand clutches at her, digging its claws painfully into her chest.

She tries to reason with the pain, telling it that it's not her fault. She has done nothing. This time. Someone else is cowering under the lacerating words, closing their eyes against the icy glare that bites into one's soul, leaving it winter-blasted and dead.

Someone else. But who? One of the servants? A friend of her husband's ~ not that he has any. She tiptoes to the banister rail and leans over it. Whoever it is, they are clearly equally angry, for they are responding, and not only responding, but actually raising their voice in counter-argument.

Lady Meriel clutches the rail so hard that her rings dig into her fingers. Somebody is actually shouting at her husband. Unheard of. What is going on down there? She hears the angry voices rise and fall. Rise and fall. Then a door opens and there is the sound of hastening footsteps in the hall below.

The front door slams.

A pause, then Hugh is in the hallway, screaming things she does not understand, though she can picture him quite clearly, his eyes diamond hard, flecks of spittle on his pale lips. She shrinks back into the shadows at the top of the stairs. The house is suddenly full of presences from the past. They are here, but not quite apparent.

A few hours later, dressed and coiffed by her lady's maid, Lady Meriel drifts cautiously into the dining room. The table is laid for two, the third place glaringly obvious by its absence. She seats herself at the foot of the table, nervously unfurling her napkin.

A maid brings in a tureen and sets it down on a side table. Then she stands eyeing the serving spoons and waiting for Sir Hugh to arrive. After a few minutes, Lady Meriel clears her throat.

"Has Sir Hugh been informed that dinner is served?"

The maid bobs a curtsy.

"Yes, ma'm."

"I think perhaps we will not wait any longer then. He may have business to attend to. Please serve the soup, Janet."

A steaming bowl of something green and glaucous is placed in front of her. Lady Meriel dips her spoon into her bowl and raises it to her lips, just as the dining room door opens and the master of the house sweeps into the room.

His face is even more waxen than usual. He scrapes back his chair and indicates to the maid that he is ready for his first course. Years of married life have taught Lady Meriel not to talk to her husband until he is well into the meat course. Thus she takes tiny quiet sips from the edge of her spoon, and tries to convince herself that the tasteless liquid is doing her good.

Eventually, when Sir Hugh has consumed several thick slices of boiled beef in uncompanionable silence, she decides the time is ripe to approach the fracas that she overheard earlier in the afternoon.

"Have you had a trying day, dear?" she ventures, as an opener.

Sir Hugh stabs at a piece of meat.

"You could say so. That blasted detective was here again. The sheer effrontery of the common little man beggars belief."

Lady Meriel's fork clatters onto her plate. Her heart begins to pound in her thin chest.

"Has he found her? Is she coming back?" she gasps.

"Oh for Christ's sake, Meriel not this again! I told you ~ the whole thing was a hoax. Once and for all: Sybella is dead. I saw her body in the mortuary. Why won't you believe it?"

Lady Meriel's lower lip trembles, but she holds her ground.

"Because I did not see it. And therefore I refuse to believe it. I know she is coming home. The spirits have confirmed it."

Her husband glares at her.

"Have you consulted one of those crazy mediums again? Against my express wishes? Have you?"

"They are not crazy, Hugh. They communicate with those who have passed over."

Wynward snorts disgustedly.

"I have a respected position in society, Meriel. One which you seem intent upon undermining with your spirit mumbo-jumbo. Enough! I have been recently mulling over in my mind a change of scene ~ London is vile at the best of times, and these fogs are clearly affecting your health, not to say your mental state.

"Italy is most pleasant at this time of year, I believe. We are leaving town. As soon as I find a suitable villa, it is my intention to close up the house. We shall winter abroad."

Lady Meriel gapes at him in horror.

"But," she stutters. "But we cannot leave. What if Sybella comes back and finds the house empty? She will not know where we are."

He bats the suggestion away.

"I have already spoken with Richmond. He agrees with me that a change of scene and climate would do you the world of good. I described your recent outbursts and various flights of fancy, and he shares my opinion that a recurrence of your old trouble must be avoided at all costs."

She struggles to stay calm, to speak levelly, not to allow the rising hysteria and fear to show in her voice.

"But I am quite fine. I do not want to leave London. All my friends are here."

"They can come and visit you in Italy. I expect we shall see them arriving in droves, given the gloomy weather."

She stares down at her plate.

"And what if I refuse?"

His expression hardens.

"I have already told you, the doctor has recommended a change of air. To set yourself against medical advice looks like sheer recklessness ... let us not forget the last time you defied medical authority, and the subsequent consequences."

She sets down her knife and fork at the correct angle.

"When are you proposing we should leave?"

"As soon as I have found a villa. I intend to depart later tonight with James to seek a suitable place. I presume you can manage without us for a short while?"

The words stick to her, consume her. She rises.

"I think I shall go to my room now. I do not want any dessert."

He shrugs.

"As you wish."

At the door, she turns.

"What did the detective want? He must have had a reason for coming to the house."

"Nothing that need concern you. He has overstepped the mark, and I have written to his superintendent expressing my opinion upon his conduct. I have no doubt that he will be severely reprimanded. Hopefully he will be sacked."

She leaves. Mounting the stairs, clinging to the smooth polished rail. Each step is a torment, a betrayal. She reaches her room, and goes straight to the window. Her hands grip the iron bars.

On the other side of the bars, the afternoon is fading into evening, though one can hardly tell from the fog filling the street. Soon it will be pitch dark out there. Everything is worse at night. She can just about endure the days, despite Hugh's occasional bursts of ill-temper, and those moments when she thinks why bother, why not just turn your face to the wall?

But as the light goes, the most quotidian sounds of London life ~ church bells, footsteps passing, the watchman calling the hours, the clop of traffic ~ all seem charged with menace. She becomes nervous, plucking at herself. She draws the curtains, but it doesn't help. Night thickens behind them, pressing at the glass like floodwater.

***

We last left the Finister family in poor lodgings, struggling to make ends meet. Since then, there has been an unexpected change for the better in their circumstances, and here they are in Southam Street, Kensal New Town, where they rent the ground floor and first floor back of a tall stucco house.

The area is one of those parts of suburban London that is newly built, the houses all having the same four storeys and classical porticoes. Most of the houses are let by the room or floor to working-class families like the Finisters. Indeed, the area is known locally as Soapsuds Island because of the numbers of women living here who take in washing.

It is a step upwards though. And here is young Bovis, quite the sartorial peacock in a thick tweed jacket that looks almost new, cord trousers that don't end short in the leg, and a pair of stout boots with unbroken laces.

He is carrying the ubiquitous basket of clean washing on his shoulder, and the client list in his pocket. One more house to call at, then his time is his own. At the start of his afternoon's errands, he passed by a pastry cook's shop. He intends to pass by it again on the way back. There were some tempting raspberry tartlets in the window.

Some time later, as Bovis comes out of the pastry cook's shop, his mouth full of warm crust, he is unexpectedly hailed by two familiar faces from the recent past. Eugenius Strictly and Jasper Thorogood have made a brief diversion via their former teacher's house to see if he has returned yet.

Finding the place still deserted, they are now taking a turn about town to walk off their frustration and by great ill-fortune for him, they have run into Master Finister and his tartlet.

"Well, well, if it isn't our good friend Bovis," Thorogood says, clapping the unfortunate Bovis on the shoulder and making him choke on his tartlet. "What brings you to this neck of the woods?"

Bovis coughs and mumbles words to the effect that he has been delivering washing.

"Of course you have! And how is Mother Finister? Still up to her elbows in soapsuds?"

Strictly, who has remained silent so far, plucks at Bovis' jacket.

"This is a nice piece of cloth. Come into a fortune since we saw you last?"

Bovis wrinkles up his good-natured face into a grin.

"Mr Dee paid for it."

This is news indeed. The apprentices eye him with sudden interest.

"Oh he did, did he? And when was this exactly?" Strictly asks.

Bovis concentrates hard.

"It was before he went away. He came round to our house and said he wouldn't want any more washing or ironing done for a while, becoz he was going abroad to look for some more of his old books. Then he gave mum a whole lot of money, and said it was payment for all the washing and the help I'd been to him."

"I see," Thorogood says, in a 'go-on' sort of voice.

"He said if it wasn't for me and the way I kept Tempering the Metall, he'd never have discovered how to make gold. And he gave me this," Bovis digs in his pocket, and produces a very small shiny golden nugget. It glows softly in his palm.

"This is some of the gold. He said he'd made a lot more since, but it was all locked away somewhere safe."

He turns to go. Thorogood steps forward and grabs his collar.

"Not so fast, Fatboy. I think anything you were given should be shared three ways, don't you agree, Eugenius?"

"I certainly do, Jasper. After all, we were apprentices too."

"Hand it over," Thorogood says sternly.

Bovis' face takes on an expression of sullen half-frightened defiance.

"He gave it to me to keep, not you."

"And now you're sharing it with us, aren't you? Like the good little fellow apprentice that you are."

Thorogood, to whom generosity came as naturally as altruism comes to a cat, nods to Strictly, who pins Bovis' arms to his side. Thorogood prises the gold nugget from his clasped hand.

"Thank you," he says, triumphantly holding it up to the streetlight. "And now be on your way; we wouldn't want Mother Washerwoman worried, would we?"

He aims a kick at Bovis' legs.

"Run, Fatboy, run ~ or we shall come after you."

With a sob, Finister drops his tartlet and takes to his heels, the basket bobbing on his broad shoulders. Thorogood watches him go, then he throws back his head and laughs. An unpleasant sound.

"Who'd have thought it, eh? So the old fool did it after all! He made gold! He. Made. Gold. Would you believe it?"

"But we still don't know how," Strictly says.

"We know ~ it has to be that last experiment, the one that exploded. Maybe it was meant to be like that ... the gold came out of the bang. Anyway, it matters not. I have the method written down in minute detail, so all we have to do is repeat the procedure."

"But we don't have the proper equipment."

"WE don't, but Dee has it in that laboratory of his. Stands to reason. He'd have replaced all the broken equipment, wouldn't he? How else could he have made more of the stuff? And I'm also betting that somewhere in the room is the rest of the gold."

Strictly stares at him, light slowly dawning.

"Are you proposing what I think you're proposing?"

Thorogood nods.

"We shall have to plan it carefully of course, but I think a special night visit to Master Dee's is on the cards for two of his loyal hardworking apprentices, don't you?" He grins, throwing the nugget into the air a couple of times, before putting it away safely in an inner pocket.

Jasper Thorogood has spent his entire life dreaming of being rich; of having so much gold that he'd have to buy clothes with reinforced pockets to accommodate it. Sometimes, on his solitary Sunday walks, he'd pause in one of the alleys behind Lombard Street, and think of the closed banks and their broad counters with a rim along the edge made for telling money out on, or the scales for weighing coins or the ponderous ledgers.

In his mind's eye, he'd picture the copper shovels for shovelling gold. He'd place himself at the counter. *"How would you like it, sir,"* the banker's clerk would ask, and he'd reply, *"In gold,"* and watch as the bright coins came pouring out of the shovel.

But then, Thorogood would return to reality and to his small rented room with its ancient bed and rickety table, with the small fireplace that always smoked, the bare floorboards and half empty cupboards, and the clothes hung at the window instead of curtains.

Now, it appears that the dream is about to become reality. He turns to his companion, "I say, what do you call that warm feeling you get inside?"

"Indigestion?"

Thorogood ignores him. They walk on until they reach the street corner, where he takes his leave. The warm feeling stays with him though, all the way to his lodgings.

***

The Great Panjandrum Music Hall just off Leicester Square is the apogee of the lavish new Music Halls currently being built to entertain the swelling populace. Constructed on the site of a former public house, and then rebuilt when an accidental backstage fire damaged the structure of the building two years ago, it now has glittering chandeliers, proper flooring and comfortable seating for over a thousand patrons.

The audience consists of tradesmen with their wives and families, respectable mechanics and a few fast clerks and warehousemen. Tourists attend in the season. There are chairs and tables by the stage. Bass's pale ale, and brandy and soda are freely available.

Here, for a modest outlay of cash you may see the variety of acts, which can include trapeze artists, magicians, singers, dancers and a drama: sixpence for the second gallery, one shilling for the pit and promenade, or two shillings for the stalls. There are private boxes for family parties, and gentlemen who wish to entertain a companion discreetly.

Outside the theatre stand the sandwich sellers in white aprons and white sleeves. They arrive at six pm, in time for the first house. Some of them will not leave their pitch until four am, though their clientele then will be very different. Their trays are piled high with huge ham sandwiches, and they are doing a brisk trade, for as everyone knows, an evening out is not an evening out without a ham sandwich.

How can you argue the merits of this or that act with a fellow audience member unless you have a sandwich in one hand to gesticulate? How can you weep at the melodrama unless your tears fall on your sandwich? And when the lights go up and it is finally time to head home, your sandwich accompanies you through the gas-lit streets like a familiar friend.

The audience is gathering, waiting for the doors to open. Look more closely. Here is someone you recognise. William Smith in a clean jacket and cap leans against the wall, chewing a straw and whistling to himself.

He is not here to enjoy the singing, the melodrama and the general ambience, though he may well do so. He is not here to drink Bass' pale ale and consume ham sandwiches, though once again, he may well do so.

William is actually here to see Miss Vesta Swann, chanteuse and one of the Hall's Brightest Stars (according to the poster that is pasted on the wall just above his head), because it was she, and none other, who sold the blue dress to 'Ole Clo'.

At least, it was her according to the small boy with very black curls and robin bright eyes to match who arrived at the livery yard earlier in the day. He chirped the message that: *'Uncle Reuben says to talk to the girl on the poster outside the theeayter in Leicester Square,'* and having delivered this cryptic communication, he ran off.

William has ascertained that Miss Swann is not on until after the melodrama, and so might be available for a quick chat. That is, if he could get through the stage door, which is guarded by a ferociously tall man in an even taller top hat.

The foyer doors open. The audience press forward, clasping their entrance money and eatables. William watches them. He is still watching them, when he sees a young lad emerge from the stage door entrance and approach one of the sandwich sellers in a purposeful manner.

William strolls over. Casually. He hears the boy ask for 'Miss Swann's special sandwich'. He is given the sandwich. He turns, and runs slap-bang into William. A few seconds later, after a certain amount of bargaining has taken place involving the handing over of some coins, William Smith, carefully carrying the special sandwich, approaches the stage door and informs the man that he is the bearer of Miss Swann's pre-performance snack.

"Where's Henry?" the man asks suspiciously.

"Had to go on anuvver errand, rather sudden like," William says. He gestures over his shoulder. "Can you let me through, guv'nor, only we're really busy on the stall tonight."

The man unfolds his arms and jerks his head in the direction of the half-open wooden door. William gives him his best 'cheeky but loveable young rascal' grin. Then he hurries through the door, before the man has a chance to change his mind.

The backstage of the Grand Panjandrum is a very different world to the bright auditorium. Here, a gloomy corridor is ill-lit by candles in wall sconces. Doors lead off the corridor, some of them bearing the names of the acts. William checks the names and when he reaches one with Miss Vesta Swann written upon it, he knocks.

"Sandwich for Miss Swan," he announces.

There is a pause, then a young woman in a long loose red robe opens the door. Her hair is tied back with a ribbon, and her face is heavily made up.

"You aren't the usual boy," she says, holding out her hand for the sandwich.

"He's busy tonight," William says, handing it over.

Vesta Swann looks William up and down. Slowly. A look that brings a blush to his cheek.

"Well, you're certainly a sight for sore eyes, I must say," she says.

She beckons him inside and closes the door.

"So Henry sent you round instead. That's kind. Very kind. Or is there some other reason you're here, eh?"

She lets the robe drop ever so slightly from her pearly white shoulders and gives him a sideways coquettish glance.

"Oh, as to that, I got a sweetheart already," William assures her earnestly.

Vesta Swann throws back her head and laughs merrily.

"Have you now, Mr ...?"

"Smith. William Smith."

"Well Mr Smith, if you aren't after what most gent'l'men usually want from a lady, and I'm guessing you don't have the tin to stand me a champagne supper after the act, what do you want?"

William tells her about Ellen, and the terrible accident, and the blue dress, and then he tells her about Mary, and the same blue dress. And after he has finished telling her, Vesta Swann smiles and says,

"Now that's a tale and a half, Mr Smith and no mistake. You could make up a song about it, and break the hearts of everyone who heard it. I'm not sure I can help you, but I'll tell you what I know. The blue dress was given me to sell by a fellow artiste: Mimi Casabianca, she called herself.

"We met when we were both booked for the pre-Panto season here at the Panjandrum, and we found ourselves sharing diggings. She was much younger than me and hadn't been in the business long, but she was good. Very very good. I saw her act one night: 'The Masked Medium' she called herself.

"She could do spirit writing, levitate objects, ectoplasm and all sorts ~ the audience loved it. Couldn't get enough of her. Two shows a night, five nights a week. Full houses every time.

"She had this older man who looked after the business side ~ I think he was her agent. Bit of a toff, always nicely dressed, and very protective of her. He used to come to our lodging house and fetch her in a cab, and then wait in her dressing room while she did her act.

"Soon as she was done, he'd make sure she went straight back to her room. I remember saying to her one night after the show: *'don't you get tired of it? Would you like to come out and have a bit of fun for a change?'* But she just shook her head. *'I'm fine,'* she said.

'Besides, I've had my fun and believe me, it stops being funny after a while.'

"Anyway, about a month ago, I was getting ready for my act when I heard them having an almighty row. She had the dressing room right next to mine, you see, and the walls are thin like cardboard. She was shouting at him that he had tricked her. He was shouting back that she knew the score when she went with him.

"Next thing, I heard a terrible scream, and furniture going over, and then there were footsteps flying down the corridor. I went to the door and looked out, and there he was running for his life, and there she was running after him, eyes like fire and her hair all down over her face. She had a big knife in her hand, and she was yelling that she'd kill him when she caught up with him.

"I shut the door and pretended I hadn't seen anything. It don't do to get involved in other people's private business, does it? But early next morning, she knocked on my door at the lodging house and said she needed to get out of town fast, as the police might be coming after her, so could she leave some of her clothes and some bits and bobs of jewellery for me to sell? She said she'd write me for the money soon as she got settled in another town.

"And that's all I can tell you, Mr William Smith. I wished her good luck. Then I sold the dresses she left with me ~ including the blue one, and the pieces of jewellery, and I have the exact money on my nightstand waiting for her letter. She clearly wasn't your Ellen though, was she?"

William shakes his head.

"No, she wasn't. But she had my Ellen's blue dress, that's for sure." He frowns, "You don't happen to know the name of the man she was with?" he inquires.

"If you'd asked me that question at the time, I couldn't have given you an answer, straight up. But now I can, for I've seen his picture in the newspapers often enough since. His name was Mr Foxx. Mr Montague Foxx. He was the same man who had his throat cut in the window of that big new department store."

By the time he quit the Music Hall, the evening had turned into a cold gloomy night with long sullen lines of cloud, and a pale dead light over the city. William hurries home as fast as he can, only too aware that though he has got not much further on his own behalf, he is now the bearer of vital information that might save Lilith from the gallows.

He finds Josephine and Lilith sitting on either side of a dying fire. Lilith looks exhausted to the point of collapse. William positions himself in front of the hearth, warming his backside after his long walk home, and proceeds to tell them what Vesta Swann told him.

"Mimi Casabianca," Lilith murmurs thoughtfully. "I have come across her name before. But I doubt if she'd have the strength to carry a man's body into a shop and place it in the window."

"Must've had help, then," William says.

"Whatever she had ~ don't you see, this means you cannot be a suspect any longer!" Josephine says, clapping her hands. "Well done, William! Now we must inform the police."

William shakes his head.

"Don't look to me. I ain't getting involved wiv the ecipol ~ I got my good name to worry about."

Josephine rolls her eyes.

"William Smith, you have to stop thinking like a crossing-sweeper. You are a respectable member of society now."

"Yeah, and I meanter stay that way."

"Then I shall write at once to Detective Sergeant Cully telling him exactly what you have found out. I believe him to be a reasonable man, and I am sure once he reads my letter, he will agree that Lilith can no longer be considered a suspect."

"In that case, I shall take my leave and let you get on," Lilith says, rising wearily to her feet. "No ~ please do not accompany me," she adds, as William reaches in his pocket for his cap. "I have a lot to think about and walking will help me think it."

"She don't look too clever does she?" William says when Josephine returns from seeing Lilith out.

"She has been under a lot of strain since this terrible murder has been laid at her door, and it is making her wretched. Let us hope that my letter will lift some of the burden from her shoulders," she replies. "And now I will light a fresh candle, and you must sit by me as I write to make sure I have it down exactly. If it is in our power to help our dear friend, we must do so."

"Wiv all my heart, Jo King," William echoes. "Wiv all my heart."

***

A few days later, Lilith Marks stands alone at the kitchen table in the Lily Lounge, preparing a bowl of egg-yellow cake batter. Light washes in from the small area window. She is enjoying the comfort of silence. She cracks the last egg into a teacup, lifting the yolk out. Then she begins to beat the batter, leaning into the motion.

In the distance, church bells chime.

The journey she has been on since her visit to the police morgue has taken her to many other places. To events and conversations that she had forgotten, and people undone by time. Lilith has ventured back down the road she came from, rediscovering old versions of herself, each one piled above the other like sacked or deserted cities.

Gambling dens, gin palaces, and smart restaurants. Women with counterfeit faces. Endless labyrinths of gaslit streets, bars where the floor was covered with blood and cock's feet and men stared at her, their eyes like weapons.

Monty's name was a drop of ink in water. Everything took on a darker shade. Night after night, she sat at her dressing table, too scared to visit the dark cupboard of sleep where dreams came at her like wolves.

Even when she drifted into fitful slumber, she knew that she would wake in the pale half-formed hours, the unreasonable time that greets all troubled minds when the longing for consolation and the knowledge of its absence are most perfectly matched.

Yet somehow her life went on. She rose, dressed, prepared food, opened her restaurant, smiled at the customers, dealt with the waitresses, did the order books and daily accounts, as if nothing had happened. And now it seems that her journey has finally come to an end.

Lilith pauses. She reflects upon Sergeant Cully's recent visit. He'd stopped by earlier and shared the contents of Josephine's letter with her, then reassured her that she was no longer under suspicion of the murder of Montague Foxx. As far as he was concerned, she was 'off the hook' as he put it.

She feels as if she has walked into a mirrored room and glimpsed herself from an unfamiliar angle. Is this really what she looks like? Is this who she really is? The wooden spoon resumes drawing smooth circles in the yellow mixture.

Lilith thinks about the young woman who is now the prime suspect, even though she has left London and her whereabouts are unknown at present. He liked them young. The younger the better. Young and innocent of the world. As she was, once upon a time. Though in all her relationship with him, she never chased after Monty with a knife.

More fool her.

Well, good luck to the young woman. At least she tried to stand up for herself. Lilith sends a silent prayer to the God she ceased believing in when she turned her back on her community: Keep her safe, wherever she is. Keep her away from men like Montague Foxx. And don't ever let her ever come back, to be arrested, tried and hung for murder.

***

Detective Inspector Stride, in contrast, could currently be described as a man without a prayer. Arriving at Scotland Yard early that morning, he'd walked into his dingy back office, placed his hat on the peg and his legs beneath the desk, as he did every morning.

A couple of hours of pointless report reading followed these manoeuvres. Then as he had nothing to do, he sat back and did nothing. He was still employed in this pursuit when his superior officer arrived, bearing the letter of complaint from Sir Hugh Wynward.

A brief interdepartmental meeting took place, during which Stride developed a facial twitch and a pencil was snapped in two. At the end of the meeting Stride was ordered firmly *'not to bother Sir Hugh Wynward again.'* After which the head of Scotland Yard left, and Stride sat on in his creaky chair, throwing paperwork on the floor and wanting to shout at somebody.

He is just contemplating his next move, which might involve either an early lunch, or possibly arresting the first person who crossed his path for crossing his path without asking his permission, when Jack Cully enters.

"Morning Jack," Stride growls. "This had better be good."

Cully observes the state of the office floor and links it silently to the recent visit from the head of Scotland Yard. Cautiously, he describes his visit to Lilith Marks.

"I took the liberty of reassuring her that she is no longer our prime suspect," he says.

Stride pulls a face.

"Well, you shouldn't have. In my book, she is still *a* suspect, at least until we track down this Mimi character and her two accomplices," he says bluntly.

"I thought you had a lead on one of them."

Stride rolls his eyes ceilingwards.

"The butler of Sir Hugh Wynward did not, could not and would not get involved with anything so sordid as murder. Apparently."

"He has an alibi for the evening in question?"

"We will never know. He has a master who refuses to allow me to question him in the first place. And furthermore, I am forbidden from bothering both man and master again."

Stride pushes Sir Hugh's letter across the desk.

"Ah," Cully says, after perusing its contents and clocking up how many synonyms there were for 'impudence' and 'effrontery'. "You'd think, wouldn't you, that these people might consider helping the police with their inquiries to be part of their civic duties."

"You'd be wrong then," Stride says acidly.

"And what about the blackmail letter ~ you'd think he'd want us to get to the bottom of it."

"Wrong once again."

"So where do we go from here?"

"We don't go anywhere, because we have nowhere to go," Stride says shortly. "So we wait."

"We do?"

Stride nods curtly.

Over the years Detective Inspector Stride had learned that there were always times when nothing happened.

When an investigation had got bogged down or, as was the case now, had stalled. When that happened, it was tempting to become impatient, but Stride knew it never worked. Ultimately, waiting it out was the best way. However frustrating. Sometimes this took days, even weeks.

Sometimes not.

**

Leaving Stride and Cully to contemplate the static state of their investigation, let us now revert to a few hours earlier. It is eight-thirty and having eaten a hearty breakfast (porridge, boiled eggs, a little kedgeree, toast and butter) Mr John Gould sallies forth for another long and hopefully profitable day at the shop-face.

Dressed in an expensive black beaver top hat, tailored frock coat, and a rather awful yellow waistcoat with red erysipelas spots, he catches the morning train, getting out at Charing Cross Station where he joins the thousands of other commuters making their way on foot to their places of work.

On the way in, Gould picks up a newspaper from the usual lad on the corner of Regent Street. Reading the latest scandals and peccadilloes was his morning treat after a walk round his little empire. Approaching the gold and glass entrance of *John Gould & Company,* he pauses, and takes a few seconds to reflect upon the events of that first fateful opening day.

Gould is a religious man, and ever since he started his first general provisions store, he has been wrestling with his conscience over the conflict between serving God and serving the gods of commerce and enterprise.

For a while, he actually pondered whether the murdered man was a sign from On High. He had overreached himself. Like Faustus, his waxen wings had mounted above his reach and melting, Heav'n was now conspiring his overthrow.

After much soul-searching however, he is reconciled to his position. After all, is he not providing employment for many poor people who might otherwise be on the streets? And to many artisans, craftsmen and food manufacturers who, without him, would not be able to put bread on the family table?

Nevertheless, Gould averts his eyes as he passes by The Window which has, even after all the elapsed time, still drawn a small crowd of the usual suspects. Other people hover hopefully outside the main entrance, though it is some time before the store will officially open up for business.

As he approaches, Gould hears snippets of conversation: *"imagine seeing a real live dead body"* ... *"my cousin was there and he swears he saw blood on the carpet"* ... *"I've been coming every day - well, you never know your luck."* He ignores them and walks up to the ornate gold and glass door, where the uniformed doorman is waiting to let him in.

Inside, the staff are gathered in an embarrassed semicircle, three deep, waiting for the morning bible reading and prayer. Gould is handed a bible on a silver salver. He opens it and reads a few verses, then appeals to the Deity for safety and a good day's business.

God and Mammon both placated, he heads for his office, stopping off first at the Servants' Clothing Department to order some black French twill that his wife wants for the parlour maid's winter dress.

Having arranged for it to be delivered later that morning, he seats himself behind the big carved mahogany desk with its green leather-backed chair. His secretary brings in the black ledger and he spends some time studying the previous day's sales takings.

All is well in his empire. He turns his attention to the correspondence. It always baffles Gould that members of the public should take time out of their busy day to write to him about matters that, on the surface, seem utterly petty and unimportant.

Today's subjects vary from a jar of potted meat that wasn't quite to the consumer's exacting taste, a door scraper so sharp that the hapless purchaser keeps barking his shins upon it, and a request from a lady who wants a job in one of his departments because she feels it is suitable to her station in life. She does not mention what that station might be.

Gould reads all the letters carefully, then summons his secretary once more and dictates the replies, one by one. He tries to be courteous, even to the most absurd complainant. He likes to think of himself as a kind of modern version of Moses, leading the shoppers of London to the Promised Land of *John Gould & Company*.

Mid-morning heralds the arrival of one of the restaurant girls. She brings him his cup of milky coffee and two arrowroot biscuits. Mrs Gould thinks they are healthier than the chocolate ones that he prefers. As he finishes chewing the first unappetising biscuit, he reaches for his newspaper and flattens it down on the desk.

Then he pauses, his hand frozen mid-air.

Gould stares at the picture on the front page, his eyes narrowed, forehead furrowed, mouth pursed in concentration. He stares at it for a bit longer, lifting the paper to his face to study it in closer detail. He tugs thoughtfully at a lock of his hair. Then he gives a shout that brings his secretary running into the room.

"Is everything all right, sir?" the secretary asks in mild enquiry.

"Pen and paper, man! Quick as you can. Then get one of the delivery boys up here. I have an important letter I want taking to Scotland Yard as soon as I've written it."

***

Meanwhile over at Scotland Yard, Stride's day slides slowly by. He fills in reports and consumes mugs of coffee and reminds himself how many times he has found himself in exactly this situation, when an investigation suddenly ceases to breathe. Like a horse that stops dead and won't go forward. Something has come to an end. Something else is yet to start.

He is just contemplating sallying forth in search of something to eat, when the new desk duty constable gives a perfunctory knock at the door and enters his office.

"Letter for you, sir," the constable says, placing it on the desk. "Delivered by hand just now. Boy says it is important and is waiting for a reply."

Stride eyes the missive suspiciously. In his recent experience, nothing but bad news has arrived in epistolary form. Especially of late. His immediate conclusion is that this is more of the same. He slits the envelope and reads the contents. Then he stares at the opposite wall for a while, his expression inscrutable.

"Tell the boy I'm on my way."

Detective Inspector Stride reaches for his hat and coat. Leaving an office which now resembles a deranged stationer's shop, he heads out into the pale morning sunshine.

***

A short while later, Detective Inspector Stride and store owner John Gould face each other across Gould's desk, which once again Stride is trying hard not to envy. Pleasantries have been awkwardly exchanged. Now Gould pushes a newspaper across the desk, folded back to the latest episode in the *Man Murdered In The Shop Window* saga.

He stabs a fat white forefinger at the picture.

"I think I may recognise him."

Stride stops staring at the desk and fixes his attention upon its owner instead.

"The one on the left?" he asks hopefully.

Gould shakes his head.

"No, t'other. He reminds me of one of Mr Bellis' men."

Stride adopts a 'please continue' expression and waits.

"Titbull Bellis was the builder who bought the original land and built the store. I and a group of investors rent the building from him on a long lease. This man, I'm sure I saw him on the site while the store was being built, and later on I'm equally sure he was one of the men fitting it out ready for business."

"And where would I find Mr Bellis?"

Gould pulls a pad of paper towards him and scribbles a few lines.

"This is his London address."

Stride glances at the address. Ah. Those sort of people. So once again he will be rubbing shoulders with the members of society who don't really want his shoulders to come anywhere near theirs.

He thanks Gould and leaves, eschewing the customer lift, which seems to be full of the same group of jolly loud-voiced youths as it was when he entered the store some time earlier.

A short time later, Detective Inspector Stride stands outside the Tyburnia residence of Mr Titbull Bellis, developer. It is an impressive three-storey house, built in various shades of yellow and red brick, ornamented with what Stride always thinks of as 'curly bits'.

A glazed glass and cast-iron awning extends the porch to the front gate. Geometric tiles in lavender, blue and grey lead from the ornate black iron gate to the front door. Everything is new, shiny, modern and showy.

Bellis built me, it proclaims. *Look upon my presence and marvel.*

Stride tugs hard on the bell rope, and hears the bell tinkle somewhere in the depths of the house. He waits. The door is eventually opened by a very small maid in a very large cap. She peers up at Stride in a slightly confused manner. He hands her his card.

"Detective Inspector Stride of Scotland Yard. Is your mistress at home?"

"If you will step inside sir, I'll go and see," the little maid whispers, bobbing a curtsey.

Stride uses the boot scraper liberally, then crosses the threshold. He spends some time hovering in the bilious green papered hallway, while he waits for the servant to ascertain what she already knows full well.

At length, she reappears.

"The mistress will see you now."

Stride follows her into a small sitting room dazzlingly awash with floral motifs. Roses riot on walls, chrysanthemums cover the carpet, pansies peek from chair backs, violets view the world from swags on the base of the oil lamps. Every conceivable surface is covered with floral tributes.

In the midst of all this heavy petal, sits a fat middle-aged woman in rusty black, her hair scraped unbecomingly back into an old-fashioned afternoon cap. She has a round doughy face with two blackcurrant eyes and a small worried mouth.

Rising to her feet, the woman wrings her hands and wails,

"Ow, it isn't Belly is it? Please tell me you ain't come about my Belly? Nuffink's happened to Belly, has it?"

Stride does a quick mental readjustment. Not the first sort of people then ~ the other sort. The ones that buy their family silver ready-plated, rather than inherit it. He can deal with them.

"Madam, let me reassure you, your husband, as far as I know is fine. I am on important police business and I need to speak urgently to one of his workmen."

The woman gapes at him.

"P'lice business? We ain't never had doings with the p'lice before. My Belly is true as a die ~ you can ask anybody you meet; they'll tell you the same."

Stride puts out a reassuring hand.

"My good woman, my business is with one of his employees, not with him. Now if you can just tell me where I might find Mr Bellis, I shall be on my way and trouble you no further."

The woman gives him the last known location of 'Belly' then sits down heavily, causing the carved legs of the floral sofa to creak.

"Ow my! A p'liceman! In my parler! I'm all of a lather!"

She produces a large and rather grubby lawn handkerchief from the recesses of the sofa and starts fanning herself vigorously. Stride observes her for a few seconds, then in the absence of the little maid, he quietly shows himself out.

***

Victorian London. The greatest city on earth, capital of empire and commerce, a vast market into which the world pours. It is the ultimate consumer city. New shops and department stores spring up everywhere, destroying the old gabled shops, quaint inns and galleried courtyards.

Wide streets, magnificent monuments, law courts, great hotels and huge new thoroughfares flatten all before them. Blocks of flats in burnished brick, brilliant limestone or terracotta advance across the terrain like invading armies.

But there is more to Babylondon than this. There is also poverty and suffering. The poor have always been part of the texture of the city, like the stones and bricks. Look more closely: women sit with their arms folded, hunched over. A beggar family sleeps upon stone benches in the recess of a bridge, the dark shape of St Paul's looming behind then.

The interiors of the poor are filthy and crepuscular. Rags hang among reeking tallow lamps. The inhabitants seem to have no faces, since they are turned towards the shadows. All around them, dilapidated wooden beams and staircases rise in crazed confusion.

Meanwhile, a few footfalls away, the streets are filled with teeming and struggling life, with the mad pursuit of getting and spending, with brutal indifference. There is something eerie and ghostlike about the endless procession of faces that flit by. Sad faces, happy faces, merry or haggard.

They flit from gloom into light, and back into gloom once more. Dislocation and relocation follow, nothing ever stands still. Nothing is constant. The noise is hard and unyielding, like an unending shout.

***

And nowhere is the noise more unyielding, than behind these hoardings in Kensal New Town, where Bellis the Builder is running up houses like there is no tomorrow. Posters proclaim that 'residences for sale or rent' are being constructed behind the wooden barricades, (which are also plastered with other posters advertising pills, potions, biscuits and dubious nocturnal entertainments).

Not that these houses can be compared to the magnificent mansion Stride has recently quit. Here is no *rus in urbe*. These serried ranks of terraces belong to the miserly two up two down stock brick variety. Once built, they will be sold to absent landlords, who will then subdivide them into as many short-term lets as possible, adding them to that surprising feature: the brand new suburban slum.

Stride locates the entrance to the building-site, and raising his voice to be heard above the din of earth moving equipment and workmen with picks and shovels, demands to see Mr Bellis. The message is conveyed across the site in a series of shouts and gestures, until it produces a bow legged little man with a flat cap, a round stomach, and a cushiony nose the colour and texture of a strawberry.

He struts towards Stride with the aggressive bantam-cock attitude of all small men who'd like to be big men, only nature hasn't permitted it.

"Wozzup squire?" he demands. "Ain't nothing to do wiv my Nance is it?"

Touched by the mutual concern of husband and wife, Stride hastens to reassure him that the Angel in the House was, when he left her, alive and well and sipping a restorative glass of sherry wine. He shows him his card.

"So what's going on? Never had any Scotland Yarders visit one of my sites before in all the years I bin building. No dead bodies here as far as I know ~ though there might be if these men don't work a bit harder."

He grins, showing a row of uneven yellow teeth. Stride pretends to find this equally amusing. He checks the workmen, who are beginning to gather at a discreet, but well within earshot distance but does not recognise the man he is looking for amongst them.

Picking his words with care, he explains that he is looking for somebody who might possibly be able to help him with a small matter. Nothing serious. Just something he needs clearing up. He gives Bellis a description of the man he is seeking, but does not show him the picture in the paper.

"Oh I know who you mean: Billy Furness. Wait now, let me consult my little black book ~ that's what I call it. I keep the names and addresses of all my regular workmen in it."

Bellis riffles through a small notebook, then stabs a finger at a particular page.

"Here y'are. 51 Angel Court. He should be there. Mind he should be here, but he ain't turned up for a couple of days. When you see him, tell him I need him back on-site toot sweet, as the French say, will yer?"

Stride thanks him, then returns to Scotland Yard where he finds Inspector Lachlan Greig (five foot seven inches) and a couple of tall constables. When you're bringing somebody in for questioning who isn't expecting to be brought in for questioning, it's always best to arrive mob-handed.

***

Stride and his posse make their way through a squalid maze of streets, courts and alleys in the November rain. Everything here is cheap and nasty. A wilderness of dirt, rags and hunger.

Pawn shop and public house repeat at regular intervals.

They pass small shops full of stale bread and slabs of grey cake. A butcher's window contains buzzing flies and bony pieces of meat. Baskets of bruised vegetables line the thoroughfare, but look only fit for consumption by the pigs that rootle aimlessly around in the gutter.

The whole neighbourhood is infused with a miasma of grinding, vicious, unwholesome poverty. The air smells of it. The houses sag with it. The children kicking a scrawny cat are rendered dull-eyed and sullen by it.

Finally, they reach a tiny alleyway at the end of a street of dead-coloured brick buildings.

It is no more than a stagnant channel of mud, so narrow they have to pick their way and walk in single file, until they arrive at a small court paved with broken flagstones covered in breadcrumbs and general litter. Ducking under lines of discoloured washing, they approach number 51.

A woman is sitting on the doorstep. She leans against the door, holding her hand against her left cheek. As the men come closer, they all see the livid bruising. The woman doesn't seem to notice their approach at first and only raises her face when they are standing right in front of her.

Stride and Greig exchange a quick glance. The left-hand side of the woman's face is swollen to twice its size, a raw and purple bruise closing the eye. There are bare patches in her scalp, as if her hair has been roughly torn out.

"Good day, madam. We are sorry to disturb you," Stride says. "We are looking for Mr Billy Furness. Can you tell us where we might find him?"

The woman tries to rise, but Greig shakes his head. He crouches down beside her so that his face is on a level with hers.

"That must hurt," he says, indicating the bruises.

She drops her eyes.

"It is sore, sir, but I've had worse."

"Did he give it to you? I know some men can be cruel to their wives."

She opens her mouth, as if she would deny her injuries are referable to such a cause, but seeing the kindness in his face, she nods.

"He did it when he came back from the pub a couple of days back. Then he collected his traps, threw me out of the 'ouse and locked the door. I don't know where he went."

"I am very sorry to hear it. Where have you been sleeping?"

"Here sir. Where you find me. I spend the day going about. But I come back when it gets dark."

She raises troubled eyes to his.

"My Dicky is still in there. He hasn't had a bite to eat for three days now."

Greig stands up.

"Constables ~ there may be a starving child in the house: break down the door, quick as you can!"

The woman utters a feeble protest, but is lifted bodily off the step by one of the men. The door yields to a couple of swift kicks, sagging sideways on its rusted hinges. The group stand back as she goes into the house.

"Best follow her," Stride mutters.

They cross the threshold. Inside, the house smells of stale food and damp. Paper is peeling off the walls, and the bare floorboards curl up in places. The woman runs straight to the back kitchen, where she unhooks a bird cage hanging in the window. It contains a tiny linnet lying on its side, claws extended. Its eyes are open but glazed.

"Oh Dicky, my poor Dicky," she sobs, bending over the cage. "No wonder you died. There's not a grain of seed nor a drop of water in your cage."

Stride pulls a face and turns away. He stares out through the cloudy window into the mean little back yard. There is a spade lying on the ground by the wall. It is coated with sticky clay soil.

"Someone's been digging," he murmurs to Greig.

Greig points to a small patch of newly-turned earth. "Maybe over there?"

Side by side, they consider the small mound of earth.

"Are you thinking what I'm thinking?" Stride asks.

"Probably," Greig agrees.

Behind them, the woman's sobs rise to a crescendo of uncontrollable grief.

"Might be worth taking a look," Stride says.

"It might well be."

They go out, followed by the constables. Stride picks up the spade and hands it to one of them.

"Come on then, let's see if there's anything down there."

The constable begins to dig. After a couple of seconds, he stops.

"You're quite right, sir: there is something here."

They all gather round and stare down at what looks to be a bit of old cloth protruding from the shallow hole. The constable digs carefully round it, eases the earth back, then squats down and lifts out a bundle of clothing. He unrolls it to reveal a pair of men's cord trousers wrapped round a short pea jacket. Both are spattered with a dark brown stain.

"Ah," Stride says nodding thoughtfully.

"Yes indeed," Greig echoes.

The clothes are brought into the house.

"Do these things belong to your husband?" Stride inquires of the woman, who has taken the linnet out of the cage and is now stroking its plumage lovingly. She gives the jacket and trousers a cursory glance and nods silently. Stride asks,

"Do you know why they are covered in blood?"

She shakes her head.

"Can you recall him coming home in these clothes?"

Another shake.

"I don't suppose you remember when he buried them?"

She looks down. Her expression is half-stupefied.

"She knows nothing, poor soul," Greig murmurs.

"We are taking these items with us," Stride tells the woman firmly. "If your husband returns, you are to go to the nearest police office at once, and tell them at the desk. Do you understand."

She stares at him, dull-eyed.

"Oh he ain't coming back," she says. "He took his bag o' tools. There's just me an' my Dicky now."

She places the tiny bird gently on the table, then sits down in the only chair, crooning softly to herself. Stride and Greig watch her for a couple of seconds in silence. Then they signal to the constables and together they walk back through the broken house and out into the noxious smelling court.

***

It is a moonlit night, but the moon, being past the full is only just rising over the great wilderness of London. Lady Meriel Wynward stands at the dark window with its bars and watches the street, where solitary figures creep through the gloom. But the one she seeks is never among them.

In her mind's eye she sees the night landscape with its bright moon and multitude of stars, stretching out before her. All its roads lead back towards her door. And somewhere out there, on a dusty highway, sheltering in the lee of a bridge, or maybe in a barn or by a millpond, is the solitary form of a young woman, weary, footsore, her dark eyes fixed on her ultimate destination: her dear long-lost childhood home.

Midnight arrives, but still the longed-for one does not come. Now the carriages in the street are few, and the other late sounds in the neighbourhood are hushed. It is so still that listening to the immense silence is like looking at intense darkness.

She holds her candle to the window, as if there might be some answering glow, as if somewhere in that black dripping night, another light is being held up, another pair of eyes staring out across the void.

Lady Meriel stays at her post until the frosty night wears away. Dawn breaks, and the ghosts of trees and hedges, rooftops, steeples and towers grow less ethereal and cede to the realities of day.

Only then does she fall to the floor with a despairing cry. She will be found, lifeless and cold, her hair wildly scattered about her chalk-white face, by one of the servants who will put her to bed before sending out for the doctor.

And yet astonishingly, some hours later and fortified by beef tea and determination, Lady Meriel rallies. She sits up and demands paper and pen. The servants confer on the landing. The doctor has prescribed absolute rest and quiet.

More importantly, the master has given instructions they are not to indulge his wife's whims and fancies. But the master is currently abroad, and while the cat is away, it is decided, the poor mouse may write letters to whomsoever she please.

So, paper is presented, pen is provided, ink is offered, and a short while later, Lady Meriel Wynward hands a sealed envelope to one of the maids with instructions to "take it to the post-box at once".

And as there is no butler present to intercept the communication, Lady Meriel's wishes are carried out ~ to the letter! A few hours later, her missive is delivered to the recipient. Some time after that, dressed and veiled, Lady Meriel Wynward opens the front door of the magnificent town house and flutters away like a leaf in the wind.

***

It is said that travel broadens the mind, a sentiment with which Felix Lightowler, antiquarian bookseller, mage and alchemist, would most certainly concur. His travels, since he quit the shores of his native land, have taken him all over Europe. He is now definitely broader of mind, though somewhat lighter of wallet.

He has been to Wittenberg and viewed the magnificent cathedral. In Paris, he dined on strange soup and meat from some animal he'd never heard of called a cheval. But the best place he visited was Prague.

Lightowler will never forget his first sight of Prague from the jolting coach window, as the city rose up out of the early evening mist, all turrets and towers and steeples, its oil lamps glowing like eyes. Prague. An unopened present.

Red pantiled roofs and ancient painted buildings. Its ancient cobbled streets trod by Tycho Brahe and Johannes Kepler and so many other famous seekers of truth. The great alchemist and magician John Dee was also a visitor.

Here, in the sixteenth century, the Jewish mystic Rabbi Loew created a golem out of clay and brought it to life. Lightowler remembers standing on the Stone Bridge with its thirty statues and feeling that Prague was a city with so much history that there was almost no room for the present.

But all good things must come to an end, so now here he is, perched precariously on the roof of a coach travelling through Bohemia on its way to the coast. At his feet, corded and wrapped in waterproof cloth, are all the books he has purchased while on his travels.

It was easy to find the 'right' sort of bookshop. All you had to do was turn down a quiet backstreet, and there it was. Bulks of yellowing volumes out front, dead flies on the grimy windowsills.

Inside the shop, there was always dust on the counter, dust on the floor, dust on the shelves of books. The bookshop owner standing behind the dusty counter wore a dusty velvet jacket. Even the bell over the door gave a dusty jangle as you walked in.

The coach forges on, the horses galloping through dark pine forests, clattering past tiny villages. In two days' time, he will take ship for England. As soon as he gets home, he intends to make a thorough study of the new books.

Maybe within one of them lies the recipe for the elusive Elixir, the precious liquid that grants eternal life. Let it be so, Lightowler prays, and I will return to Prague and live there for ever, treading the cobbles with the ghosts of the past.

**

A restaurant on the first floor of a West End department store is a far cry from the woods and forest glades of Bohemia, yet that is where Detective Inspector Stride is even now directing his footsteps.

Crossing the threshold, he hears the tinkle of teacups, the rise and fall of well-bred voices. A piano plays discreetly in one corner (another of Gould's innovations). Stride looks about him, and sees a lone woman in a veil sitting at a corner table. He goes over.

"Lady Wynward?"

She lifts her veil.

Stride is struck by the change in her appearance. Lady Meriel's face is death-pale, the hollows at the temple more pronounced. Her nose and cheekbones look as delicately ridged and fragile as meringues. But there is a hectic flush upon her cheeks, and her eyes are bright and feverish.

"Please sit down, detective inspector."

He sits down. The waitress brings some tea.

"I took the liberty of ordering. I hope you like Indian tea."

He does not, but accepts the cup anyway.

She plays with her gloves, pulling compulsively at the finger-ends.

Stride waits patiently for her to explain why he is here; why, out of the blue and in clear contravention of her husband's express wishes, she has written to him suggesting this clandestine meeting.

"My husband is from home," she says, as if reading his thoughts. "He and James our butler have gone to Italy to find a suitable villa to rent. My doctor says I cannot survive another London winter. I need sunshine and tranquillity."

"I see." Stride shovels a couple of spoonfuls of sugar into his tea in the hope that it will render it drinkable.

"While he is absent, I have taken the opportunity to consult with some friends who have the ability to communicate with those on the other side."

"I see."

"They have conveyed many messages from the spirits, from whom I have learned that my daughter is not there."

"Is not ...?"

"There, detective inspector. On the other side. She has not passed over. Therefore she is still alive."

Lady Meriel reaches into her bag and hands Stride a small pasteboard oblong.

"Here is a photograph of Sybella. It is the only one that I now possess of her. We had some taken just before she left for her holiday. My husband made me throw all the other pictures of her away after she ... he said they would only lead me to morbid thoughts. But I kept this one. Now I should like you to take it."

Stride is completely out of his depths. He stares down into his teacup.

"She did not die in the train accident. I know that. I have always known that. A mother ... detective inspector ... a mother knows these things. The letter and the lock of her hair was her way of telling me."

Stride takes a deep breath.

"Lady Wynward, I am at a loss to know what you require of me. Your husband clearly does not share your opinion and indeed has gone so far as to write to my superior to request that I cease investigating the origins of the letter."

"But he is not here. And now I ~ I am requesting you to continue."

She fixes her eager over-bright eyes full on his face.

"I am aware that many people are sceptical about the world of the spirits, detective inspector. Maybe you are one of them. To you I say: there are so many uncanny things in this world. Consider the instant communication through telegraph wires? How do the words get from one end to the other? The miracle of a photograph. How can the image of a person be translated from what they are into an identical picture? So why should the spirits not speak to us?"

Stride is just racking his brains for a suitable answer that won't cause offence, when he suddenly sees John Gould standing at the restaurant entrance. He is glancing intently from one table to the other, as if searching for somebody.

When Gould spots Stride, his face lights up and he hurries over. Stride feels a flicker of annoyance. Can't the man see he is busy? Gould stops at the table, rubbing his hands together.

"Lady Wynward," he says in a fawning voice, ignoring Stride completely. "What a pleasant surprise. One of the floorwalkers overheard a customer mentioning that you were honouring my little restaurant with your presence."

Lady Meriel looks up at him in bewilderment.

"I am sorry ~ you must excuse me, have we met before?"

Gould is unabashed. He draws himself up to his full height.

"I am the proprietor of the store, my lady: Mr John Gould, at your service," he announces, deliberately avoiding Stride's go-away stare. "I hope you find everything to your satisfaction, Lady Wynward?"

Lady Meriel inclines her head.

"It is very pleasant here."

"You think so? Good. Good. I am delighted to hear you say it. And Sir Hugh Wynward, he is well?"

"My husband is out of the country at the moment," she replies stiffly.

"Is he? Well, well. A little change of scene does us all good from time to time ~ ah, I see the good inspector is indicating that I have outstayed my welcome. I must therefore leave you. Please enjoy your tea."

Gould bows low and backs away, still smiling fatuously.

Stride gives her a quizzical look.

Lady Meriel sighs and stirs her tea.

"My husband owns shares in the store, I believe. I take little interest in his business concerns." She leans forward, fixing her eyes earnestly upon Stride's face. "Detective inspector, my request to you is very simple. You have her likeness there in your hand. Find Sybella and return her to her mother. That is all I ask."

***

"A hamper?" Stride exclaims. "A joke, surely?"

Jack Cully folds over *The Inquirer* and points to the headline which reads:

Catch This Man! Christmas Hamper Reward!

Underneath the headline is the 'Wanted' picture of Billy Furness recently circulated to all police offices. Under that, is an article stating that Mr John Gould (prop.) of *John Gould & Company* has generously offered a *lavish* Christmas hamper to anybody assisting in the apprehension of the man suspected of murdering a well-liked member of London society, and leaving his corpse in his department store window.

The article then goes on to lament the inefficiency of the Metropolitan Police Force who, the reporter suggests, could not catch a cold, let alone a murderer.

"But I was in his blasted store yesterday. He never mentioned this!" Stride exclaims. "For God's sake! Why does everything nowadays have to come with payment of some kind or another? What happened to good old-fashioned public spirit and just doing your civic duty?"

"Too old-fashioned," Cully says.

"And since when was Montague Foxx a *'well-liked member of society'*?" Stride continues indignantly. "I thought you told me nobody liked him."

"Journalistic licence."

"I *told* him about not speaking to the press," Stride mutters. "Why does nobody listen to me? You know what this means, don't you?"

"If it's anything like the last time *The Inquirer* offered a reward, I should imagine the outer office will shortly be full of people claiming they've seen Mr Furness, might have seen Mr Furness or swearing that they aren't

Mr Furness even though they bear a striking resemblance to him," Cully says laconically.

"Exactly. Meanwhile the real culprit is probably long gone."

Wearily Stride reaches for pen and paper.

"I shall write and remind Mr Gould of my instructions. And the editor of that populist rag. For all the good it'll do," he adds disgustedly.

Cully departs.

Stride sits on, chewing the end of his pen. The meeting with Lady Meriel Wynward has thrown up an unexpected link. Previously, he was unable to see any connection between the two individuals at the centre of Foxx's murder. A building site worker and a butler? It was too far-fetched. They moved in different worlds altogether.

But after the disclosure that her husband was actually one of the store's shareholders, Stride is beginning to see how it might have worked. Furness was around when the store was being refitted. Sir Hugh might well have called by from time to time to check on his investment. Perhaps accompanied by his man.

All police work dealt with drawing conclusions, which were later discarded or built on. The precipitate departure of both individuals was adding credence to his theory. How to go about translating theory into fact however, was still eluding him.

***

There are people in this world who will do something for the sheer fascination of doing it. Or because they shouldn't. Behold, therefore, Jasper Thorogood and Eugenious Strictly, fortified by strong drink and avarice, standing in the pale moonlight outside the empty house of Felix Lightowler.

They carry various small bags containing the bottles of chemicals and packets of other substances they require for their great experiment. They also carry a box of lucifer matches, a device to pick the lock, and a couple of candles. When engaged upon nefarious purposes, it always pays to come suitably well-equipped.

Now, under cover of darkness, they gain entrance to the house, light a candle and make their way up the creaky stairs to the laboratory. Everything is still and silent and covered with a thick layer of dust.

They place their bags down on the table.

"Right, you get everything ready and start the furnace. I'll weigh out the lead and the oil and sulphur," Thorogood says.

"Lucky for us the old fool left everything set up."

"Luck does not play a part in it," Thorogood reprimands him. "We've spent enough hard-earned money and listened to enough boring lectures. Now we are finally going to get what we deserve. No more, no less."

They work in silence for a while. Strictly checks the water temperature and tempers the flame. Thorogood consults his notes and mutters to himself as he weighs and carefully mixes the lead and the various chemicals. Finally, he transfers them into one of the closed glass vessels and attaches it to the beaker of water bubbling on a trivet.

"Now let the Transmutation Beginne," Strictly intones, and is silenced by a Looke.

Meanwhile, not far away, a small furtive man in a long black cloak climbs out of a cab and lifts down a heavy case, which he hauls to the door of a deserted book shop. Fumbling in his pocket for the key, he unlocks the door and heaves the case over the threshold.

The door closes. A few seconds later, the flickering light of a candle can be seen through the wooden shutters. Felix Lightowler aka John Dee is back in town.

***

Gold was not made in a day. Time must be given for the Worke to proceed, so that nature may be granted convenient space to work in. After a couple of hours, the Metall has gone from black (Nigredo) to white (Albedo) and yellow (Citinas). But no sign of the final stage, the red mixture (Rubedo) that signals the transmutation into gold.

The fire has had to be constantly tempered, a tedious job that was previously the provenance of Bovis Finister but has now fallen to Strictly's charge, and the air in the room has thickened to an almost fog-like opacity.

"I say, Jasper," the bellows-blower gasps, "maybe you'd like to take a turn at tempering the flame?"

Thorogood folds his arms and regards him sternly.

"I think not," he says. "It is my job to watch the Metall closely. We are almost there, my friend. The final stage is about to arrive, and then finally, we will have our gold!"

Strictly shoots him a glare, the effect of which is lost in the darkening gloom and the thickening smoke. Surreptitiously, he turns up the heat. After all, if they are nearly there, what harm speeding up the process? The sooner they make their gold, the sooner he can go home to his lodgings.

The fire burns, the water bubbles, and the Metall begins to Quicken.

***

Meanwhile, having reassured himself that all his books have arrived safely and intact, Lightowler snuffs out the candle and emerges into the street once more. He locks up the shop, and heads in the direction of hearth and home.

It has been a long day's travelling and he is ready for bed. It has been many weeks since he slept in his own bed. East, West, home's best, he thinks, stepping up his pace. Tomorrow he will open the shop and resume the business of life.

Passing a late-opening public house, Lightowler stops off to refresh himself with a quick nightcap, which is why he isn't around to hear the massive explosion. His first inkling that something is wrong comes as he turns the corner into his street, and sees the strange sight of the unpleasant elderly man who lives next door capering in the middle of the road, eyes bulging, his hair blowing in the night wind. He is dressed in a ragged night-shirt and slippers.

"I told 'im!" he shrieks to nobody in particular, pointing to the wreck that was formerly Lightowler's house and alchemic laboratory. It is now a smoking ruin of bricks and rubble emitting small explosions, with bright green and yellow flames shooting up into the night sky. "I said they was Up to No Good! Maybe now he'll listen to me!"

As shocked neighbours start to pile into the street and form a bucket chain to the nearest pump, Felix Lightowler, aka John Dee decides that discretion is the better part of valour, and absence the best part of both.

He turns on his heels and skeddadles back the way he has come, leaving the ruins of his former dwelling to be picked over by scavengers once daylight comes. His black-clad figure will not be seen in the street again.

It will be some weeks before newspapers publish the report of the subsequent police inquiry into the explosion and its possible causes. The report will conclude that, as the house was empty at the time, the event was probably caused by some sort of spontaneous combustion.

***

In the meantime, let us return to more pleasant places. It is a few days later and here are Constantia Mortram, twins Dorinda and Veracia Davenport, Pugsley and a selection of delicious cakes and small crust-less sandwiches. The setting is the Mortrams' parlour, where the newly-engaged one is holding a small afternoon tea party to celebrate her forthcoming nuptials.

The gathering is awaiting the arrival of Olivia May Hanchard, younger sister of the betrothed. She is a very sweet girl, country-bred, convent educated and newly arrived in London to be fitted for her bridesmaid outfit. Best behaviour has been tacitly agreed upon by all.

And here she comes, dressed in a simple pink dress, her fresh girlish complexion and winning smile reminding the three, rather pointedly, of how they inhabited, once upon a time, that innocent fairy tale country of the past.

Constantia rises, steps forward and begins to greet her young guest with a few well-prepared words of welcome. Then she stops, the words of welcome dying in her throat. Her gaze suddenly focuses in hard on Olivia May. The twins frown gently, tilt their heads in symmetric puzzlement.

What could possibly have upset their worldly-wise, socially adept hostess? They eye the newcomer with interest, but see nothing in her demeanour or appearance to suggest more than the sweet young thing they have been led to expect.

Recovering herself quickly, Constantia leads the sweet one to the sofa and indicates to the lurking maid that tea is to be poured and plates distributed. She positions herself next to Olivia May and inquires how she is finding London.

"Oh, it is so wonderful," Olivia May replies, rolling her baby-blue eyes and clutching her plate of sandwiches. "I have never seen so many lovely things! Paintings and waxworks and last night we went to the opera!"

"I am so pleased," Constantia says in her best verbal wallpaper voice.

"And the shops! So many lovely shops!" the sweet one continues. "My brother has been so generous," she says. "Look, he bought me this carnelian agate locket soon after I arrived. He said it was identical to the one he'd seen you wear so often, dear Constantia. So when he saw it in a jeweller's shop window, he knew he had to buy it. Because we are soon going to be sisters, you see?"

"I see," Constantia says in a low voice. "It is very like my own, you are right. May I inquire where he found it?"

Olivia May shakes her head.

"He did not say."

For a moment, Constantia Mortram looks as if she has seen a ghost. Then she rises swiftly to her feet, murmuring, "Please excuse me for a moment," and leaves the room.

By the time she returns, the guests are tucking into the cakes and the matter is not mentioned again until the sweet one departs. Then the twins turn on Constantia.

"Explain!" Veracia orders.

"Yes, what happened?" Dorinda demands. "Why did you leave the room so suddenly?"

Constantia bites her lip.

"The locket was Sybella's ~ I am sure of it."

Dorinda shakes her head.

"That cannot be. Maybe it is very like, but it can't be Syb's."

"It is hers," Constantia counters. "We bought them that summer when we went to Scotland together. The jeweller said he only managed to make two matching lockets out of the original stone. Olivia's locket had the same coral streak running through it as mine."

She produces her own locket for them to look at.

"I have a lock of Syb's hair inside my locket, and she had a lock of my hair in hers. Don't you see? It means she must still be alive."

The twins examine the locket very carefully.

"I must say they do look exactly the same," Veracia says thoughtfully. "But how do you explain Syb's locket being in a jeweller's shop window?"

"Maybe she needed the money?" Constantia looks from one twin to the other. "We all think we saw her in town. Her mother received a letter containing a lock of her hair. Now her locket has turned up. It is a sign. I think we must tell the little detective after all. Imagine if Syb was in some sort of trouble, and we alone had the power to save her?"

"What sort of trouble?"

Constantia puts a finger to her lips and leans forward. The twins copy her.

"Remember *Belinda's Lovers*?" she whispers.

The twins give a gasp, followed by a shudder of horror.

"Oh ~ but surely Syb didn't have any male admirers. None of us did. It wasn't allowed."

"Not at school. But she did receive those letters, remember. She tried to hide them, so I know they weren't from her mother."

"Oh Con! So you think Syb might be ... might have had ... oh no ~ it is too awful to contemplate!" Veracia gasps.

"But if it *has* happened, and she is even now alone and abandoned, do we not owe it to her to try and rescue her?"

"Oh, well, when you put it like *that* ..." Veracia says.

"All for one, and one for all," Dorinda adds.

"Then we are agreed. I shall write to Scotland Yard at once," Constantia says. "When I receive a reply, I'll let you both know. Until then, we will continue to say nothing to our parents."

"Absolutely."

"Our lips are sealed."

"Oh poor, poor Syb," Veracia adds.

"But she has us now," Constantia says firmly, getting up to show them out. "She is no longer alone. Nor poor. We will save her."

***

Regent Street on a chilly, but sunny afternoon in late October. The broad pavements and glittering passages swarm with people jostling each other at every step. The air is redolent with cigar smoke, pomade and perfume as the worthy and unworthy take the air.

Saunter past the brilliant plate-glass shop windows. Here are gloves, shawls, cambric pocket-handkerchiefs, patent leather goods, Strasburg pies, ormolu clocks, Vanille chocolate, bonbons and barley-sugar cages to tempt the passer-by intent upon purchasing.

Irreproachably polished boots, successful moustaches, beautiful bonnets, rich tresses, mulberry-coloured coats and velveteen shooting-jackets promenade side by side. Dealers in poodles, penknives and prints display their wares along the kerbstones.

Look more closely. A tall sallow man, his head somewhat devoid of hair, has just drawn alongside a pretty belle who is eyeing some dainty cakes. The man has prominent eyes and a deeply-lined face.

There is something powerfully combative in his look ~ as if it would not take much to stir him to anger, a chafing, irritable manner that might break out into violent deeds and words. Suddenly, the man reaches out and cuts the string of her bag. Catching it as it falls, he spins round and is off, helter-skelter through the crowd.

Instantly the cry of 'stop thief' goes up on all sides. A few gallants give pursuit. The man glances over his shoulder and ducks down a convenient alley leading to the maze of tiny side streets running off Carnaby Street, where his luck runs out, or rather runs slap bang into the flesh mountain that is Bovis Finister, fruit pie in one hand, basket of washing on his shoulder.

There is a cry, followed by a crump, as skull meets pavement. The pursuers pelt round the corner and skid to a halt in front of the prone and very unconscious man.

"He went straight into me," Bovis tells them laconically.

A constable steps out of the serried rank of onlookers and rolls the man over with his boot. The man begins to stir. Bovis looks down at him.

"He made me drop my pie," he adds sadly.

The constable hoiks the groaning man to his feet and examines his features closely.

"Well done, my lad. I think this man is wanted by Scotland Yard no less, and you have only gone and apprehended him."

He digs out his whistle and gives three short blasts. A few moments later, two other constables appear on the scene. The crowd parts to let them through. They handcuff the man and half walk, half drag him back to the main thoroughfare, where the belle and her entourage are waiting.

"Here you are miss," the constable says, handing her the bag, "All safe and sound, thanks to this brave young man here."

The belle dimples her thanks. Bovis goes bright red. The constable whistles up a cab and the miscreant is bundled roughly inside. The constable lays a hand on Bovis' shoulder.

"Now then my boy, you give me your name and where you live, and I'll hand it to the detective inspector. There's a nice reward for doing what you've just done, and he'll want to make sure you get it."

Utterly confounded by the turn of events, Bovis stammers out his details. The constable writes it down. Then he jumps into the cab, telling the driver to whip up the horse. The cab rattles off.

The crowd, seeing that nothing more is going to happen, melt away, leaving the hero of the hour standing on his own. Bovis goes back to the alley to retrieve the washing basket.

"He still made me drop my pie, though," he murmurs, as he sets off back home.

***

The arrival at Scotland Yard of a murder suspect is always a cause for rejoicing. Billy Furness is frog-marched into the police station, where his presence is logged by the duty officer. Then he is escorted to one of the bare whitewashed cells to await developments.

The developments turn out to be Detective Sergeant Cully and Inspector Greig. The extension to the developments comes in the form of every free officer, who gather outside the cell door, which is quietly eased open just enough for the interrogation to be heard.

"Ain't I gonna have a cuppa tea or nuffink?" the suspect complains. "My head's fair bursting."

Cully and Greig look him, then at each other. They both shake their heads.

"Maybe when you've told us what we want to know, we'll think about it," Greig says crisply.

The suspect mutters something about 'ferkin pigs', then catches Greig's eye and clamps his mouth shut. Greig and Cully lean forward.

"So, your name is Mr Billy Furness, you live at 51 Angel Court and you work for a builder and developer called Mr Titbull Bellis, is that correct?" Cully asks.

After a pause, the suspect admits reluctantly that this might be the case.

"Would you like to tell us where you were on the night of September the twelfth?"

The suspect shrugs. "Dunno. Prob'ly down the King's Arms."

"We can check that," Greig says to Cully sotto voce, but loud enough for Furness to hear.

"Let's think about later on that evening. Maybe you went for a little walk after your night down the pub," Cully suggests. "Perhaps you met a pal on the way, let's say his name might be James Oxley. Perhaps you both met another man: his name being Montague Foxx and all three of you went for a stroll down Oxford Street together. Then you and your friend murdered Foxx in cold blood and dumped his body in a shop window. How does that sound for a night out?"

The suspect assumes totally blank expression.

"Dunno what you're on abaht. Nivver met either of them. Wasn't there and you can't prove I was."

"Really?" Cully says. "I'd be very interested to know why you buried a pair of bloodstained trousers and a jacket in your back yard. Can you explain that?"

The suspect gapes at them.

"You can't prove they was mine."

"Your wife identified them as belonging to you."

Another pause. A fly buzzes frantically against the window.

Greig and Cully sit back and fold their arms.

"Well, you can't prove I was in Oxford Street that night."

Greig and Cully lean forward.

"Ah, but we can. You see, we have a reliable witness who saw you in the company of Oxley and Foxx on the night in question. They are waiting just outside the door to identify you ~ shall I invite them in?" Greig says sweetly.

Furness swallows.

Greig and Cully sit back, arms folded, and wait.

"Look, maybe I was where you said I was when you said I was, but I din't do nuffink. It was him ~ he done it all, I just helped a bit."

Greig and Cully lean forward.

"Really? Suppose you tell us all about what he did and your 'help'?" Cully suggests.

The suspect sucks in his breath.

Greig and Cully sit back and fold their arms.

They wait.

The story, when it slowly emerges, runs like this: Furness encountered Wynward's butler when Mr Bellis had sent him round to the house with a note for the nob the butler worked for. Well, it was more of a re-encounter, because as soon as he opened the door, Furness had recognised Jimbo Oxley from way back when they were both growing up. Arses hanging out of their trousers and now look at him: smart uniform and lording it like you'd think he was born to the life. Which he bloody well wasn't.

Amazing how things turns out. There was him, scraping to find the rent, working every hour Gawd sent, and that Jimbo opening and closing doors for a living and eating three square meals a day. Weren't fair, was it?

They met again when Furness was working on the fixtures and fittings for the new store, only this time Jimbo took a bit more notice of his former playmate ~ stood him a drink, chatted about the good old days. Which they weren't as far as he was concerned.

A few other meetings followed. Also with drink. During which Jimbo confided that his master was having a bit of trouble with a 'cove' demanding money off of him. He didn't go into details, just said if Billy was prepared to help him teach 'the cove' a lesson, there'd be something in it for him.

So Furness said yes and one night ~ the one Greig and Cully'd asked him about, he agreed to meet Jimbo and 'the cove'. Well, he could see straight off someone had put something into the man's drink, because he wasn't acting normal. Slurring his words and staggering around, he was.

Jimbo told Furness not to worry, it was just a little something he'd given him from home. Sort of relax him a bit. Smart clothes but a nasty piece of work though, Billy could see that from the off.

They'd walked him down Oxford Street and when they reached the side alleyway of the store, Jimbo'd said, *"Let's put him in one of the windows, then everyone will laugh at him tomorrow when he wakes up."* So they'd strolled down the alley, and as the staff door was still open, they'd gone in.

Furness knew the layout of the store from having fitted it up, so he guided them to the back of the display window. But then, just when they'd got the man placed like he was asleep at the table, Jimbo had suddenly picked up a carving knife and cut the cove's throat. *"That'll teach the bastard,"* he'd said, and he'd grinned up at Furness as if he'd just done something really clever.

There was that funny glint in his eye, and Furness suddenly remembered it from when they were kids and Jimbo had cut the tails off of puppies and drowned kittens for fun, and thrown stones at a poor mad old woman who lived in their court.

Furness hadn't thought it'd be like that, on account of he'd understood 'teaching a lesson' to mean handing out a beating, so he turned and scarpered. Only noticed the blood on his clothes when he got home. Didn't get a penny in the end.

Some time later, Jimbo had turned up at the building site where he worked and told him the police was onto them and he'd better make himself scarce.

"That's God's honest truth," Furness says in the tone of voice of one who knows their only hope is now reliant upon the goodwill of people who have no pressing reason to have any. "Look, I bin lying low, starving to death for the past few days. Had to steal just to keep body and soul together."

After Furness has excused and exonerated himself to a standstill, Greig and Cully confer outside the interview room.

"If that man is innocent, I'm the Lord Chancellor of England," Cully says.

"Do you intend to charge him?"

Cully thinks about the poor battered woman crooning over her dead bird, and something deep and dark inside him turns.

"He deserves more than just charges, but it's a start. Let's arrest him for theft, and aiding and abetting a murderer," he says grimly.

Still protesting his innocence at full volume, Furness is escorted to the cells at the back of the building. Then Cully retires to write up his notes on the interview. After completing them, he goes to find Stride. He needs to update him with what he has just heard.

But Cully's news will have to wait, for his colleague is not in his office. Nor is he to be found anywhere else, for Detective Inspector Stride has left the building and gone to hunt ghosts.

***

The hunt has taken Stride via a letter from Miss Constantia Mortram ~ a letter he wasn't expecting at all ~ to an interview with the same young lady at which she was unexpectedly forthcoming, and her mother was not present.

After the interview, he took a cab to a small jeweller's shop in Ludgate Hill, and asked the jeweller certain pertinent questions on the back of information gleaned from the interview. From thence, he has travelled across town to the district of Whitechapel to visit an extremely unsavoury boarding house run by an equally unsavoury woman in a precarious red wig.

There, he has spoken to 'One of the Hall's Brightest Stars' before finding a quiet, decent public house, in which he'd refreshed himself with a glass of ale and a plate of chops while he had a good long think.

It is early evening before Stride returns to Scotland Yard, where he finds Cully's report of Furness' capture and subsequent interview waiting for him on his desk. Stride reads the report in the gathering gloom, nodding to himself thoughtfully and scribbling notes in the margin.

Having read it, he sits back, a smile of quiet satisfaction on his face. Events that appeared random are now coalescing. There is the sense that an investigation that had stalled is now moving forward. All he needs to do now, is patiently follow where it leads.

***

Lady Meriel Wynward sits at her open window staring up at the vast empty scoop of night sky. Waves of sleep are pulling at her body, but she refuses to give in to them, even though her nerves are wound tight by too little sleep and the oily slick of fear that clings to her skin.

There is a pain behind Lady Meriel's eyes in the place that only exists before tears come. She is unspooling. In her lap is the letter from her husband. A villa has been found and taken. The arrangements for her departure are being finalised. She leaves London shortly.

The illusion that she had control over her life, if only for a short time, has been shattered. How can she speak to Sybella in a strange land and under a different sky? How will Sybella know where she has gone? Her hands start shaking and there is a clattering sound somewhere. She wonders if it is rats, then realises it is her own teeth.

Lady Meriel recalls watching her daughter walk towards the carriage that will take her to the station. She stands at the drawing room window, her hand raised in farewell. Sybella turns and smiles radiantly. Then she climbs into the carriage and is borne swiftly away.

The memory forces itself up. The sense of Sybella is so strong, it is like an actual presence. She sits on in silence, thinking about the many secret night time conversations she has had with her daughter since her death. As in any conversation, sometimes Sybella answers, sometimes she doesn't.

***

Detective Inspector Stride drums a pencil on the edge of his desk.

"The French have a word for it," he tells Cully, "'*cherchez la femme.*'"

Three words actually, Cully thinks.

They are in Stride's messy office, the morning after his ghost hunt.

"There's usually a woman at the heart of every crime," Stride continues. "Sex or money, Jack. The two oldest and most powerful motivations in the world."

"And here we have ...?"

"Here we have Miss Mimi Casabianca. The mysterious medium. I've been putting together all the strands of the case, and this is what I think happened: Wynward was having an illicit affair with Miss Casabianca and gave her his dead daughter's carnelian locket as a gift. Foxx, who was her theatrical agent, found out about the relationship and decided to use the gift as a way of extorting money from him.

"The way I see it, the first letter was a declaration of intent. Remember me. The second, a reminder that Foxx wasn't going to give up. *'Be sure your sin will find you out'*. He didn't have time to send it, but it was clear he was going to. Nothing like quoting the Bible for putting the wind up someone, is there?

"Given Wynward's standing in London society, he wouldn't want any knowledge of his affair with a much younger woman who was not of his class nor his social equal, to get into the public domain would he? A knight committing adultery with a member of the theatrical profession? It'd wreck his career, let alone his marriage.

"So he asked his trusted butler to give Foxx a 'warning'. Looking back, I remember seeing a copy of *The Times* on Wynward's desk shortly after news of the murder broke. It's clear that's why he called off the investigation. He knew there was no point continuing. The blackmailer had been dealt with.

"He certainly didn't want me asking awkward questions that might end up drawing attention to his actions. I'm also prepared to bet good money that the Wynwards have a conservatory containing a Datura plant, which is where the seeds Robinson found in Foxx's body came from."

"What about the lock of hair in the letter?"

Stride points the pencil at him.

"Ah. Now. Glad you brought it up. I asked Miss Vesta Swann, the young woman who sold the locket to the jeweller to describe Miss Casabianca. She said the young woman had long coal-black hair. Very striking. Apparently, it came right down to her waist. It was pure coincidence that the letter arrived when it did. Nothing more."

"So the letter and the hair weren't from Sybella Wynward after all?"

Stride rolls his eyes.

"Sybella Wynward is dead. She died in a train smash a year ago. I have seen her grave."

"Is that what you're going to tell Lady Wynward?"

Stride stares hard at the opposite wall.

"Well, I'm working on a way of putting it slightly more diplomatically, but basically, yes. The poor woman has been suffering under a delusion that her daughter is alive and will come back one day. The shock of the accident has clearly turned her brain."

"I don't envy you the task."

Stride's expression hardens.

"And some time after I have imparted the sad news and returned the photograph she gave us, I intend to have Lord Wynward's butler James Oxley arrested for murder and Wynward himself brought in for questioning, as he is clearly complicit in the whole business."

Cully whistles.

"The press will have a field day," he remarks dryly.

"Indeed they will. I think this may be one of the few occasions when I won't be cursing Mr Dandy Dick and his brethren. Sex and money, Jack. As I said at first. The most potent combination. And here we have the two inextricably linked, with disastrous results."

"And Miss Mimi Casabianca?"

Stride shrugs and shakes his head.

"Who knows where that young lady is now? We can hazard a guess at what part she played in the whole sorry affair, but alas, we may never find out the full story."

***

The evening fog races through the streets on its journey to the river and the docks. The late trains rattle past, their steel wheels drumming rhythmically. The city is always secretive, even more so at this time of night, with its walls and hoardings dimmed by the fog, its acres full of unseen courts and cloisters, its lodging houses and stairs full of lives held in waiting until morning.

The young woman sits at her mirror, streaks of dirt running across her white dress. Her eyes are round and wide, painted black. Her hair is coiled in snakelike plaits around her head, her lips stained with carmine.

In the darkness of the shabby backstage dressing room, it feels like both no time and forever. She is here, but part of her is still waiting back there. And yet it is impossible to imagine herself back there now. The harder she tries, the fainter it becomes. Everything fades away from her, like the fog.

Who are you, she asks the pale reflection in the mirror. The face stares back. It does not reply. She hears it speaking, though. *I am a liar*, it says. *A liar like you. I hide as much as I reveal. And I tell nobody, not even myself, who I really am.*

***

The importance of the gentlemen's club cannot be overstated. It is a sanctuary from the cares and woes of business. It is a convivial meeting place for members of the male gender. It is a forum for the discussion of news and sharing the burning topic of the day.

Mostly however, it is a refuge from the trials and tribulations of the marital home. *'I'm just calling in at the club after work,'* is the *lingua franca* that has rescued many a hapless husband from the beady stare and unreasonable demands of his Angel in the House.

Here is Colonel Mortram in the smoking room of his club. He is entertaining some select chums to brandy, some fine pipe tobacco and his considered opinion. The first two are always welcome. The third is tolerated in respect of the first two.

"Saw from *The Times* that your gal got engaged," one of the marital refugees remarks. "Nice fella?"

"Guards," comes the laconic reply. "Based at Knightsbridge. Family owns land in Hampshire. Comfortable little place. Father's going to buy him a commission, so he should be pretty well set-up."

"Good for him. I heard one don't get much change out of £5,000 for a commission nowadays," the other refugee remarks.

"Not my problem, thank God," Mortram says. "Just got to steer the wife and girl away from the frills and furbelows. Never believe the amount of clothes womenfolk need for a wedding! May have to sell some shares to pay for it."

"Hope he don't see any service … remember my boy … he left for the Crimea a couple of months after he was wed."

There is a respectful pause. The speaker's 'boy' lost his life at Sebastopol.

"Pam's not going to brook any more of that nonsense," Mortram says firmly. "He put Johnny

Foreigner in his place then, and he ain't going to try it on for a long time."

The chums nod their agreement about the superiority of the current Prime Minister, and for the next few minutes, pipes are puffed in companionable silence. Then one of the chums remarks idly,

"I gather Wynward's selling up?"

"Really? Where did you hear that?" Mortram inquires.

"Talk of the 'Change. That Dominion Diamond Mine Company business cost him a fortune. He'd invested in it heavily. Lost a pretty packet. Found it hard to hold his head up when it all went smash and his losses came out."

"Where's he going?"

"Gone. Italy, I gather. Washed up."

Mortram pursed his mouth.

"Have to say I always found him a hard man to like. Got a way of looking at you. Cold and calculating. The wife says he always reminds her of one of those tigers at the Zoo ~ you wouldn't want to turn your back on him. Oh well, maybe it's for the best. Fresh start an' all that. After that tragic train smash."

He levers his bulk out of the easy chair.

"Right. Better make a move. Wife expecting me home for dinner. No doubt there'll be a nice little pile of bills waiting for me to settle. Weddings, eh?"

***

Across London, Lady Meriel Wynward lies awake, listening to the noises outside her window. An insomniac bird shrieks in an outside aviary. Jarring strains of some popular song drift in from a passing wolf-pack of revellers.

Since the detective inspector's visit, she has ceased her nightly watches. Not that it does any good. She still falls asleep with archaeological slowness, as if descending through intricate strata of consciousness, sub consciousness to final unconsciousness.

Today she left the house to visit Sybella's grave for the final time before the house is closed up. As her carriage bore her through the thronged London streets, she thought how the city always had a gleaming, hurrying coldness that reminded her of Hugh.

Lady Meriel had stood at the graveside of her dead daughter, her thoughts circling like a flock of dark brooding birds. They came to rest finally upon her husband. The man to whom she has been married for so many years. The man whose child she had given birth to. The man who treated her as if she were a child herself, lecturing her, and installing bars on her bedroom window to stop her jumping out.

How many years has it been since he commanded the door between her room and his to be sealed? Since he employed *that man* to intercept her letters and spy on her comings and goings? Oh, she knows full well why James always inquires so solicitously after her well-being. Over time she has come to fear him almost as much as her husband. And now?

She recalls the detective inspector's visit. He'd suggested they sit in the conservatory to catch the last warm rays of the sun. They'd discussed the plants that she grew, and then when he'd set her at ease, he had broken the news, so very gently, that he had not been able to find her beloved daughter.

She had not given way, she remembers that. She had been strong. She had not cried out in despair nor fallen to the floor. Not then. Lady Meriel remembers how the visit continued. The careful questions. Not telling her anything, but telling her everything in the not telling. She isn't as stupid as her husband and his friends think she is. She has learned to read between the lines.

There is something going on. It is serious. And her husband and his man are at the centre of it. That is why they have gone abroad so suddenly, and why he has not told her or anyone else in their set exactly where he is. But it matters not. Once she has arrived at the Italian villa, she will send a telegram to Scotland Yard giving the detective her address. Now that her final hope of finding Sybella has gone, she has nothing left to lose.

She has promised herself that she will do this. It will be her last and greatest act of defiance. Let him hang or go to gaol. She can live without Hugh. After all, she has lived without him for years and years.

Lady Meriel Wynward lies awake in the bedroom with bars on the window and thinks about everything she has lost. Reflecting back over her life, it seems to her that she must have gone wrong somewhere. She has turned down a wrong road without realising it, so that now she is headed towards some dark and unknown destination.

***

Dawn breaks over the vast city. In her small dingy rented room, Vesta Swann, chanteuse, opens her eyes, teetering on the edge of the moment as *then* becomes *now*. Rain is lashing down against her window. Somewhere in the distance, church bells chime and a cockerel crows. A carillon of bells and cockerels, accompanied by the gurgling of an overflowing gutter.

She has slept well, rested wonderfully, thanks to the good supper bought and paid for by one of her many admirers. A mischievous smile lurks at the corners of her mouth as she remembers how cleverly she managed to elude being included in the bill of fare.

Vesta sits up, curling her arms round her legs. The bed is hard and the room is spare as befits theatrical digs.

Mimi's letter lies on the floor. She had been reading it before getting into bed. Now the contents snag at her thoughts.

She slides her legs from between the thin darned sheets and goes to the window. The view is of nothing washed in rain. She hears the opposite door open, and footsteps going downstairs. Professor Antimony and his Ingenious Fleas are heading for the breakfast table.

Vesta picks up Mimi's letter and flattens it out. Mimi writes that she is now settled in one place at last, having been booked by the management of the Theatre of Varieties for the Winter Season. She writes that she is well and hopes Vesta is also, and please to send by return to the above address, the money for the things she left to be sold.

Vesta Swann gathers together the money and wraps it up. She thinks about William Smith and the story of the blue dress. She had told him that if she ever heard from Mimi, she'd let him know.

But then she'd also given the detective from Scotland Yard the same promise. Both promises were given in the sure and certain knowledge that she was unlikely to hear from Mimi again. In their line of work people came and went, and you rarely saw or heard from them.

And now this letter. She opens her writing case. She has two envelopes left.

Vesta Swann thinks long and hard, as she eats Mrs Frost's flabby damp toast and drinks her weak coffee and tries not to notice the Professor staring at her cleavage. She is still thinking when she returns to her room.

By the time she has washed and dressed, ready to go out, she has made up her mind. She encloses Mimi's money in one envelope, with a brief note saying how she hopes it finds her friend as it leaves her. Then she scribbles another note and puts it in the second envelope.

She will post both letters on her way to the morning rehearsal. She hopes she has made the right decision.

***

While Vesta Swann is making her way to her place of employment, a certain department store proprietor is surveying his latest window with satisfaction. In the centre of the display is a tall fir tree decorated with candles and strings of nuts (Seasonal Gifts). Piles of gaily wrapped parcels are strewn in merry profusion underneath the tree on the bright Turkey floor covering (Carpets & Rugs).

A fake fire blazes in the iron hearth (Hardware). The *pièce de resistance* however, is The Hamper. It stands alone on a large dais, lid raised to show the goodies inside.

In front of the hamper is a framed photograph showing Gould shaking hands with a portly youth wearing a tightly buttoned short jacket, a starched white cravat and a totally bewildered expression.

A notice pinned to the centre of the dais reads: **His Reward For Bravery: A Hamper from John Gould & Company**. and below, in slightly smaller letters: **Similar hampers may be ordered from our extensive Grocery Department.**

Thanks to the extensive coverage in the daily newspapers, hampers are flying off the shelves (metaphorically). Gould rubs his hands. It was his innovative idea to link the reward offered for the capture of Billy Furness with the upcoming Christmas season.

He eyes the little crowd standing in the rain and looking at the window. '*All shall be well and all manner of things shall be well*'. He has read that recently in one of his devotional books. He makes a note of it in a little octavo notebook (Stationery). He may well add it to tomorrow's bible reading and short homily.

In the meantime, he will go and discuss the current window arrangement with de Lesseps. He is sure there are plenty of other things that could be added in the run-up to the festive day. Indeed, if it proves to be as popular as it seems, he may well do a Christmas window every year.

***

Detective Inspector Stride is enjoying a walking breakfast. In one hand he has a mug of treacly black coffee, in the other, a doorstep of bread thickly spread with butter. The mug will be returned to the coffee stall holders on his homeward journey. It always is. Some people you never let down. Especially if you need a caffeine kick to start your day.

Stride turns the corner. He is a man at peace with the world. It has been a while since Rancid Cretney and his foul-smelling trousers have ambushed him. Also he has slept peacefully, for Mrs Stride and her nocturnal nasal noises are temporarily imposing their presence upon a sick relative.

He takes a bite of bread and slows to the familiar speed known to every street constable as *proceeding*. Eating on the go is something Mrs Stride does not approve of, citing various medical authorities as to the dire effects upon the digestive system. But as she was not present to cook his breakfast this morning, he has had to improvise. He may well improvise this evening and dine at Sally's.

Detective Inspector Stride strolls into Scotland Yard, feeling happier than he has for some time. Today he intends to write up his report on the Montague Foxx murder. The case is not yet closed as one of the criminals remains at large, but he has a constable keeping an eye on the Wynward residence, and as soon as Sir Hugh and his man return, he will be on their doorstep with a police vehicle.

Stride is looking forward to presenting the snooty aristocrat with a warrant for the arrest of his butler. And this time, he won't be turned off like a dog that has outlived its use. Wynward has questions to answer too, he thinks grimly. He intends to ask them. And he will go on asking them until he gets satisfactory answers.

He barrels through the door of Scotland Yard, greets the desk constable and heads for his office where a selection of the morning papers has been placed on his desk for him to shout at. Pushing them to one side, Stride reaches for pen, ink and paper. A busy morning lies ahead of him.

***

Felix Lightowler, bookseller, aka John Dee, alchemist, is having a busy morning as well. Having been deprived of his former accommodation via a freak accident, he has had to take up residence at the back of his shop. Now, thanks to the moonlight flitting of the upstairs tenants, he has taken over the first floor and the attic as well.

There are three rooms. In two he lives. The attic is being fitted out as a laboratory. For the Great Worke must go on. This morning he is being helped to add the finishing touches by Master Finister, apprehender of criminals, receiver of hampers and now, fetcher and carrier of chemical equipment.

"Is it dinner time yet, Master Dee?" Bovis asks, puffing slightly after hauling a couple of heavy crates up two rickety flights of stairs.

Lightowler shoots his cuffs and surveys the room. The benches are in place. The tall carboys are filled. The shelves are stacked with strange shaped bulbous glass instruments. The table is piled with old books and trivets. On one sits a beaker of cloudy liquid. The liquid is bubbling gently and giving off pungent smoke.

"I think we may call it a day, Master Finister," he says, reaching up to clap Bovis on a meaty shoulder.

"Shame the other two can't be here to see your new laboratory, in't it? I wonder where they have got to?"

Lightowler has his suspicions on that front. But he reminds himself that the police found no trace of anything human amidst the rubble of his house. And even if they had, he wasn't there when Big Bang Two happened, so no blame could possibly accrue to him.

"They are probably somewhere else," he says vaguely, staring at the already smoke-blackening ceiling.

Bovis nods slowly. Lightowler gives him a couple of small coins for his trouble and a bundle of washing for his mother.

"See that thou art returned tomorrow night, Master Finister, for wee have Muche to accomplish here," he says in the high-toned voice of his alter-ego.

Bovis clatters down the stairs and leaves by the back door. It is a long time since he ate breakfast, and he has just remembered that there is some fruitcake left in the hamper. He adjusts his cap to a jaunty angle and steps out cheerfully in the direction of home.

Meanwhile, Lightowler opens one of the books and runs a finger slowly down the page. His lips move silently. Then he turns down the flame under the liquid and adds a teaspoon of yellow powder.

If Tensibility Hellicatus and his '*Meditions uponne Chrysopoeia*' are to be believed, he is even now slowly and painstakingly approaching the Elixir, the magnum opus and achievement of gnosis.

And if that is so, and he prays nightly that it is, then he will be bidding adieu to these dusty and cramped quarters and setting sail for Prague, where he will live ... and live ... and live for ever.

***

The achievement of a different kind of gnosis is happening in the constables' day room at Scotland Yard, where Jack Cully is inducting two of the newest recruits into the mysteries of punctuation.

He has just about managed to achieve commas, when he is brought to a full stop by the entrance of Stride, jubilantly waving a piece of paper.

"You'll never guess what this is?" he says.

Cully is an old hand at this game.

"The Prime Minister is putting your name forward for a knighthood for services to Queen and country?"

Stride rolls his eyes exasperatedly.

"I don't know why you keep suggesting that. No, it's a letter from Miss Swann ~ the singer. She has news of the elusive Mimi. Get your hat and coat, Jack. It looks like we might be about to discover exactly what part Miss Casabianca played in the murder of Montague Foxx after all."

A short while later, Stride and Cully approach the Grand Panjandrum Music Hall, where the posters for the new show are being affixed to a hoarding by a man up a ladder with a paste pot. It is Pantomime Season, and not to be outdone by its rivals, the Grand Panjandrum is presenting, for the delight and delectation of its audiences, *Cinderella and the Fight for the Fairy Kingdom* (on the basis that if one pantomime plot is good, a combination of two must be a solid winner).

Who does not tremble with delight at the mention of the Pantomime? The joyous anarchy and unwonted excitement! The happiness as one leaves the theatre with parents, governesses or other domestic guardians, having enjoyed three hours of wondrous spectacle and enchantment.

Certainly Jack Cully's memories are stirred by the promised extravaganza being uploaded before his eyes, and as they pass through the theatre doors and apply to the front of house manager, he remembers the Cave of Gloom that always opened the pantomimes of his youth, and the Dark and Good Fairy, and he has a vague memory of hiding under the seat when the Evil Baron appeared to a chorus of boos and hissing.

Stride and Cully are escorted across the foyer and into the stalls of the part-lit theatre, where a small Shetland pony is being persuaded to leave the stage, having been spooked into immobility by the antics of the limelighters overhead in the flies.

The manager signals to a stage-hand, who disappears into the wings, shortly reappearing with Miss Vesta Swann. She wears the traditional costume of rags and patches and carries a broom, for she is playing the part of Cinderella, and they have arrived just before the transformation scene that will see her re-clothed in a sparkling dress, ready to be carried to the Ball in a golden coach pulled by the small Shetland pony that is still refusing to shift.

The two detectives accompany her to the back of the stalls, where they will not be overheard. They sit down, Vesta Swann arranging her rags in such a way as to display as little leg as possible out of deference to her interlocutors.

"Thank you for coming so promptly, gentlemen," she says.

"I gather your friend has now sent you her present address," Stride says.

"She has. I have to say I wasn't sure whether to write to you or not at first, but the way I saw it, Mimi left town believing she had killed Montague Foxx and the police were after her, except from what you said, you weren't and she didn't. It was two other men. So I thought if you could get a message to her that she is in the clear and not wanted for murder, it'd set her mind at rest."

Stride and Cully exchange glances. There are several other reasons why they want to talk to the elusive Miss Mimi Casabianca. Setting her mind at rest is pretty low on their list of priorities.

"Tell me a bit about her," Cully says. "How old is she?"

Vesta Swann considers, head on one side.

"Well I reckon, having seen her without her paint, that she must be quite young. And she ain't been in the business for long, because I'd never heard of her before she arrived."

"Do you know where she came from?"

She shakes her head.

"She wouldn't talk about her past. Clammed up as soon as you asked her anything about it. She'd always change the subject. Which is odd, because most of us like to share where we've been, the theatres we've played. Not Mimi though."

Cully nods.

"And her relationship with Montague Foxx?"

She shrugs.

"He weren't her fancy man, I know that. Never seen them kissing or anything. I thought he was her manager, though sometimes it seemed that there was more to it. Don't know. But then she certainly took off quick after they had that bust up. Didn't hang about to see if he was alright."

"What did you think about that?"

"She had a temper on her. Went with the black hair and the Italian name. Fiery. She'd get into these moods too. I often saw her after her show leaning against the ropes with a look on her face as if the world was weighing on her shoulders."

"Sounds definitely foreign to me," Stride remarks.

"Well, I don't think she was. She spoke quite normally; there was no trace of any accent with her. I think Mimi was just a stage name she adopted. It made her sound more mysterious, if you get what I mean."

"So, you never heard her called anything other than Mimi?"

She shakes her head.

Stride nods. Then he gets to his feet, signalling to Cully that the meeting has finished.

"Well, thank you very much for your help, Miss Swann. We will certainly be following this up."

Vesta Swann pauses.

"Hold up a bit though. I did hear Foxx call her something else. It was just the once, mind. When they were fighting like cat and dog before he was murdered, and she did a flit."

They wait, looking down at her expectantly.

"He called her Essie," she says. "Yes, that was the name he used: Essie."

***

"Essie was the name of Mrs Marks' baby," Cully says, when they are clear of the theatre and heading back towards Scotland Yard. "And Montague Foxx was her husband. Interesting."

Stride glances at him.

"I thought you told me the baby died."

"That was what *she* was told."

"But surely ... no ... it couldn't be ... could it?"

Cully frowns.

"It sounds pretty unlikely. After all, nobody we interviewed about Foxx ever mentioned he had a daughter."

"So who is this girl?"

"I don't know. Perhaps she just has a similar sounding name? Miss Swann might have misheard, remember. Clearly, we need to speak to her though."

"Cardiff," Stride muses. "It's quite a journey."

"But not an impossible one," Cully reminds him. "There are trains. And we have a contact in the local police office."

Stride glances at him, a puzzled expression upon his face. Then he breaks into an unexpected grin.

"So we do, Jack. So we do. I had forgotten about that. Well, why don't you send a telegram to our good friend and former colleague."

"I shall. I'd also like to go there myself, if you don't mind. Somebody needs to talk to the girl ~ and it ought to be someone who knows the background to the case."

"Do you think Mrs Cully can spare you for a night or two?" Stride smiles.

Cully thinks of the broken nights with Violet. His constant feeling of grey draining exhaustion. It would be good to have a whole night's undisturbed sleep. Maybe even two nights if he can swing it.

"I'm sure she can. When I've explained the position."

"Then telegraph Cardiff and make your arrangements. Well, well," Stride rubs his hands in satisfaction. "It looks as if we're finally going to get to the bottom of the case. And not before time too."

***

Emily Cully folds a couple of clean shirts and places them in the travelling bag. Supper is cleared out of the way and Violet is sleeping in her crib, replete and clutching a small rag blanket, her current constant companion.

Jack Cully sits by the fire, watching his wife prepare his bag for the early morning start.

"What if the young woman turns out to be your Mrs Marks' long-lost daughter after all?" Emily asks.

Jack Cully smiles indulgently at her.

"I don't think it is very likely, Em."

"Stranger things have happened," Emily counters. "There was that story in the newspapers about the boy who was found in an orphanage after his mother said he'd been missing for five years. So it could be her. What will you do if it is?"

"I don't know. How on earth do you set about telling a woman that the child she thought was dead, is alive?" Cully asks, shaking his head.

"Gently and with great care," Emily says.

She regards him with a serious expression on her face.

"It's not a man's job, Jack. It needs a woman's touch. If it turns out to be so, maybe Miss King might be the person to break the news? What do you think? She is Mrs Marks' friend. I'm sure she would be overjoyed to tell her."

Cully stares thoughtfully up at the ceiling.

"Ah. Yes. Indeed. She might be."

Emily suppresses a smile.

"You could telegraph Lachlan and ask him to go round and explain things to her first," she suggests, innocence hanging like loops of toffee from her words.

Cully has told her of the spark of interest in the young inspector. And that, if he wasn't mistaken, there was the same spark of interest in Miss King also. Emily smiles at him.

"Now, I'm going to put a few little dresses into the bag for the new baby," she says. "How old did you say he was?"

Cully tells her.

"Oh ~ he'll be sitting up and cutting his first tooth."

Ah, Cully thinks. A teething child. From one broken night's sleep to another. Just his luck. As if she could read his thoughts, Violet mutters, then whimpers, then wakes up with a roar. Emily hurries over and picks her up, laying her soft head against her shoulder.

"There, there, little one. Are you hurting? Never mind, Mama will make it go away," she murmurs, rocking backwards and forwards. "You get off to bed, Jack," she says over Violet's damp curls. "I'll settle her down, and then finish your packing. You have an early start tomorrow and you need your sleep."

Jack Cully makes his way to the small bedroom at the back of the house, takes off his day clothes and rolls into bed. Tomorrow, he will be travelling into unknown territory. In many more ways than one.

***

The last time we encountered Sergeant Tom 'Taffy' Evans, he was reaping the rewards of his diligent policing in the form of twenty guineas and the promise of possible promotion. And here he is now, an inspector based at Glamorgan Constabulary. He has a shared desk at the Bridgend headquarters, and six constables who report directly to him.

More importantly, he has finally married his childhood sweetheart Megan and they have both settled down happily to married life in a tiny rented terrace house in Talbot Street. And to complete his joy, he is the proud father of William Thomas Evans, possessor of the loudest pair of lungs in the street.

It is a cold brisk afternoon as Inspector Evans waits patiently by the platform barrier in Cardiff Station for the train from London via Gloucester to arrive. He has not seen, nor heard from Jack Cully since he himself left London well over a year ago.

In Evans' coat pocket is the telegram from his former colleague. It does not say much, but Evans knows it must be something serious for Cully to make the long journey to Wales. And now the train is pulling into the station, filling the air with smoke and the smell of steam, and through the smoke comes Jack Cully, hefting a bag and looking exactly as he remembers him and not a day older, and the months fall away as Evans steps forward to greet him.

A hired trap attends outside the station, ready to convey the two officers to Evans' house where Megan is preparing a hot supper. He is sure Cully will be ready for it. And when they have eaten, they will talk.

And so it is that, as evening settles gently over the town, Cully and Evans sit on either side of the glowing hearth. Stew and dumplings have been eaten and enjoyed. Emily's gift has been unpacked and admired. Now, with his baby on his knee, and the small black and white cat curled up on the rag rug at his feet, Inspector Evans of the Glamorgan constabulary learns what has brought his former colleague all the way from Scotland Yard.

By the time Cully has finished, the fire has almost died and the cat has left for a nocturnal prowl outside. Evans stares into the glowing embers, his big honest face screwed up with the effort of trying to understand what he has been told.

"A beautiful young woman with a mysterious past. It sounds like the plot of one of the cheap novels my Megan likes reading. Except that it's not a novel, is it?"

"Whoever she is, she has to know something about the connection between Foxx and Wynward. Especially if she is, as we suspect, Wynward's mistress. Though as for the notion that she is Mrs Marks' long-lost child, I think it is unlikely. Jessie, Essie and Tessie all sound very much the same when shouted along a corridor."

"You don't like this Sir Hugh character, do you?"

"I never met him," Cully says. "But from what I gather, he's a nasty piece of work. He mistreats his wife and if we can prove that he ordered the murder of Montague Foxx ~ well, that's a crime and he's not going to get away with it just because he has a title, a big house and a position in London society. Wherever he's gone, we'll track him down eventually and bring him before the courts."

Evans gets to his feet, filling the space in the small room. He dampens down the fire and chirrups out of the back door to fetch in the cat.

"I'll leave you to sleep now," he says. "I hope the baby doesn't wake you, but he is getting his first teeth at the moment."

"Believe me, I am well used to being woken by a teething child," Cully says, rolling his eyes. "But after that excellent supper and our talk, I'm sure I shall sleep like a log. Good night to you."

Jack Cully unfolds the blanket and the patchwork quilt Megan has left by the sofa and makes up his bed. It is very quiet. An owl hoots; something scuffles in the pantry, but there are no chiming church clocks, late night revellers or passing carriages to jolt him awake.

Cully closes his eyes. His last thoughts, before dropping into a deep and dream free sleep, are of Emily and the child asleep in their terraced house, so far away they might as well be on the moon.

***

Lady Meriel Wynward has also spent the day travelling on a train from London. Now, she has arrived at her destination: Dover Harbour, where she is boarding the night packet for Calais.

She is not alone, of course. A lady cannot travel unaccompanied. A nurse, hired by her husband, and one of the house maids, accompany her. The maid is there to help with her clothes, to brush and arrange her hair and make sure she arrives at her destination looking presentable.

The nurse is there to make sure she takes her medicine, for Lady Meriel has not been well again ~ indeed she has declined most markedly over the past week. It is a recurrence of her 'old trouble' says the doctor, who has visited the house on a daily basis, and then wired Sir Hugh to alert him of her regress.

The doctor has advised utmost delicacy in the way she is handled, citing Lady Meriel's rationality on many topics, a rationality which only falters when the one particular circumstance and event suggests itself to her mind. He recommends a stay in the country and has sent Sir Hugh details of a first-class establishment, where the latest treatments are available.

But Sir Hugh has already made alternative arrangements, so here is Lady Meriel stepping onto the gangplank, supported on either side by the maid and the nurse, because the gangplank is slippery underfoot. The gaslights of the Marine Parade twinkle in the distance, and the windows of the Lord Warden Hotel glow bright and warm and welcoming, but her eyes do not see them.

The last passengers mount the gangplank, clutching their hatboxes and travelling bags, and now the hawsers are thrown aboard to cries of *'Half a turn ahead,' 'Stand by,' 'Stand by below'*. Then the South Foreland lights flicker as the boat shudders and heaves and heads out into the open sea.

The wind blows stiffly from the North-East, but it is a fine night with a bright silver moon and a plethora of stars. The moon shines upon the sea billows, painting them silver, and the only sounds are the wind, the slapping of the waves and the pounding of the paddles as the boat sails onward towards France.

Lady Meriel stands at the stern of the boat, holding onto the iron railings. She stares down at the white wash that follows in the wake, while her maid and her nurse go below to prepare her cabin, for the doctor has prescribed rest at all times.

They unpack her medicine bottles, her silver-backed brush and a travelling rug, and having got all ready to their satisfaction, they sit on the hard plank bed and chat, as servants do whenever they get a moment of peace and quiet on their own.

Meanwhile Lady Meriel remains alone upon deck. The moon shines on the water and the sea runs high, tumbling by the boat with deep sounds. Suddenly, she stares down into the roiling depths, her expression fixed and rigid. She grips the railings even tighter, the colour draining from her face.

Below deck, the maid and the nurse chat on.

The passengers are all at the other end of the boat, watching for the first sighting of the French coast. Unobserved, Lady Meriel climbs onto the top rail and stands poised for a split second, perfectly balanced, silhouetted against the night sky. Her gaze is fixed upon something she sees in the water. Her eyes are alight with joy, and her mouth moves, framing a single word. A name. Then she is gone.

The boat ploughs on towards the lights of Cape Grisnez, finally entering Calais Harbour at the top of the tide. All the lights along the quay shiver in the wind, and the bells of Calais ring out. The sea washes in and out among planks and piles with a dead heavy beating sound. The carriage ordered to carry Lady Meriel Wynward to her hotel is lined up waiting, but it will wait in vain.

For my Lady is not coming, nor will she ever come, for she has found a softer bed and a kinder home than her harsh husband could offer her, and she will never be seen again on ship or shore, or anywhere else in the hard and relentless land of the living.

***

Jack Cully wakes to the smell of bacon frying and a dim recollection of a cat trying to get under his blanket in the small hours. He yawns, then sits up and stretches. The fire is lit and the table is laid with a red check cloth. Two places are set.

He rises, as Evans comes into the room, holding a frying pan.

"Good morning. You slept well, I hope?"

"Like a log."

"Breakfast won't be long. Megan has taken the baby out for some air, but she will be back shortly with milk and the bread. There is hot water in the kettle and a cake of soap in the scullery if you care to wash and shave."

Cully pours the water into a china bowl and prepares himself for the day ahead. After breakfast, he and Evans will head back to Cardiff to track down Miss Mimi Casabianca and hopefully persuade her to talk.

It is mid-morning by the time the two men arrive outside the Royal Victoria Palace of Varieties. They stare at the billboard which, like theatres the length and breadth of the country, is now also advertising the forthcoming Christmas pantomime.

"*The Fate of Frankenstein*," Cully murmurs. "*With a chorus of vampires & featuring the amusing antics of Ratzbarn and Tiddliwincz. A family entertainment.*"

He pulls a face.

"I hope we are in time," Evans says.

"Let's ask at the stage door: from my experience, theatre performers often come in during the day to rehearse."

The man in the small wooden kiosk has an accent so liltingly incomprehensible that Cully is grateful for Evans' company. After some verbal to-ing and fro-ing and hand-waving, Evans steps back from the window.

"He says Miss Mimi Casabianca should be in after lunch. I told him we were Spiritualists and we wanted to book her for a séance as we'd heard so much about her. It was either that or he wasn't going to tell us anything. Why do people always assume we are from the police?"

"Because we are," Cully replies wearily. "Even if we're not wearing uniform. Don't ask me how they know. They just do. Stride says he just has to enter a public house for everybody to start staring at the table and looking terribly innocent."

He digs out his watch from a waistcoat pocket.

"Why don't you show me round Cardiff while we wait? I'd like to buy Emily a little present to take back. We haven't spent a night apart since we were married."

A few hours later the two men return to the theatre. Cully is carrying a parcel containing a Welsh tartan shawl and a wooden love-spoon. They present themselves to the stage door keeper and are told that Miss Mimi Casabianca is on stage. The man directs them up a set of unswept stairs and along a dimly-lit corridor. The air smells of damp and human sweat and violet powder.

Eventually the two officers arrive in the wings. It takes a few minutes for their eyes to adjust before they can make out the scenery for the new show, the backdrops and curtains, and the wooden flats.

Sets and curtains and ropes lie piled all around, like discarded things in a cellar. The front of the stage is a little rectangle of light. Beyond the stage row after row of unoccupied velvet seats stretch into unlit blackness. On either side are boxes, and above the boxes curves a gallery with an empty chandelier hanging in space, waiting to be filled with candles.

There is something uncanny about an empty theatre, Cully thinks. Something ghostly. He steps towards the lighted stage. A table has been placed at its centre. A young woman sits behind the table, facing out towards the invisible audience. She wears white; her dark raven-wing hair is studded with diamond clips and hangs down her back. As the two officers watch, she picks up a quill from the table and begins writing in the air.

Strange ethereal music immediately fills the theatre. From where he is standing, Cully can see it is being played by a man with a flute, who stands in the shadow of the opposite wing. The young woman rises, and glides to the front of the stage. The music gets louder. She stretches out her arms. Strands of shiny white material seem to rise up from her finger ends.

Motioning Evans to stay hidden, Cully tiptoes to the back of the stage. The young woman's eyes are closed tight. She sways backwards and forwards, moaning softly as if in some sort of trance. Cully stands a few steps away, watching her intently.

After a few minutes she stops and turns round, giving Cully a glimpse of her features for the first time. Cully feels the breath leaving his body. I'm imagining things, he tells himself. I'm seeing ghosts where there aren't any ghosts.

The young woman opens her eyes and realises suddenly that she is not alone on stage. Her carmine painted mouth falls open in shock. Her dark painted brows come together in a frown. Her hands clasp the sides of the table.

"Who are you?" she demands in a low voice. "What are you doing here?"

"I am Detective Sergeant Jack Cully from Scotland Yard in London," Cully says, advancing towards her. "And I think, if I am not very much mistaken, that you are Miss Sybella Wynward."

***

Sybella Wynward was a high-spirited, well-bred sixteen-year-old, the leader of a group of similar-natured young women, when she first received a letter from the man who would change her life forever. She was a weekly boarder at an elite Girls' Academy, and it was there, one Wednesday morning, that she was given an envelope that bore her name, but was not in a hand that she recognised.

Sybella took the strange letter out to the garden, where she sat on a bench and opened it. The letter proved to be from somebody she did not know. The man (and why should a man write to her?) informed her that he had some most important news to tell her.

This man (his signature said he was called Montague Foxx) wrote that he would be at a certain tea-room the following day at four o'clock and would wait for her there. If she could not come, he would be in the same spot the day after. He begged her not to tell anyone, not even her closest friend, but to come on her own.

At first, Sybella was inclined to dismiss the letter as some sort of joke. Then as the day wore on, she started to feel intrigued. Who was this Mr Foxx? How had he found her out? What was the important news he had to tell her? And why had he sworn her to secrecy?

In the end, curiosity got the better of her. She kept the appointment. Mr Foxx turned out to be a respectable looking gentleman in a tailored suit and immaculate linen. But what Mr Foxx told Sybella over tea and a selection of cakes, was anything but respectable.

He told her about a rich aristocrat, whose wife had been left a huge inheritance, kept in trust for the first female child of the marriage. He told her how the wife eventually gave birth to a baby girl, but tragically, the baby only lived for a few days, and its death drove the poor unfortunate woman mad.

While she was incarcerated in a lunatic asylum, out of her mind with grief, the aristocrat persuaded a friend to give him his baby girl, so that the money wouldn't be lost. That baby girl, said Foxx, looking straight at Sybella, was you. I, Foxx said, am your father. Your real name is Essie.

Had she not noticed how different she was from her mother and father, he went on? Had she never compared her dark hair and eyes to her mother's mousy hair and pale complexion? Had she never wondered where her own wild spirited nature came from?

She was not their true child. She had been handed over to the Wynwards to make sure the fortune remained in the family. Foxx then produced a 'contract' drawn up between Wynward's lawyer and himself to prove it.

And my real mother? she had asked, trembling.

She was my former wife. A nobody, said Foxx. She left me and abandoned you when you were born. If I could have kept you, I would ~ but I saw a chance for you to have the best of everything that I was not in a position to offer you.

Sybella returned home that weekend a different person. Her eyes had been opened. Outwardly, she acted just as she had always done. Inwardly she started to feel a growing sense of injustice. She had been treated as a chattel. The people who were supposed to love her only wanted to use her to get money.

Shortly after the revelation, Sir Hugh told her of his plan to marry her off to her cousin. She tried to run away, but was brought back in disgrace. Sir Hugh beat her and locked her in her room. Her rage against her treatment, and her deep sense of unfairness increased.

Sybella met with Foxx several more times, always in secret. Little by little, word by treacherous word, he managed to distance her from her family. It was he who suggested how she might punish them for what they had done.

Sybella would arrange to go on holiday with a friend who lived in Brighton. She would insist on travelling to the friend's house by train, rather than in the family carriage. Only she wouldn't arrive at her destination.

Instead, she would leave the train at the first station outside London. Foxx would meet her and escort her to a safe place. After enough time had elapsed for her parents to suffer her loss, she would return. Upon the fulfilment of certain conditions. He didn't say exactly what they would be.

And so it was that Sybella Wynward, accompanied by Ellen, her faithful maid, and their luggage, boarded the Brighton train on that fateful day. Foxx had given Sybella something to put in the girl's drink to make her drowsy.

As soon as the maid fell asleep, Sybella covered her with her own shawl, and then when they reached the appointed station, she simply picked up the luggage and stepped out onto the platform. She was not to know that the train would crash. That her 'body' would subsequently be identified by the remains of the burned red shawl.

Next day, she read of the terrible accident in the morning papers and wept. She had been instrumental in causing Ellen's death. She wanted to return at once, but Foxx dissuaded her. A few days later, she read about her own death, then later, her funeral service. She realised that that there was no going back. Dead people don't go home.

And thus Mimi Casabianca, the Mystic Medium was born. Sybella loved acting. And she had attended enough séances and spiritualist meetings with her mother to know how the business worked. Together, she and Foxx created the act, trying it out on small groups first, then gradually moving to actual performances.

It helped that Sybella was young and beautifully exotic with her slender figure, dark eyes and coal-black hair. With Foxx as her business manager, she toured the country, appearing in public rooms, and small halls.

It was a strange peripatetic existence, far from her former privileged and cosseted lifestyle. But Sybella reminded herself, when the digs were dingy or the meals mundane, that she had chosen to recreate herself as a stage artiste.

And at least her 'real' father did not shout at her, or stare at her with those cold grey eyes. He never locked her in her room or beat her or suggested marriage with her cousin. In fact, he pretty much let her do what she wanted.

Then, some months short of her eighteenth birthday, Foxx told her he'd secured a booking at a London theatre. Sybella was reluctant at first. London was where her former family and friends lived. What if somebody recognised her? Once again she was reassured. Nobody would be expecting to 'see' her. Besides, Foxx had a particular reason for moving her to London.

She was soon to discover what it was.

Sybella knew Foxx had another existence outwith his life with her and the shows. Sometimes he'd disappear for days on end, never telling her where he was going. But he always returned, and she never questioned him about it. Lodging at Mrs Frost's, it didn't take long for her to learn where he had probably been and what he had been up to.

Mrs Frost seemed to take a perverse delight in disclosing all the unsavoury background details of the man she thought was Sybella's manager. The women, the gambling, the drugs and drinking, it was all poured into her ear like poison.

But there was worse to come. Sybella learned that Foxx's intention was to use her initial disappearance to extract money from Sir Hugh. The train accident had put paid to that little scam. But now that Sybella's eighteenth birthday was approaching, he had come up with an even better and more audacious plan.

She heard him discussing it with Mrs Frost one night, when they both thought she was safely tucked up in bed in her room. Foxx was intending to blackmail Sir Hugh over the faked adoption. If the aristocrat refused to split Sybella's inheritance with him, as he'd promised, Foxx would go to the newspapers and give them the story of the aristocratic man who had forced him to give up his beloved child.

Sybella sat on the landing, wrapped in a shawl, her blood running cold as she listened. Foxx had already sent several letters to Sir Hugh's club. So far, the man was stalling. But if the aristocrat refused to give in to his demands, Foxx intended to reveal Sybella's true identity ~ the poor little rich girl reduced to performing séances and spirit-writing to earn a crust.

Sybella bided her time, waiting until her next performance had finished. Then, when Foxx arrived to escort her back to her room, she told him what she had overheard. He laughed and replied that he was meeting Sir Hugh later to finalise the arrangements, and if he tried to wriggle out of it, Foxx had already posted what he called 'a little gift' to Sir Hugh's wife that he was quite sure should do the trick.

Once he had got hold of his share of the money, he then informed her, he intended to leave London for America and begin a new life under a different name. *And me?* she had asked, *what about me?* And Foxx had shrugged and replied that they'd had a good innings together but all good things came to an end eventually.

That was when she saw red. She shouted at him that this was not what they'd agreed. Then she picked up the knife she used as part of her act, and ran at him. Foxx turned and fled into the corridor pursued by his daughter with all the furies of Hell at her heels. She managed to stab him in the back, but he got away.

Sybella went back to the sordid lodgings that night, her mind in a turmoil. She had attacked her father, for all she knew dealing him a fatal wound. If he succumbed, the police would track her down with little difficulty. She was scared and alone and terrified. She decided to flit.

"And the rest you know, detective sergeant," she said. "I gave my clothes and jewellery to my friend Miss Swann to sell for me, and I left London. It was hand to mouth for a while, then a kind friend in the business got me the booking here. And now you turn up out of the blue, and tell me that I didn't kill my father after all; it was the work of two other men."

"Two other men doing the bidding of Sir Hugh Wynward," Cully says.

She shudders at the mention of his name.

"That may be so. But I'm not going back. Never. I'd rather die penniless and an orphan than return to that cold house and that evil man."

Her eyes glance at him sideways, feral and dark.

"Listen, detective sergeant, I'll tell you your fortune for nothing. Lie, flatter and cajole the fools in the world and you're booked for a soft thing. That's my experience."

Cully looks into the hard, set face, and his heart bleeds for her. He thinks of his own small daughter surrounded by love, growing up between walls that will always be a shelter, with parents who would do anything for her happiness.

"It doesn't have to be like that, you know," he says gently. "Sometimes, maybe when we least expect it, wonderful things can happen. Things that will change our lives for the better."

The girl stares at him, her eyes dark and remote and hostile.

"Yes? What sort of wonderful things?"

So Jack Cully tells her about Lilith Marks and her marriage to Foxx. He tells her about the baby that was taken away, and the grief and pain it caused. He tells her how Lilith wandered the streets for months and months looking for her child. How she has never ever forgotten her. And when he has finished telling her everything Lilith told him, there is a very long silence.

Cully waits, holding his breath.

At last Sybella heaves a great sigh.

"Come back tomorrow morning, Mr Cully. Then I'll give you my reply."

She catches the edge of his expression.

"I promise I'm not going to run away. There's been far too much running away in my life. But I need to think carefully about everything you've said. That's alright, isn't it? You will give me one night to make up my mind?"

"Of course," Cully says.

She turns her face away from him and towards the dark space of the empty auditorium. An eloquent gesture of farewell. Cully and Evans bid her farewell, and receiving no reply, walk out into the street, where the light is beginning to fade.

"What an amazing story," Evans says. "I cannot begin to imagine what that poor young lady has been through."

"I must telegraph Scotland Yard at once," Cully tells him. "And then I have to write an important letter that will need to catch the night mail."

"Not a problem. We'll use the police office. It's only a step away from the post office. Will she return to London with you do you think?"

Cully shrugs, "If I were a betting man, after all she's been through, I'd give it odds of 50:50."

Evans smiles seraphically at him. "Well, I'm a praying man, my good friend. And I believe in the power of love. So I think my odds are a little shorter."

***

Emily Cully is spooning sweetened warm porridge into Violet's mouth by candlelight, as the sun has not yet penetrated the city fog, when she is startled by an unexpected knock at the door. Placing her daughter on the floor, she goes to answer it. A scarlet-coated postman stands on the step. He hands her a letter.

Emily Cully's heart almost stops beating. She does not receive letters. In her mind letters are always associated with very bad news. Somebody is dying, or has died. Fearing the worst, she returns to the kitchen and slits open the envelope. Relief floods through her as she sees the communication is from Jack.

Emily continues feeding Violet her breakfast while she reads her letter, her eyes widening as they skim the lines of neat copperplate. By the time she has reached the end of the letter, and read the loving message from her husband, her face has taken on a fixed, determined expression.

She scrapes the last spoonful of porridge and gives it to Violet. Then she sits the little girl down by the hearth with her toys. She needs to think carefully about the contents of Jack's letter, and what she is going to do about it.

A few minutes pass in companionable silence. Then Emily's frown of concentration clears. She washes and dresses Violet. She packs her basket with the deliveries she needs to make. Then she places her best bonnet on her head and puts on her coat.

Emily Cully locks her front door and places the key in her basket, after which she and young Violet set off to find an omnibus. They are on a mission. The outcome is uncertain, but for Jack's sake, Emily will do her level best to succeed in her quest.

***

Meanwhile, many miles away, Jack Cully opens his eyes and peers into the dark geography of a room he doesn't know. The sky outside has the blacklight tinge of darkness on the edge of dawn. He rises, crosses to the scullery and ducks his head to the tap in the sink. Raising his face, he sees his reflection in the window's doubled glass, faint as a ghost.

Cully dresses, packing his spare clothes, and the gifts for Emily. Then he folds the quilt and blanket. By the time he is ready, Evans and his wife have risen. The fire is lit and breakfast placed on the table. They sit down and eat together.

After they have finished eating, Jack Cully says his final good-byes. His last sight of Evans is of the tall uniformed officer standing on his doorstep with Megan, so small in comparison, tucked into his side. Evans holds up the baby to bid him farewell.

The sight of the little family rejoices Cully's heart and sends him on his way with a lightness of spirit. He hopes it is a good omen for what is to come.

***

The Lily Lounge has just opened for business, when a slight pretty woman with a small child enters the restaurant. She secures a window table so that the child can amuse herself by watching the people and carriages passing by.

The woman orders a pot of tea and a scone, and when they arrive, she whispers something to the waitress, who gestures towards the high wooden counter. She nods her thanks. The waitress returns to the counter.

"The customer at the window table with the little girl says she would like a quiet word with you, ma'am."

Lilith glances quickly over to the window table. Emily Cully meets her gaze and smiles politely, controlling her nerves by clasping her hands together in her lap. Violet stares out of the window, still hypnotised by the ebb and flow of traffic. There is a plate of buttered scone fragments in front of her for when she gets bored.

Lilith crosses over to the table.

"Good morning. I gather you wish to speak to me. Is there a problem?"

Emily rises, smiling a little nervously.

"Good morning Mrs Marks. You do not know me, but my name is Emily Cully ~ I am the wife of Detective

Sergeant Jack Cully, whom you do know, I believe. I have received a letter this morning from Jack and we both think you should read it."

She resumes her seat. Lilith remains standing.

Emily indicates the vacant chair opposite.

"It is the sort of letter best read sitting down."

Lilith sits.

Emily fishes in her basket and passes the letter across the table. Then she cups her chin in her hands and waits. Violet eats her scone. Lilith reads and rereads the letter. Slowly, silently, tears begin to stream down her cheeks.

Emily stretches out a gloved hand and places it on top of Lilith's. To her surprise, for she feared that her gesture might be repudiated, Lilith grasps the hand and looks up, her wet eyes meeting Emily's clear-eyed gaze.

"I do not know what to say. This news, now, after all these years. It is almost too much to believe."

"I can understand," Emily nods. "The reason Jack asked me to break it to you is because last year, I almost lost my little girl. She was taken by one of those terrible baby-minders. It was only for a few minutes, but the thought of losing my child, of never seeing her sweet face again, was so agonising that I have never forgotten it. And you have carried the same agony inside you for many years. I don't know how you have managed to bear it."

Lilith wipes her eyes.

"I have borne it because I had no choice," she says brokenly. "And now, I feel as if I were dreaming. Essie is alive? I do not know what I should do. Tell me, Mrs Cully ~ you seem a wise woman. What should I do?"

"Emily, please. And I think you should do nothing. Jack writes that he is meeting Essie this morning at the theatre where she works, and she will tell him whether she wants to return to London."

"But what if she doesn't want to?" Lilith gives her a stricken look.

"Then at least you will know that your daughter is alive in this world. That she didn't die after all. It has to be some consolation. But I am sure she will want to meet you, her real mother. Consider her situation: she is alone; she has no friends where she is living. Nobody to confide in. How much must she yearn for her mother's love?

"You asked me a moment ago what you should do. I think you should prepare a room for your daughter, and bake her a homecoming cake." Emily smiles. "If Jack does not bring her back with him tonight, then as he says, I am the Lord Chancellor of England."

She rises and gets out her purse.

"Now I must pay you for the delicious scone and tea and be on my way. Come Violet, we have deliveries to make."

Lilith waves the money away.

"May I keep the letter?" she asks.

"Of course. It is meant for you."

Lilith folds the precious sheets of thin paper and puts them into her apron pocket.

"We are both mothers," Emily says, buttoning Violet's coat and tying her tiny bonnet. "We know what it is to love a child. Our love ~ your love is the strongest thing on earth, and it will bring Essie back home."

Emily picks up her basket and takes Violet by the hand. Mother and daughter head for the door. Lilith follows them, never taking her eyes off them.

She watches, hungry-eyed, as Emily scoops up the little girl, pressing her cheek to Violet's soft one, and feels a sharp stab of pain around her heart. As soon as they have gone, Lilith flips the open sign to closed and returns to the counter, where the waitresses are gathered in a little knot of anxiety.

"Please don't worry," she says, trying to keep her voice level. "It wasn't bad news. But I must close the Lily Lounge for a while. Serve the customers who are still here, but do not let anybody else in. When you have finished, you may get your things and go home."

Lilith descends to the kitchen, where she falls straight into one of the Windsor chairs. Holding the side of the worn worktable with both hands, she stares into the middle distance. So this is joy, she thinks. This feeling that grasps you tightly, until you feel you must die. This feeling that throws you up into the air and sets you down before you know what has happened.

Lilith knows the pain of a headache, a twisted ankle, a broken heart; pain one can bear and pain one can't bear, but one has to. Now out of the blue, she has been ambushed. Suddenly, unexpectedly, life has delivered her this wondrous, joyous revelation. And the pain of it is almost more than she can bear.

***

Inspector Lachlan Greig approaches Stride's office, carrying a telegram in one hand. The door is firmly shut, although several day constables are gathered outside in a gleeful huddle.

"Morning gentlemen. Is there a problem?" Greig asks.

He is answered with a line of innocent faces bearing a set of delighted grins.

"No problem at all, inspector."

"Not with us. We're just listening to Mr Stride expressing his opinion, aren't we, boys?"

"He's expressing it sure enough."

"Such a fine turn of phrase."

"Troopers have got nothing on Mr Stride once he gets going."

Greig pulls a face. He gives a discreet knock on the door, the sort that you use if you secretly hope it won't be answered.

"Damn it! What d'you want?" Stride yells back.

The posse regard Greig in a man-about-to-enter-a-lion's-den manner.

"Ooh, I wouldn't disturb him right now, inspector," one volunteers.

"You haven't been here long have you? He can be awfully... tetchy."

"Tetchy? More like that apple thing."

"Apoplectic?"

"That's the word."

Greig ignores them. He opens the door. Stride is standing behind his desk glaring at a selection of the morning papers.

"Telegram from Jack Cully," Greig says, placing it on top of the offending front pages.

Stride brushes it to one side.

"Take a look at this," he commands.

Lachlan Greig glances down at the top headline, which is from the *Times*.

Missing at Sea! Unexpected Disappearance of London Aristocrat!

He reads the subheading:

An impenetrable mystery surrounds the disappearance of Lady Meriel Wynward, wife of Sir Hugh Wynward, from the Dover to Calais boat.

He looks up.

"Oh dear. That is most unfortunate."

"Indeed. Most 'unfortunate', as you put it. It looks as if the good lady has either thrown herself overboard, or accidentally fallen over the side. Either way, her husband now has no reason to return to this country. He can stay abroad indefinitely, as can his damned butler. And they will, mark my words, I know these bloody people and their ways.

"They are off the hook. We've lost them, Lachlan. And it grieves me. It grieves me mightily. He's going to get away with murder, and so is his man. Justice has not been done."

"We still have one of the perpetrators under lock and key," Greig reminds him.

"But not the other one. And more importantly, not the man who masterminded the whole thing."

Stride strikes the desk with his fist.

"Damn him to hell! I was so close ..."

Greig leans forward and shuffles the telegram back into Stride's eye line.

"Jack Cully sent this telegram. I think you should read it," he says.

Stride picks up the telegram and scans its contents. He frowns.

"Really?"

"So it would appear."

"This is very unexpected. I had not anticipated it at all."

"Indeed. What will you do?"

Stride waves the telegram in the air.

"I shall do exactly as he asks, of course." he says loftily. "As I always do."

***

Jack Cully approaches the Royal Victoria Palace of Varieties, noting that the bill of fare has now been entirely replaced by posters for the upcoming pantomime. He goes to the stage door, telling the doorman that he has an appointment with Miss Mimi Casabianca, and is admitted.

Cully climbs up the same dusty stairs and along the corridor towards the stage. She is there, sitting with her back to the metal pulley system and resting her head against the ropes. She has taken off her stage costume, and has wrapped a cone-patterned shawl around her shoulders.

Her hair is now coiled snakelike around her head; her face is bare of the lurid makeup that defined her on stage. Without it, the similarity to Lilith is striking. She leans her head into the darkness, her hands clasped in her lap. Her face is unreadable.

"Well, Essie, here I am as we arranged yesterday," Cully says.

She acknowledges his presence with a brief nod of acquiescence.

"Have you made up your mind?" Cully asks gently.

She continues staring into the darkness, not looking at him. "Essie. How strange it feels to be called that name once again. It is as if I have died and become somebody else."

"Sybella 'died'," Cully reminds her. "She is buried in Highgate Cemetery."

"She is. And now Essie has returned to life. What does she want from me, I wonder?"

"Does she want you to meet your real mother ~ who has always loved you and never forgotten you for a single day of her life? Does she want you to feel your mother's arms around your neck, and her tears of welcome on your cheek?"

Now she turns her head to look at him, and Cully sees that her face is lit up by a half-smile, like the faint beam of light from a waning moon.

"I think she does."

He holds out a hand.

"Then let us set out together and bring her home."

***

London in winter. The first heavy frost of the season has arrived. A city that was black with soot and dirt is transformed overnight into a city of almost silver beauty. It glitters with glacial architecture. Every housetop seems newly thatched with frost flakes.

The roads and pavements are as white as a wedding-cake. The omnibuses leave glistening trails behind, as if some monster snail has crawled along the route. Hay is wound round their stepping-irons, while the gents on the knife-boards and roofs are wrapped in thick railway rugs.

In parks, trees are ashy-grey. Ducks huddle together for warmth on the banks of the Serpentine. The cheeky sparrows seem almost to have disappeared, while the few that remain have a sleepy look and have gone all fluffy, turning into a mere ball of brown feathers.

Those that can, put on warm flannel and encase their bodies in thick greatcoats or fur, and talk about the 'healthy bracing weather' as they go about their business. They eye the West End shop windows, filled with spices, and dried fruit studded with candied peel, or pause to admire the butchers' shops piled with meat coated with thick fat, as they dream about the upcoming season of mirth and feastings, of pantomimes and parties.

In anticipation of the coming season, the windows of public houses are suddenly placarded with announcements of hot elder wine and hot spiced ale. Street sellers in caped coats offer pea-soup in fish kettles. Baked potato cans spurt out jets of vapour like miniature steam factories.

As the city clerks and office workers return home, their nostrils are assailed by the smell of baked apples and chestnuts roasted on a brazier, the fire shining in bright orange spots through the holes.

Covent Garden is awash with holly, mistletoe and laurel, and fragrant with the smell of bright-coloured fruits. And each evening, as the light fades, crimson flickering of flames can be seen in squares and crescents, lighting up parlour windows like flashes of lightning.

As he leaves Scotland Yard, Detective Inspector Stride turns up his coat collar, for the temperature in the street is already dropping fast. He makes his way towards Paddington Station where he is to meet the train carrying Cully and the former Sybella Wynward, now newly-minted as Miss Essie Marks.

In the main street, some labourers are mending a water-pipe. They have lit a great brazier, round which a group of shoeless boys and ragged elderly men are gathered, warming their hands and toasting their chilled faces in rapture.

Stride cannot help ponder their fate as winter sets in, the earth becomes cast-iron with frost and their means of living cease. How merry must Christmas appear to those whose tattered clothes offer no more protection than broken windows, or the brick arches under which they crouch?

He enters the station and scans the arrivals board. The train is due in. Stride makes his way to the barrier, as the green liveried GWR engine clanks and hisses gently to a halt by the buffers, sending out clouds of acrid grey smoke and hot steam into the air.

Stride peers into the smoke, until he spies the familiar figure of Jack Cully making his way along the platform towards him. He carries two travelling bags, and is accompanied by a slender dark-eyed young woman who glances around her, biting her lower lip nervously.

Stride steps forward and raises his hat.

"Miss Marks, I presume. A pleasure to meet you at last."

The young woman's gaze takes in the passengers striding determinedly towards the exit, the smoke, and the porters rushing to and fro with trolleys laden with luggage.

"I never thought I'd come back," she says wonderingly. "And now ... now ..."

"Now I have a cab in attendance, and with your permission, we shall both accompany you to Hampstead and your real mother. Your arrival is eagerly anticipated," Stride says, as he offers her his arm.

***

Emily Cully stirs the big pot of stew, then lifts out the wooden spoon and tastes the gravy. She adds a pinch of salt, and covers the pot with a lid, turning down the heat. By the time Jack gets in, the meat will be tender and flavoursome, falling off the bone the way he likes it, and the vegetables soft and cooked to perfection.

She banks up the fire, then goes to the dresser where she keeps her work. Christmas is coming and so are the orders. Emily pulls out her basket of cottons and pins, followed by her patterns, and finally yard upon yard of pastel coloured cloth.

She lays the material flat on the washed kitchen table, and begins pinning on the paper patterns, her fingers automatically smoothing out the material as she pins. Tonight, she will baste the tiny dresses, ready to hand out tomorrow to her home workers.

There is sufficient here to ensure that everybody will have enough money to feed their families over the Christmas period. She thinks of Alice and her little ones

~ she will make sure Alice gets the best bits of the piece work. Her family will eat well this year.

While she cuts and bastes, Emily Cully sings softly to herself: songs she recalls her own mother singing, songs that she now sings to Violet to send her to sleep. The scissors shirr through the material like a hot knife through butter.

Eventually Emily finishes cutting out the tiny clothes. She gets to her feet, placing a hand to the small of her back. Then, as she breathes in and out quietly, she feels it for the first time: the tiny butterfly-wing flutter in her stomach.

Emily smiles to herself. Now she will have good news to tell Jack when he gets in later. She thinks of her husband approaching London on a train (she has never been on a train in her life), and sends out a silent prayer that he will also be bringing back good news for someone.

***

The hansom whirls them up the Edgware Road, through Marylebone and St John's Wood, and then on towards Hampstead. The two detectives attempt to engage Essie in conversation, but with each mile that passes, she becomes less and less communicative, staring out of the window at streets and sights that they guess might be bringing back unwelcome memories of her former life.

The cab finally sets them down outside a pharmacist in Hampstead High Street. Stride pays off the driver. Then he and Cully accompany the young woman across the road. Even at this hour, many stores are open for business and thronged with shoppers. They walk down the narrow side street until they reach the Lily Lounge.

The sign on the door reads 'Closed', but a single candle burns brightly in the window. Stride knocks and

Lilith opens the door at once. She takes one look at the young woman, then clutches the door frame, gripping it with both hands as if it is suddenly the most important thing in her life. As if she is drowning and it is her only life-preserver.

"Essie! Oh my god, Essie! My little girl ~ my beautiful daughter ~ come back from the dead!"

Essie stares back at her, eyes wide. "Mama? Is it really you?" she whispers.

Placing a hand on the small of her back, Stride propels her towards the open door.

"In you go, young lady. And now, if you would please excuse us, we shall be on our way. You both have much to talk about, and I do not think either of you need us here right now."

He touches his hat lightly and turns from the door, which closes behind them. A few seconds later the single candle is blown out, and the blind is lowered.

"An exceedingly good result, Jack," Stride says, nodding in satisfaction. "Though not one either of us could have predicted, I believe. You did well to persuade her to return."

Cully looks back at the darkened window and sends up a silent prayer of gratitude to his wife. She has played an equally important part in preparing Lilith for her daughter's arrival.

"What will you tell Sir Hugh Wynward?" he asks.

"If he ever returns to England and after I have arrested him? Nothing. We were tasked with finding a missing girl and returning her to her mother. We found her and did exactly as we were asked. As far as I am concerned, this case is now closed."

The daytime edges of the city are gently blurring into dusk as Jack Cully follows Stride to the High Street. It is that hour of a winter's afternoon when the lamplighter starts on his rounds a little early, because the darkness thickens fast, and so one by one the street lamps are coming on.

Cully glances up to where the roofs of buildings frame a corridor of sky, distant and already dusted with stars. A road leading to anywhere, he thinks. But his road lies elsewhere, and now it is going to take him home to Emily, and the hot supper awaiting his arrival.

Finis

Thank you for reading this novel. If you have enjoyed it, why not leave a review on Amazon and recommend it to other readers? All reviews, however long or short, help me to continue doing what I do.

Printed in Great Britain
by Amazon